Damon Runyon's Boys

"Damon Taylor is a flawed but likable protagonist, and Cain keeps the action moving along at a very nice pace indeed. *Damon Runyon's Boys* is exactly the sort of complex, hardboiled, vividly written novel that I really enjoy, and I had a great time reading it. Highly recommended." —James Reasoner, *Rough Edges*

"Cain effectively portrays the settings and ambiance of post-War New York, with its flashy dress styles, vintage cars, and endless nightlife celebrated at nightclubs and bars throughout the city…[his] third-person prose style is energetic and engaging."
—Alan Cranis, *Bookgasm*

"A simply riveting novel from first page to last… replete with unexpected twists and turns."
—*Midwest Book Review*

"Author Michael Scott Cain places the reader squarely in the center of the Damon Runyon era of gamblers, bars, big bands, and gangsters… a tough, fast-moving novel… Cain gets the dialogue right and pulls no punches (literally)…"
—Ted Hertel, *Deadly Pleasures*

"Opens quickly and keeps you interested by grabbing your lapels and not letting go. Good stuff. Very good stuff." —*Men Reading Books*

A Net of Good and Evil

a Damon Taylor novel by

Michael Scott Cain

STARK
HOUSE

Stark House Press • Eureka California

A NET OF GOOD AND EVIL

Published by Stark House Press
1315 H Street
Eureka, CA 95501
griffinskye3@sbcglobal.net
www.starkhousepress.com

ISBN-13: 978-1-951473-08-2

Book design by Mark Shepard, shepgraphics.com

*The publisher and the family of Michael Scott Cain would
like to thank Rick Ollerman for all his help in the final edit.*

First Stark House Press Edition: September 2020

Humans are caught—in their lives, in their thoughts, in their avarice and cruelty and in their kindness and generosity too—in a net of good and evil.

—John Steinbeck

1

Damon Taylor was having trouble keeping his attention focused on the little man who stood primly before his desk, his hands clasped in front of him, face as serious as a newborn's. The man babbled at him in a monotone, barely audible over the clatter of typewriter keys sounding throughout the newsroom. Taylor could see reporters working on their copy. Every couple of minutes, someone would rip a page out of his typewriter, spike it on top of a fistful of other pages, wave his arms over his head and shout for a copy boy. Taylor wondered what they were all writing, what stories they were working on. Right now, since he hadn't caught a story, he couldn't lose himself in the thinking, researching and writing process. He had to sit here with the little man's droning voice dripping on him like an unexpected snowfall. His hands were clenched into tight fists, even though he had no memory of tightening them.

He couldn't decide whether the little man looked more like a ferret or a weasel. Both buttons on the man's suit coat were fastened and his sharp-nosed little face stuck out of his collar as though he were lying in a field peeking over a log. Taylor expected him to clean his face with his paws.

"This is serious, Mr. Taylor," he said.

It was hard to see anything serious coming out of this guy. Irritating, maybe, and certainly boring, but serious? Taylor doubted it.

"What exactly do you want out of me?" he said.

"Do you mind if I sit down?"

"Go ahead."

The little man glanced around. "There's no chair."

"Ever occur to you there's a reason for that?"

"But I need to talk to you." The little man strove for a dignified expression.

"Pull one over."

The ferret-faced man—Taylor decided he was more of a ferret than a weasel—considered that for a moment, then nodded, walked over to the next desk, got a chair and carried it back. When he walked, he showed just the slightest hint of a waddle and he had the look of a person who waged a constant war for dignity. The battle was reflected in his clothes. Expensively dressed, he wore a suit that looked tailored, dark gray with a barely visible light pinstripe. His white shirt was starched and his tie perfectly straight, its dimple perfectly centered. The topcoat he had folded over his arm appeared to be woven of cashmere.

Taylor figured it must take him hours to get out of his apartment in the morning; he had to spend a lot of time primping, adjusting his presentation like a model.

His posture and behavior screamed of a longing for dignity. When the ferret-faced man had the chair exactly where he wanted it, he sat down primly, protecting the creases in his pants. When he had first come in, he'd stood at attention in front of the desk and said, "My name is Russell Wallace." He acted as if he expected the name to be recognized.

"I'm Damon Taylor."

Taylor glanced around the *Crime Scene* magazine offices; reporters and copy boys were everywhere, hustling to get their stories done so they could go for a drink. Over by the elevator, Lou Marsczyk, the managing editor, was chewing out a rewrite man. Everything was ordinary, the way it was every day.

Back during the summer, he'd stormed out of this place determined never to set foot in a magazine office again and now it was fall, the city was getting ready for another winter and he was back. He had to admit it, he was glad to be here. In the couple of months he'd been gone, he'd missed the place terribly, had felt lost and alone in the world. Now, surrounded by all the familiar confusion, he felt safe again. He caught the eye of a copy boy and mimed drinking coffee. The boy waved and scurried over to the pot.

"I know who you are," Wallace said. "You could say we're in the same business, Mr. Taylor. I'm an investigator for *Counterattack*. You've heard of it, I assume?"

Taylor looked across the desk at the little man, who was puffed up with serious intent, looking a lot like a cop about to spring a trap on a suspect. Placing his hands on the desktop, Taylor felt his facial muscles tighten.

"Sure, I've heard of it and there's no way in hell we're in the same business. You're the guys who run around looking beneath the furniture for Communists and when you find somebody you think might be one, you haul his ass outside and throw him under a bus. When you don't find one, you make up a bunch of rumors about somebody whose reputation you want to ruin and print them."

"You don't approve of our mission?"

"No, I don't. It's nobody's business what a man's politics are."

"Even if the man's red?"

"Even then. There's no law against being a Communist. The Party's on the ballot, isn't it?"

"For the moment." Wallace puffed up like an adder.

The copy boy brought the coffee over, placing it on Taylor's desk. He was a kid, no more than sixteen, as red-faced and gawky as a circus clown. He pulled up the waist of his pants and started to turn away.

"Thanks," Taylor said. "I don't think I know you. You new?"

"It's my third week, Mr. Taylor."

"What's your name?"

"Paul. Paul Carter."

"Good to meet you, Paul."

The kid grinned. "Same here," he said. When he spoke again, his words were rushed, at the same time shy and enthusiastic. "It's really good to meet you, sir. I'm a big fan of yours."

"You want to be a reporter?"

"Yes, sir. Like you, Mr. Taylor."

Russell Wallace looked at his watch, frowning. He drummed his fingers on his thighs impatiently, a mannerism that encouraged Taylor to continue talking to the copy boy.

"You're here to be a reporter, let me teach you your first lesson right now. You don't want to be a reporter like me or anybody else. You want to be you."

Carter frowned, taking that information in. After a moment, he brightened again. "Oh, I get it. Yes, sir. Thank you."

"Talk to you later, Paul." He turned back to Russell Wallace, who had begun squirming in his chair. "What do you want here, Wallace? Are you investigating me?"

"No. Of course not. I just want to ask you a couple of questions about a neighbor of yours. Do you know Bob O'Bradovich?"

"He's a good friend of mine. What about him?"

"We've got reason to doubt his loyalty."

That's when Taylor first wanted to boot him out of the building. He leaned back in his chair, working to loosen his fists. When he felt under control again, he stared at Wallace.

"Loyalty to what?" he said.

"I beg your pardon?"

"What exactly is he not loyal to? He's always been loyal to me. He's always been loyal to his job and to his art. I'm having a hard time figuring out just what he's not loyal to."

"You know what I'm talking about. We hear he's red."

Taylor took a sip of his coffee. It was delicious, fresh and hot. He'd gotten lucky and asked for a cup when a new pot had just finished brewing. Or had Paul the copy boy made a new pot for him? He'd have to find out.

"Tell you what, Wallace: for about the last five minutes or so, I've been toying with the idea of throwing you down the stairs. Why don't you just get out of my office before I go ahead and do it?"

"Are you threatening me?"

Taylor stood and took another sip of his coffee. Paul was watching him from across the room. Taylor saluted him with his coffee cup and, though it was hard to tell for sure from this distance, he could have sworn the kid was blushing. Wallace drew himself back in his seat, not liking the way Taylor was towering over him.

"I don't need to threaten you, Wallace. I know who you are. You're the little kid who was terrified of the big kids on the block. You're the kid who never got chosen to play stickball, the kid who was scared to go to the park because you were afraid you might get beaten up by all the other kids. You're the guy who squealed on the kids in your class who acted up in school. You're the guy who never had a bit of power in the world and now you've found a way to get back at everybody that made your life a living hell. You're not only getting back at them, you've found a way to ruin their lives and you're going to take advantage of it. All because you were a limp little kid who was afraid of his own shadow. Why would I want to threaten you? You're not worth it."

"Don't you talk to me like that."

"Why not? You going to tell me it isn't the truth?"

"You know," Wallace scribbled in his notebook, "all I have to do is say the word and we'll be investigating you, too. If we go back far enough, I'm pretty sure we'll find some stuff you don't want to see in print."

Taylor waved to a man across the bullpen. "Hey, Fairstein, you want to come over here for a minute?"

Fairstein was a balding man with a beer belly; in his fifties, he was close to retirement, happy to do research and rewrite so he could keep himself out of the field. He stood next to Wallace, his shirt hanging out and his tie loose. He looked down at the little man, who reacted as if he'd been exposed to a virus of some kind.

Taylor pointed to Wallace and said, "This here's Russell Wallace."
Fairstein nodded at Wallace and then looked back over at Taylor,
waiting for instructions. He wasn't impressed.

"I need you to do me a favor," Taylor said. "I want you to take a good
look at Wallace here's background. I want to know everything there
is to know about his past. I want to know what he ate for breakfast
when he was eight, which dime store he was too afraid to shoplift
from, what girls he had a crush on who didn't even give him a glance.
I want it all." He waited, while Fairstein made a couple of quick
notes. "And I especially want to know all the dirt, everything shady,
everything he did wrong, everything he thought about doing but did-
n't have the nerve to actually try. Got it?"

Fairstein grinned. "Got it."

"Oh, and make sure that new kid, Paul, gets a shot at some of the
research."

"Not a problem." He looked at Wallace as if the man weren't worth
noticing. "When do you want it?"

"Soon as you can get it. Thanks." When Fairstein had gone back to
his own desk, Taylor turned back to Wallace. "Here's the thing: we
turn a hundred or so rocks over, we're going to find everything
you've ever done, and, like you said about me, I'm pretty sure there's
some stuff you don't want to see in a national magazine."

"Why are you doing this?"

The radiator rattled as new heat came up through the pipes. A
room this size, open, undivided by walls, as big as an industrial loft,
was impossible to heat right. It was always either too hot or too cold.
Here by Taylor's desk, which was about ten feet from the radiator,
it was almost always too hot. He felt the heat and knew it was time
to get out of the office before it got too uncomfortable.

"What's the big deal?" he said. "It's the same thing you do, isn't it?"

"We go after Communists, threats to national security."

"That why you threatened to go after me?"

Wallace tried to smile. He wasn't very good at it. Waving his hands
wildly, he said, "I was upset, that's all. I wouldn't really do that to
you."

"Well, you see, that's the difference between us. I *would* do it to you.
Matter of fact, I'm doing it. And the minute I hear you're looking into
Bob O'Bradovich or any other friend of mine, I'll use it. I'll do exactly
what you do, use your own history to destroy you."

"Mr. Taylor, I'm afraid we may have gotten off to a bad start here."

"It's not going to get any better," Taylor said, "so maybe you leave before it actually gets worse."

The little man squirmed in his seat, scanning Taylor's face as if looking for a sign of weakness. He squinted and his face curled into a frown that made his eyes recede until they looked like slits in a pumpkin. Then, slowly, he got up and left. As the little man waddled toward the elevator, Fairchild wandered back over to Taylor's desk.

"You want me to go through with looking at that guy's past?" he said.

"Yeah. We'll sit on whatever you come up with in case we need it."

Fairchild grinned and said, "Damn, remind me never to get you pissed off at me, will you?"

2

After Taylor told him about the visit from Wallace, Lou Marsczyk said, "You ever hear of John Rankin?"

"The congressman from Mississippi?" Taylor said. "Sure. What about him?"

The sound of Hollywood gunfire came from the TV set against the left wall of Marzscyk's office. A Hopalong Cassidy movie was showing. Hoppy was crouched behind a cardboard boulder, shooting at one of the bad guys who was conveniently standing in the open on top of a hill. Hoppy leaned against the boulder, resting his shooting arm on an edge to get better aim and Taylor could see the boulder move. He doubted if any of the kids the show was meant for would notice, though. Marsczyk had always said he installed the TV in his office so he could watch the fights while he worked at night, but the set was always on, tuned to stuff no one over ten years old would watch.

"Why are you watching this crap?" Taylor said.

Marzscyk shrugged. "Passes the time. I find it amusing. Let's focus on Rankin, though. He's on the House Un-American Activities Committee. I take it you know what's they've been doing?"

"Looking for commies? Like Wallace does?"

"That's a fact. They were set up to look into any kind of un-American activities but they gave up on that a long time ago. When they were going to look into the KKK, Rankin blocked it, said the Klan was a treasured old American institution. He suggested the committee go after Albert Einstein instead. Claimed he was a commie agitator."

"Einstein?"

"That's right. Rankin's one of the greatest minds of the nineteenth century." Marzscyk began stuffing tobacco into a pipe, a meerschaum with a bowl big enough to eat soup out of. "Remember the Port Chicago incident?"

"I was overseas but I remember reading about it in *Stars and Stripes*. Bunch of munitions being loaded on a ship blew up?"

"Three hundred sailors killed. Congress decided to give each of their families five thousand dollars." He took out an Army lighter, a black Zippo whose lack of reflection was supposed to make it harder for an enemy soldier to see—and shoot at. Marsczyk tried to get the pipe going but it was tough and took some time. "Rankin was all for the payment till he found out most of the dead sailors were negroes. Then he insisted the payment be cut to two thousand."

"He get away with that?"

"They negotiated up to three grand a person." He took a drag on the pipe and frowned; it had gone out. Putting it down, he opened his desk drawer and pulled out a pack of Lucky Strikes and lit one up. "That's what we're up against. Guys like Wallace see what's happening down in Washington and they think, hey, our time has come, let's go get everybody we don't approve of."

"Aren't you exaggerating a little?"

He flicked his ashes onto the floor. "You tell me if I'm exaggerating. A few years back, they went after Shirley Temple."

"You kidding me?"

"Listen to me, Damon. *Shirley Temple*. She was ten at the time. A ten-year old commie terror."

"That's impossible."

Marsczyk pointed his cigarette at Taylor and said, "Damn it, Damon, nobody knows the city the way you do and there ain't many that can equal you when it comes to what's going on at City Hall, but you got to start paying some attention to what's happening in DC."

"Last time I paid attention to what Washington was doing, I wound up chasing Germans all over Italy. There's also the fact that it bores the hell out of me."

"Develop an interest. If this shit keeps up, you're going to need to be fucking fascinated by it." He took a deep drag on his cigarette and stared out into the city room, a sure sign he was thinking. "You say you put Fairstein on this Wallace guy?"

"Yeah. Too early?"

"No, not at all. What I do think is he's small potatoes. We need to be looking at who he's working for."

"What for? They haven't committed a crime."

"Let's just say I'm curious."

"I'll take a look at it, but the fact is all this stuff's going to fade away like fog. The American people aren't stupid enough to keep buying into this crap."

"Son, no politician ever got voted out of office for underestimating the American people. Like Lincoln said, you can fool most of the people most of the time and all the people some of the time and that puts the odds way in your favor."

"That's not what Lincoln said."

"Maybe not, but I'll bet the fucking farm that's what he was thinking."

Bob O'Bradovich was working and couldn't get free for a drink, so he asked Taylor to drop by the studio. Taylor went down to the NBC headquarters at 30 Rockefeller Center, checked in with security and took the elevator to the seventh floor, where he found O'Bradovich making up an actor, a pudgy man who had eyes as big as phonograph records and a head of wild black hair that gave him a slightly demented look.

"Hey, Damon, how you doing?"

"Fine, Bob. You?"

"Couldn't be better." He rubbed greasepaint lightly on the actor's cheeks. "You know Zero Mostel, Damon?"

"Saw you at Café Society a while back. You were very funny."

"Thanks."

"Zee, this is my friend, Damon Taylor."

The actor held out a hand. It was cold to the touch. "Damon Taylor," Mostel said. "I know that name. You the writer?"

"Reporter. *Crime Scene* magazine."

"I've read your stuff. You're good."

Mostel was excited, leaning forward in the makeup chair, waving his hands around, but Taylor got the feeling that he was always excited. O'Bradovich appeared to be used to it. Grabbing him by the temples, he pulled the actor back in the chair and said, "Hold still," while he continued to coat his face and neck with cosmetics.

"You said it was important, Damon," O'Bradovich said as he dusted Mostel's cheeks. "What's going on?"

"I said it *might* be important. Can't say for sure. You know a man named Russell Wallace?"

"Nope. Can't say I ever heard of him. Why?"

"You sure you don't know him?"

"Doesn't ring a bell."

"I know him," Mostel began squirming in his seat again. "I was at a Henry Wallace for President rally and he was there taking names. He's one of those guys that sees a Communist on every corner. Anything or anybody he doesn't like is red and he's on a crusade to rid the world of anything smacks of red."

"What's that got to do with me?" O'Bradovich said.

"He was in my office today, asking about you."

"He thinks I'm a red?" O'Bradovich, who had been bending over Mostel, stood straight and, wiping his hands almost angrily on a towel, said, "Jesus, you're right, this *could* be trouble."

Mostel checked himself out in the mirror. Nodding approvingly, he climbed out of the chair and removed the barber's apron that covered him from neck to knees. He still had tissue tucked into his collar keeping the makeup off his shirt.

"What's the big deal, Bob?" Taylor said. "Like Mostel said, Wallace thinks everybody's a red."

"You don't know what he's up to, do you?" O'Bradovich said.

He reached behind the curtain on his makeup desk and came out with a bottle of bourbon and three glasses. He poured each of them a shot and handed the glasses around. Tossing his off, he stared at the bottle as if he wanted another one already.

"Something I need to know about this guy, Bob?" Taylor said.

"Have you read *Counterattack*?"

"Why would I waste my time on crap like that?"

Mostel reached into his briefcase and pulled out a cheaply mimeographed copy. Its stories hinted that people it did not name were Communists and Communist sympathizers. As far as Taylor could see, it read like Walter Winchell's column:

> *What big time movie director insists that a member of his cast whistle the Communist theme song in every movie he makes?*
>
> *We're not ready to name names, but rumors are flying about a producer of Broadway musical comedies. It seems he is using Communist Party money to finance his shows and is funneling the profits to the Party. That means American audiences are unwittingly financing Communist espionage.*

"Who's going to take this crap seriously?" Taylor said.

"A lot of people," Mostel said.

"They want to publish the names of everybody in show business that they think is red," O'Bradovich said. "That could be messy."

"Well, relax. You won't be on the list."

"Damon, I went to some meetings before the war. Everybody did. It was the thing to do."

"You ever join the Party?"

"You kidding me? I'm like Groucho Marx: I'd never join an organization that would have someone like me for a member." He stared at his makeup case for a long moment. After taking a sip of his drink, he said, "Back in the thirties, Damon, being on the left was the thing to do if you were any kind of an artist. Everybody went to meetings, to parties thrown by the reds, folk music concerts, all kinds of gatherings. If you wanted to meet free-spirited girls, that's where you went. I must have been in a hundred different places where some curious anti-red right wing son of a bitch could write my name down or take my picture."

"But you were never a Communist?"

Mostel said, "A commie? All Bob was was horny."

"That's about it," O'Bradovich said. "I never bought into the ideology. It was too simplistic, just downright stupid, really. The girls, though? That was another question. Still if *Counterattack* prints anything about me, I could be in big trouble."

"Wallace and I reached an understanding. He comes after you, *Crime Scene* goes after him. We'll destroy him."

"Oh, I'd like to see that." Mostel rubbed his hands together.

"I'm not in trouble?"

"I don't think so. I just dropped by to let you know what went down. I believe I handled it."

"Thanks, I owe you a big one. Listen, I get through here about nine o'clock. Want to get a drink?"

"Sure. How 'bout Costello's?"

"Great. See you there."

"Maybe I'll join you," Mostel said. "Unwind after the show."

"Good."

"You want to stay and see the show, watch me work the old magic?" Mostel said.

"Can't. I got work to do myself. See you later at Costello's, though."

As he walked toward the elevator, Taylor thought back to when he'd been a kid growing up on the Lower East Side, back after his father had left and his mother hadn't been able to find work. They were hungry, going under, about to be thrown out on the street when Mitchell Goodman and his wife, Miriam, had dropped by. His mother was not to worry, the Goodmans said, the rent was covered and food would be delivered to the door for as long as they needed it. They and their friends would take care of it, the way they'd done for other people in the neighborhood who fell on hard circumstances. It was at times like this, Miriam said, that people needed to take care of each other. Mitchell and Miriam Goodman had been members of the Communist Party, USA.

Back then, everybody in the neighborhood had been supporters of Russia. All of that good will and cooperation began changing, though, when news of the Stalin purges hit the States. When that happened, it became impossible to deny what a horror Stalin was. And when Russia got the bomb, America decided to forget they'd been our allies just a couple of years before and had helped us bring down Germany.

Now they were our mortal enemy and people like Russell Wallace were saying the Russians were like a cancer, striking from within and that they were going to bring us down unless we stayed eternally vigilant.

Taylor wondered if the whole country was losing its collective mind.

3

"You went where and talked to who?" Anthony Hayden said.

Wallace felt an almost delicious shiver run through him. He was a capable man, he thought, able to take a person by surprise and get the job done, whatever it was, but Hayden was so strong, so powerful, that standing before him Wallace felt as small and unimportant as an ash tray. He felt grateful just to be in the man's presence. If he had been a dog, he would have dropped to the floor and rolled over, showing the bigger man his belly.

"I had to go see him. He's O'Bradovich's best friend. If anybody knows about O'Bradovich, it's Taylor."

They were in Hayden's office. He ran one of the biggest advertising agencies in town and his corner office was sheer luxury. You could tell he was *somebody* just by looking at him. He had a shock of gray hair, expensively cut, that Wallace thought made him look distinguished, along with a matching mustache. Wallace prided himself on being a stylish dresser, too, but Hayden's suits made his own look drab, old, the sort of things an out of work appliance salesman might wear. If you looked at the advertising man in his office, you felt as though he had just inherited the world and unless you were very careful, he wouldn't let you live in it.

Hayden's office was every bit as impressive as he was. At one end of the room, matching brown leather couches with gold-tacked trim faced each other, a glass-topped coffee table between them, with a freshly polished brass floor lamp lighting the area. His desk, centered in the room with a huge window behind it so the city could be seen sprawling beyond, was huge, piled high with folders, papers, sketches and mockups of ads. The man radiated success.

"Did it ever dawn on you that Damon Taylor's at the apex of a dozen magazines, so he can turn his reporters loose on whatever or whoever he wants to?" Hayden's voice was soft, little more than a whisper, but that only made it more threatening. As he spoke, he took off his glasses and pointed them at Russell as though they were a revolver. "Did it cross your mind that he can make life very unpleasant for all of us? Did you think about those things when you threatened to investigate him?"

"Well, no, but…."

"Wallace, we are in a very precarious position here. Right now, we're cranking up an offensive that will bring the reds to their knees. This time next year, there won't a Communist left in show business. If anything happens before we're ready, it can set the cause back for years. Now, here's what I want you to keep in mind: you are a very small cog, a very unimportant part of a huge operation and you will do nothing to jeopardize it. You get me? Nothing. You'll do what you're told and nothing else."

"Yes, sir."

Wallace told himself he wouldn't have let anyone else talk to him that way. Anybody who tried it would find they were up against a person who could make life hard for them, who could, as he had several times in the past, ruin a man. But Hayden? He was no ordinary man. Wallace respected Hayden because he was a person who commanded respect. And he feared him because the man generated fear in whoever was opposite him.

He'd been in the office close to half an hour now and Hayden hadn't asked him to sit down, so he was still standing in front of the desk like a flunky waiting to be fired. It wasn't right. He was a good field agent, a valuable part of the operation, yet here he was, being treated like a junior copywriter, a man who wasn't allowed to exercise his own initiative.

If Hayden knew exactly who he was dealing with, then he might have treated Wallace a lot differently. Wallace was an important man, in many ways as big as Hayden—bigger, even—but for reasons of his own, he felt he had to hide his power. Now he told himself he was getting fed up with this whole situation. If it hadn't been for his plans and, of course, the money coming in from a dozen different sources, he'd walk from this job.

"Anything to say for yourself?"

"Mr. Hayden, I'm committed to the cause. That's all I can tell you. I made a mistake, I guess. Maybe it was too soon to go see Taylor. I should have checked out his politics first. But I want you to know I'm one hundred percent behind what we're doing here. I'm faithful and I'm true to the cause."

Hayden cocked his head slowly to one side and studied Wallace. Then he broke out in what looked like a practiced smile, the kind you'd give a client when a pitch was going poorly. Before he spoke, Hayden glanced over at his two colleagues. Since they were behind him, Wallace couldn't tell what their faces were showing.

"All right," Hayden said. "We'll leave O'Bradovich alone for now.

There's always plenty of reds to bring down."

"Yes, sir."

"Here's what I want you to do: there's an outfit called People's Songs. They're as pink as a monkey's ass. They share office space with a theater group called Stage for Action, which bills itself as a radical group but by God, radical doesn't begin to describe them. Between those two groups, that whole building is loaded with commies. Look into it."

"Yes, sir."

"And, Wallace?"

"Sir?"

"Let's use a little subtlety, all right? Don't go getting carried away and screw this one up."

"Yes, sir."

As Wallace left Hayden's office, Kenneth Murphy followed him through the door and gripped him by the arm. He led Wallace into his own office, carefully shut the door and said, "Sit down, Russell."

"Yes, sir." He sat at attention, hands propped on his knees, leery but his face bright with anticipation.

"Russell, I know the boss was pretty rough on you. He's got a point, though. This is a tricky time for us. We can't afford any bad publicity right now. Still, he didn't need to speak to you like he did. I just wanted to tell you not to take it too seriously. You're doing a good job for us and we appreciate it."

"Thank you, sir."

"Anything you need? Anything that'll make your work easier?"

It felt so good to be respected, to be treated like a human being. He felt bigger, as though his very muscles were swelling. Murphy made him feel like a member of the team, as if he recognized that what he was doing was every bit as important as he himself thought it was. Right now, he felt that if it came down to it, if the situation called for it, he would kill for a man like Kenneth Murphy. Why wouldn't he? he thought; after all, he'd killed for less than that.

Actually, to be truthful about it, he hadn't really done the killing but he'd been there when it happened. He'd been party to it. It wasn't a thing he was proud of but it was a part of his life, one of the things that gotten him where he was now, so he couldn't deny it. The plain truth of it was he'd been ready to kill for a big bunch of money.

And if he was willing to kill for something like that, shouldn't he be ready to kill for the cause?

The door to the People's Songs office was locked, so Wallace banged on it with his closed fist. When no one answered, he checked his notes which said the offices were at 141 W. 42nd Street and that's where he was standing. He was uncomfortable here on this block and wondered why anybody would want to operate a business in this neighborhood, no matter how cheap the rent.

At one time, Times Square had been the center of the theater district. Actually, Wallace thought, it still was but that fact didn't mean very much anymore. Movies and TV were killing live theater; it was now a dying art and by God he for one wouldn't miss it; these days the producers made money feeding leftist crap to an unknowing public that thought they were only in for a night's entertainment.

With the decline of live Broadway shows, most of the theaters on this strip had taken to showing movies, and not always the kind you wanted your family to see. A lot of them couldn't bring in a crowd that way—theaters had abandoned films and were presenting burlesque shows. Down the block, the theater that Oscar Hammerstein had built, the Republic, now housed Minsky's Burlesque.

Other forms of entertainment, each more shallow and tasteless than the other, were springing up all over Times Square. Hubert's Museum had opened next to the Amsterdam Theater. Wallace snorted at the mere thought of the place. It wasn't much of a museum, featuring as it did Olga the Bearded Lady and Lady Estelline the Sword Swallower. This whole area had gone creepy and Wallace didn't like it one bit. He felt filthy just being on this block.

The changes had brought a new population to Times Square. On the surface, it was still a tourist destination, like the Statue of Liberty and the Empire State Building, but beneath the surface it crawled with gamblers, thieves, drunks, dopers, strippers and prostitutes, all of the degenerates you didn't want anything to do with. When he absolutely had to be there—and he didn't go near the area unless that were the case—Russell Wallace walked quickly, almost marching, with his eyes straight ahead and his jaws clenched.

In some circumstances Wallace resented his situation, like when he was ordered to do the work in place he did not want to go. Sometimes this really bothered him. He was doing everything right, doing the it for the people, but so many of them acted as if he were the enemy, as if he were the one working to bring the country down to its knees. It wasn't fair and he didn't like it.

He arrived at the address and knocked on the door. He waited a moment and then banged again.

A short man, no more than five-six or seven, with tight curly hair and a cigarette stuck in the corner of his mouth, opened the door a few inches and peered out.

"Who are you and what do you want?" he said.

"My name's Russell Wallace. I'm from *Counterattack*...."

"The magazine?" the little man said.

"That's right. I need to see...."

"That right wing sack of shit magazine that's always trying to hurt people's good names?"

"Just a minute, mister. You can't...."

The little man pulled the door open and stormed through it. "The hell I can't. Mister, you got a brain in your head, you'll haul your ass out of here right now before I get a good temper up. Right now it ain't nothing personal but I'm just pissed off at that sack of shit you call a magazine. You give me a minute or two and it'll get personal, all right. I'll be in a rage you never seen the likes of and I'm here to tell you, that ain't a pretty sight."

He had an accent, southern something, and stood bowlegged, like a banty rooster. He was wearing Levi's blue jeans and a flannel shirt and had a red bandana tied around his neck. Wallace fell back, holding a hand out. This guy was likely to jump him and the last thing he needed was to get beaten up by a crazy cowboy.

"You still here?" the little man drew himself up to his full height and looked at Wallace through squinted eyes.

"Please, mister," Wallace said, "all I want to do is talk."

"We don't have a damn thing to talk about." The little man was shouting now. "Who the hell do you think you are to go around calling people red and acting like there's something wrong with their politics? It's people like you that shot up the good union men back before the war and tried to break the miners union and now you're going after the CIO? You get the hell out of my sight."

Wallace looked around. A crowd was gathering but there wasn't a soul in it that was going to help him. All they wanted to do was watch him get humiliated, maybe seriously injured by this crazy cowboy. He tried to raise his voice but could only swallow nervously. God, what was going to happen to him?

He made one more effort to avoid being driven off. "I just want to talk."

"Well, I ain't got a thing to say to you. You get the hell out of here before you get yourself into trouble you can't talk your way out of, you hear me?"

"Yes, sir."

"Don't you go calling me 'sir.' I ain't nothing but a man just like you. I ain't no sir."

"Yes, sir."

"What'd I just say to you?"

"I'm sorry." People in the crowd were laughing now. Laughing at him. If he hadn't been so frightened, he'd've been angry. "I don't know what you want," he cried out.

"I want you to go on and get the hell out of here."

"Yes, sir. I mean, I will."

He turned and scurried back toward Broadway. Looking back over his shoulder, he saw the crazy cowboy going back into the building as the crowd began to break up. Again, it wasn't right. People had no idea what was going to happen to this country if he didn't help drive the reds out into the light where they could be exposed for what they were.

Why was it the people who made the moral choice, that stood up, were the ones that got all the trouble dumped on them?

When Russell Wallace got home, he quickly prepared a pitcher of martinis and poured himself one. After the afternoon he'd had, he needed a drink. Carrying his martini carefully, he settled into his favorite easy chair and settled back, letting his body feel its way into a comfortable position. He took a sip of his martini, which was perfectly dry, the way he liked it. As he swallowed, he felt something in the air, something he hadn't noticed when he'd come in. The energy was disturbed, as if the air was filled with charging electrons, and he felt that he wasn't alone. He looked around and jumped to his feet suddenly as the tall woman came out of his bedroom.

"Where is it, Wallace?" she said.

Wallace froze, his martini glass suspended in front of him. "You're dead."

"Evidently not."

"We heard you were dead. All of us. We heard you were dead."

"Oh, no. I'm very much alive and if you don't tell me where it is, you won't be."

"I don't know," he said, shaking his head. "I haven't got it."

As she walked toward him, the tall woman took a knife out of her peacoat. "It would be a shame if you didn't have it or didn't know where it was."

"Listen, I had it, yes, I did but somebody stole it. One of the others."

"Wallace, do you think I can't make you tell me the truth? Do you really think that?"

His shaking hand spilled his martini all over his shirt but he had an ominous feeling that it really didn't matter.

4

The patrolman led Taylor over to a jowly man with a crew cut, whose mashed-in nose made him look like a former boxer who'd stayed in the ring too long. He appeared to be in his late fifties and as Taylor approached, the man focused all of his attention on him, staring at him through hooded beady eyes. Because he covered crime, Taylor knew a lot of cops but this guy was a stranger.

"You're Damon Taylor?" the detective said.

"That's right."

"I'm Danny Murphy. Homicide. I guess you know why I brought you over here."

"Matter of fact, I don't."

Although he'd never met Murphy, the man's name resonated. He tried to place him, to recall what he'd heard about him but he couldn't quite bring it into his active memory.

Taylor had been packing up his stuff to leave the office when the phone rang. The caller had been a patrolman who'd said homicide needed him and was sending a car. "Be waiting outside your office. We'll pick you up."

"What's this about?"

"I don't know. I was just told to alert you. Fifteen minutes, okay?"

"There been a killing?"

"The detectives'll tell you what's going on. The car's leaving here now."

Homicide detectives did not call you with tips. If you were invited to a murder scene, then it was a good bet the murder had something to do with you. He backtracked through his mind, wondering how he was connected to whatever was going on, but came up blank. Still, you didn't turn down an invitation from homicide. If he didn't go down and meet them, the detectives would haul him down to headquarters and park him somewhere to make him sweat, the passing hours softening him up for an interrogation. No, it was better to cooperate. There was also the possibility of a story. He told Marsczyk what was happening and went down to the street to wait.

As the uniform drove him north Taylor asked, "Where are we going?"

"Midtown."

This just gets better and better, he thought.

Now he stood next to Murphy, who didn't seem to regard him very highly and appeared to think Taylor was barely worth his attention. After introducing himself and studying Taylor as if he were a specimen, he had turned his face away and looked over his notes. Taylor noticed that his lips moved a little when he read. When Murphy hadn't spoken for several minutes he asked himself why the guy was sweating him.

The room had been torn apart, quickly, thoroughly and messily searched. Everything had been ripped out of its place and left wherever it landed. Sofa cushions had been slashed open and white padding was everywhere. From what he could see of the bedroom, it too had been tossed.

"We were talking about why you brought me down here?" Taylor said.

"You know a guy named Russell Wallace?"

"He came to see me this morning. What about him?"

"Tell me about the visit."

If a homicide detective was asking him about Russell Wallace, then Wallace was in the middle of a killing, either as a suspect or as a victim. Taylor didn't see the little ferret as a killer.

"Something happen to Wallace?"

"Got himself gutted like a fish. Sliced to pieces and then gutted. Looks like he was tortured before he was killed." He pointed to his left. "He's over there in the bedroom. Now tell me about that visit."

He kept his eyes on the bedroom door. A couple of crime scene investigators were bending over the body, while a third one made notes. Simply another everyday scene.

"Nothing much to tell. He was looking for reds, figured maybe *Crime Scene* could help him. I told him no and that was about it. How you'd know I was connected to him?"

"Both your name and your office and home addresses were in his notebook. He had a little check mark next to you. Was he investigating you?"

Now he remembered what he'd heard about Murphy. The detective had a solid record but he had a reputation for being too quick to close cases. The word was that he was far more interested in building up his record by closing cases than he was in solving them. Neither his ethics nor his honesty were ever going to get him plaques to hang on the wall.

"If he was, he didn't tell me."

"I'm betting you know how what you told me sounds. Guy came to you wanting *Crime Scene* to help him find commies? Sort of weak, Taylor."

"I didn't say he was very bright."

"You're going to stick to that story?"

"Till the day you prove it wrong."

Murphy gave him a look designed to cause him to quake, to create a sense of menace as strong as an Edgar Allan Poe story. "I suppose you can account for where you were when this went down."

"Sure, if you can tell me when it happened."

"Couple of hours ago," he said.

"And he was here in his apartment the whole time?"

"How 'bout you let me ask the questions? Where were you this afternoon?"

"In my office. Maybe twenty other people were there. I can give you names and numbers."

"Write them out for me before you leave here."

Demanding the list was a pure power play. It said, remember who's in charge here; I can jerk you round all I want and there's not a damn thing you can do about it.

"Where was Wallace before he came home?"

"He was at the People's Songs office on 42nd Street. He had an argument with one of the people there...."

"Who?"

"What the hell, Taylor, you think I'm here to do your research for you? Guy named Woody Guthrie, calls himself a folksinger. His name was in Wallace's notebook also so I sent a man down there to talk to him." He watched as the coroner's men brought the body out of the bedroom and walked it out the door. "And you know something? That's the last fact I'm giving out. I didn't come here to get you up to speed on a story. I want to know what you know."

"Well, that's easy enough. I don't know a thing."

"I can't buy that. The man had to come see you for a reason. I need to know what that was."

"I told you...."

"I know what you told me and it's a crock of shit. You're holding out on me, Taylor."

"Why would I do that?"

"Maybe because you're a writer and you think going to press with stuff the police don't have will sell a couple of copies of that shit rag you work for. I heard about you, Taylor, you don't give a damn about nothing but your story. You'd sell your mother for a scoop."

"We don't call them that anymore, Murphy. You get it first, it's a *beat.*"

"I don't give a damn if you call it Harry. You hold out on me, I'll have your ass."

Lou Marsczyk pulled the scotch bottle out of his desk drawer and poured them each a shot. The TV on the cabinet was tuned to a show where a woman with an odd hairstyle chatted with a dragon puppet. Marsczyk walked over and turned the volume down. Settling himself behind his desk, he took a sip and clasped his hands over his belly.

"Well, tell me about it."

"I think we got ourselves a story here."

"Like I said, tell me about it."

Taylor checked his notes. "Russell Wallace looks for reds for *Counter Attack*, a mimeo rag that some advertising guys put out. Occasionally they call somebody a commie but most of the time they just hint at stuff, planting suggestions like a bunch of gossip columnists. He comes here wanting me to rat out my friend Bob O'Bradovich...."

"This O'Bradovich guy a commie?"

"I got no idea. Says he isn't. Went to a couple of meetings back before the war, when he was a kid. You remember, all the intellectuals in town and everybody in show business flirted with the Party back then. Says he never joined, though. Anyway, Wallace has his name from somewhere, and wants me to say Bob's a commie. I turn him down...."

"Turned him down big time, from what I heard through the wall."

Taylor took a swallow of his drink. "I was mad, you know? Anyway, later on, Wallace went down to 42nd Street. An outfit called People's Songs and a leftie theater group share an office there. He goes there and has a run-in with a guy named Woody Guthrie, a folk singer. Later that afternoon, Wallace turns up in his apartment tortured and murdered. Somebody sliced and diced him like a bunch of carrots."

"This guy Guthrie handy with a knife?"

"Murphy didn't take him in. He was gone by the time I got down to People's Songs."

"Gone?"

"Girl in the office said he had a gig at a union hall downtown."

"You'll be wanting to talk to him."

"Yeah. I did a little canvassing while I was down there. Didn't turn up a thing."

"This fight they had, happened right there in broad daylight?"

"In front of everybody on the street. Murphy found a dozen witnesses that would talk and didn't get a damn thing out of them. Everybody's story just canceled out somebody else's story."

"Well, that narrows it down, doesn't it?" He tossed off his drink and said, "Get on it. Start with that guy Guthrie."

"I can't see him doing this. I mean, the whole street saw the argument. What's he going to do, get a knife, somehow find out where Wallace lived, go over there and cut him to ribbons before he kills him? Besides, the apartment had been tossed. Every inch. Somebody was looking for something and from the shape he left the apartment in, he didn't find it. Doesn't make sense this Guthrie guy did it, not unless there's more to it."

"And you figure the murderer is the one that tossed the apartment."

"Makes everything fit better."

"You know what I think?" Marsczyk capped his bottle and slid it back into the desk. "I think before you go developing all these theories about what happened, you need to go out and get a couple of facts."

5

O'Bradovich and Mostel were already seated in a booth, drinking large bourbons, when Taylor got to Costello's. Both men attacked their drinks enthusiastically. Taylor got a Jameson on the rocks and went over to join them.

"Look," Mostel said, pointing to a signature carved into the table top. "Jimmy Cannon. Best sports writer in New York. You read his stuff, Damon?"

"Every day. He comes in here a lot."

"Really? This a writer's bar?"

Mostel was way too enthusiastic. He radiated happiness and appeared to have an overwhelming interest in everything. Taylor had a feeling that if he brought up plumbing, Mostel would get excited about different sizes of pipe wrenches. The size and amount of his energy might work on a nightclub stage but here in a bar, it threatened to get a little overwhelming. His level of interest radiated in his eyes, which were expressive, huge and round, the size of saucers.

"Mostly a newspaper bar," he said. "It's close to the papers so everybody drops by when they finish their shifts."

"Nobody here now."

"It's early yet. Morning paper deadlines are around ten, so writers don't finish till after eleven. How'd your show go?"

"We got through it. You know, with live TV you set out at the beginning of the week hoping to do a masterpiece and by show day, you just want to make it through without a major fuckup. A hundred things went wrong, but they were little; the audience probably didn't notice anything. Right, Bob?"

"I think so. You were great, Zee."

"Thanks. Think I'll go for another round. You ready, Damon?"

"Just started this one."

"Be right back."

"I really appreciate you taking care of that Wallace guy for me," O'Bradovich said.

"Somebody took care of him a lot better than I did. He's dead."

"What'd you say?"

"He got killed this afternoon."

"Murdered, you mean?"

"Yeah."

"Oh, my God. Who did it?"

"No idea."

"Well, I can tell you," a voice to his right said.

He looked over. Fred Osbourne stood there, a beer in one hand, a full pitcher in his other. Osbourne, an editorial page editor for the *Journal-American,* was one of the reasons Taylor wouldn't write for that paper anymore. As soon as the House Un-American Activities Committee began its search for Communists, Osbourne took to writing anti-Communist editorials and managed to shift the paper even more sharply to the right, continuing to crank out editorials and commissioning other editorial page stories that implied Communists were in every closet and that the nation was on the verge of losing its freedom forever.

"Okay, Osbourne," Taylor said. "I'll bite. Who did it?"

"One of those Commies down at that Stage for Action group. Wallace was onto them and they killed him."

"And your proof for this charge is?"

Osbourne waved the hand that held the pitcher, spilling a little of the beer. "Everybody knows that's how it went down and, by God the cops are going to prove it."

He walked away, sitting down by himself at a booth near the restrooms. Mostel, carrying a couple of drinks, slid back into his seat and passed one of the drinks over to O'Bradovich.

"Who in the hell was that?" he said.

"That was one of those newspaper guys you were so excited about. Fred Osbourne, from the *Journal-American.*"

Mostel shook his head. "Way too old to get that worked up. His heart might explode."

"He's been that worked up since I met him," Taylor said.

"Damon," O'Bradovich said, "this whole anti-commie thing is getting out of hand. People's entire livelihoods are going to get wiped out."

"It's happening already," Mostel said. "You know that TV show I'm doing, *Off the Record*?"

Since Mostel was an actor, when he mentioned the name of his show, his eyebrows raised and he searched Taylor's face with anticipation, waiting to be praised. That was the thing with actors, Taylor thought, they all had this need to be noticed. In truth it went beyond that: they needed to be worshiped, they were always calling attention to themselves, always breaking into song, reminding you of their credits, or letting you know what great parts they were up for.

"I don't have a set," Taylor sad.

"You don't have a television set? Get one. Tomorrow. There's some wonderful stuff on television." He hesitated and then said, "As I was saying, though, it's getting bad out there. A major sponsor just bailed on my show."

"Sponsors are always bailing on shows," O'Bradovich said.

"Not for political reasons. All a sponsor usually cares about is ratings. These guys jumped because they didn't like my politics."

"You think it's going to get serious?" Taylor said.

"If they put out that list they're talking about, a lot of people are going to find themselves in trouble."

"There's a list?" O'Bradovich said.

Mostel leaned forward, cradling his hands around his drink. "Well, what I hear is that list you were talking about back at NBC? I hear the people that put out *Counterattack* are getting ready to put out a book naming everybody they think is a Communist in show business. Doesn't make any difference to them whether it's true or not. They're going to use their little book to drive anybody on the left out of the business."

"Why would they want to do that?" Taylor asked.

"You know how they are about the *red menace*." He bit down on the phrase. "The very idea that somebody might have different politics from them just drives them crazy."

"Doesn't make sense."

O'Bradovich grinned at Taylor. "Fact is, you don't give a damn about the political side of this, do you?" Turning to Mostel he said, "See, Damon doesn't really care about big issues. He just likes to turn over the rocks, see what's underneath. He wants to know what's beneath the surface."

"Yeah?"

"Oh, yeah. If something's happening and he doesn't know the truth about it, he can't stand it. Drives him crazy."

"Truth?" Taylor said. "I might not know much but here's one thing I know: no two people talking about the truth are talking about the same thing. Seems to me we don't have *the* truth. What we have is *your* truth, *my* truth, *Zee's* truth. The truth is different for every one of us."

"Like I said. Drives you crazy, doesn't it?"

Taylor sat still for a moment, and then he knocked back a big slug of his drink. "Yeah," he said. "Yeah, it drives me crazy."

Mostel looked at him as if he suspected that Taylor just might be the pilot of one of those flying saucers he'd been reading about.

The next day, Taylor left the office at about eleven in the morning, took the subway up to 42nd Street and walked down to the offices of People's Songs and Stage for Action. The door was unlocked, so he went inside. A little man with a shock of tight curly hair and a cigarette dangling from the corner of his mouth sat on the edge of the stage, playing a guitar. Taking the cigarette out of his mouth, the man tucked it beneath a string at the head of the guitar by the tuning peg and began singing in a low voice, sounding as if he were testing out some lyrics. The song was about Jesse James but halfway through, the little man substituted the name of Jesus Christ. The tune and most of the lyrics remained the same.

The man's voice was rough and primitive, but it had a power and an edge to it that left you wanting to hear more. His was a unique, individual voice, one that carried the strength of truth. It made you feel you were listening to the real thing, that show business had nothing to do with the message of the song. Taylor thought this was no trained vocalist but if Frank Sinatra was your idea of fine singing you weren't going to be listening to people like Woody Guthrie anyway.

Taylor waited. The room he was in was large, a scaled-down nightclub. At the far end was a small stage, which looked more like rehearsal space than a performance place. He didn't see any chairs anywhere so he figured if the company did perform here, the audience must sit on the floor. Stage for Action appeared to be that kind of troop. Companies like this were springing up all over the city. These were groups where the play was more important than the comfort of the audience. All of them felt they had something important to say and screamed for the attention of the people. His actor friends were always dragging him to performances; a couple of weeks before, he'd seen a play staged in somebody's cramped and tiny living room. The last time he'd talked to Terry Louvin, she'd told him about a production staged in the 14th Street subway station.

Taylor picked up a brochure from the desk and leafed through it while he waited for the guitar player to finish his song. Stage for Action, he read, dramatized current social and political problems using what they called a "living newspaper" technique. They took on

Anti-semitism, atomic warfare, racism—all of the standard issues. He imagined that watching one of their productions would be about as exciting as reading the pages of *PM*.

What interested him, though, was the fact that in two weeks they were going to open a play that attacked HUAC and the anti-red scare.

"What can I do for you, friend?" The guitar player retrieved his cigarette and placed it back in his mouth.

"I'm looking for a man named Woody Guthrie."

"Lot of people looking for that guy. Which one are you?"

Taylor handed him a business card, which the little guy examined as if he suspected it was a counterfeit ten-dollar bill.

"My name's Damon Taylor. I'm a reporter."

"Says here you work for *Crime Scene?*"

"That's right."

The little man took the cigarette from his lips and walked over to an ash tray on the desk, where he ground out the butt. He walked bowlegged, as if he'd just gotten off a horse after riding in from Oklahoma. Taylor suspected that both his walk and his Okie accent were exaggerated.

"What's this Guthrie guy suspected of doing?"

"He may have witnessed a crime. I'm looking into Russell Wallace's murder."

"Who's this Wallace guy?"

Taylor decided he didn't want to play anymore. "The man you had a big argument with outside yesterday."

"Me?"

"You *are* Woody Guthrie, aren't you?"

The little guy grinned and made a motion as if lifting his hat. "That would be me," he said. "Pleased to make your acquaintance, Mr...."—he checked the card—"Damon Taylor, and even more pleased to tell you I ain't never killed a soul, not yesterday or any other time. Not that I ain't known a ton of men that needed killing and not that I ain't made up a bunch of songs about it, but I never done it. Want to hear one of the songs?"

Guthrie was a man who was going to take a little getting used to. "Well, actually...."

"'Well, actually.' That's the kind of enthusiasm I like." He began strumming. "This here's a song about some of the boys I knew when I was I was riding the rails. It's called 'East Texas Red.'"

He tossed his head back and sang in a nasally voice about a pistol-packing railroad guard who mistreated a couple of railroad bums. They gave the guard, East Texas Red, a year to get his affairs in order, vowing to come back on the same day the following year and kill him.

Which they did.

"What'd you think?" Guthrie said, when he'd finished.

"Not bad," Taylor said.

"Not bad? Hell, man, your enthusiasm don't know no bounds, does it?"

"Well, I'm more a blues fan, myself."

"Blues, huh? You know, in about an hour or so, Sonny Terry and Brownie McGhee'll be here. They'll play you some blues."

"So then you got an open hour?"

"I reckon."

"Well, how 'bout I buy you a drink and do a little interview?"

Guthrie put his guitar into its case. "You're buying, I'm drinking. Let me leave a note for Pete and Lee and the rest of the boys and we're outa here."

6

Guthrie was a man who liked his booze. He tossed off drinks as if he was lost in the desert and found a water fountain. But he also liked to talk and the whiskey loosened him up, although Taylor didn't believe he never needed much. Still he kept the drinks coming. They were in the bar at the Lamb's Club on 44th Street, a place Guthrie said he was fond of because it held onto its speakeasy attitude. Taylor agreed with the little man; you walked up to the door, you expect to see a hole at eye level where a rough looking man with a flattened nose dressed in a tuxedo checked you out and asked for the password.

"You find the real people in this place," Guthrie said. "It ain't all overflowing with tourists."

At this moment, it wasn't overflowing with anyone. Up at the bar, a couple of basketball fans argued over the season Columbia University was having while Taylor and Guthrie sat at a table in the middle of the floor. Taylor had suggested a booth but Guthrie plopped himself down at the table, saying, "I like to be out where I can see everything, don't you?" His guitar leaned against the table. He'd brought it with him, he said, because you don't leave a good guitar lying around the office.

"Tell me about the fight," Taylor said.

"The fight?"

"With Wallace. Yesterday."

"Well, friend, it wasn't what you'd call a fight. More like a dispute, I'd say. He wanted to come inside and start asking everybody about their politics and I didn't see where that was any of his business, even if nobody was there for him to harass, and I told him so, right to his face. He didn't appreciate it and got kind of uppity, so we yelled at each other a little bit. I reckon I yelled louder than he did 'cause he up and left in a huff, so I went back in the office. What happened to him anyway? You said something about a murder?"

"You didn't hear?"

"Soon as Pete and Lee—that's Pete Seeger and Lee Hayes—showed up, we headed downtown and played a gig. I ain't heard a thing."

"Wallace got himself slashed to pieces with a knife back at his apartment right after you two were arguing. Anybody in the office with you?"

"Nope. Till my friends come along about an hour or so after that Wallace fellow left, I was the only one there."

"You realize that makes you the number one suspect, don't you?"

"Hell, man, what you're telling me, I'm flat out amazed I ain't in jail right now."

"Cops haven't been around to see you?"

"Nope. Wonder what's slowing them up? Listening to you, you'd think they'd be swarming all over this place, waving guns and shoutin' through bullhorns, wouldn't you?"

"Could be they're building a case. When they do show up, it might be with handcuffs out."

"Like I told you, I didn't do it."

"Where you from, Woody?"

"What's that got to do with the murder?"

He signaled the bartender for another round. "Woody, I don't write about murders. I write about people. The crime's secondary. Where you from?"

"Oklahoma. I was born in Okemah, Oklahoma."

"What sort of town was it?"

"First ten years of my life, it was just an ordinary little farm community. Then, in 1922, they found oil and everything changed. Folks started getting rich overnight. Back home, we call it 'found money' and the thing you can count on is it never lasts. Oil ran out, town went to hell, so I drifted on down to Pampa, Texas." He stopped, his face distant, as if memories were rising faster than he could keep up with them. "Come the dust bowl, that place dried up, so I joined up with everybody else going out to California. Wandered around with my guitar, wound up here." He shrugged. "Ain't nothing out of the ordinary."

The bartender put the fresh drinks on the table. Guthrie smiled approvingly. Studying Taylor's face for a moment, he reached down and stroked his guitar, as if he wanted to make sure it was still there.

"Tell you what, Mr. Damon Taylor," he said. "I'm pretty good at sizing folks up. Reckon it comes from my time on the road, where you got to be able to read people just to stay alive." His face grew more serious and he said, "You're a man that loves to dig up the graves. You're telling me you're just a man looking for a story—well, that's a load of horse shit and we both know it. If the cops came in here and hauled me out right now, well, that'd be a story, but that ain't what you're after. The story's the box, that's all. You, well, you want to unlock the box, open it up and see what's in it. You got to know what folks are hiding. You were in the war, weren't you?"

"Yeah."

"Well, you ain't a big enough fool to believe you fought a war for justice or any of that crap, but you do believe that you have to live by a code and that code has to include honor and as much freedom as can be had in this world. A man's politics are his own and a person who would make you suffer because of your politics ain't interested in them at all, he's interested in making folks suffer. It's a power play and you won't go along with it. You know why you're writing up this here story?"

"How 'bout you tell me."

"Well, that's just what I had in mind. It's 'cause that Wallace fellow and the folks he works for are trying to tell other folks how to live, trying to punish people for what they believe in. He's trying to take away their freedom and, to you, that's about the biggest crime of all, ain't it?"

"You might be onto something there."

"Might be? Hell, man, we both know I am."

Guthrie was a little unsteady on his feet as they walked back down to the People's Songs office. As they neared the front door, Guthrie pointed at the cop car parked at the curb. Danny Murphy must have seen them in his rear view mirror. He opened the door of his squad car, which gave a loud squeak, and climbed out.

"Looks like they done caught up with me," Guthrie said with a laugh.

Murphy followed them into the office, his wide body almost filling the opening, blocking the light behind him so that he looked like a standing shadow.

"Might have known you'd be here, Taylor."

"And I might have known you'd be showing up."

Murphy stood with his hands on his hips, facing Taylor, ignoring Guthrie. "Well, I got some questions for our friend here."

"And I got one for you. When can I take a look at the case file on Russell Wallace?"

"Why should I let you see it?" He looked like he wanted to slug Taylor.

"How about because it's the official policy of the New York Police

Department to cooperate with the press and share information whenever possible? Which means if you hold out on me I can file a report on you."

Murphy drummed his fingers on the tabletop. "Come down to the precinct this afternoon. About five or so. Right now, though, I want you out of here so I can talk to your friend in peace."

Taylor knew it wasn't worth it to argue.

"So," Marsczyk said. "What you got?"

Taylor was cranking out his first story about the murder. He shook his head, lifted his hands and let them drop. "I got nothing. I'm pushing the political angle, suggesting that somebody he was investigating might have done it, but it's all as speculative as a starting hand in a poker game."

"Let me see your copy." He took Taylor's pages into his office.

Taylor had some time to kill while his editor went through his work, so Taylor picked up the phone and called Ken Bierly over at Kirkpatrick, Keenan and Coleman. Once he'd talked his way past Bierly's secretary, he said, "Hey, Ken, this is Damon Taylor."

"Damon. I figured you'd call."

"One of your boys gets killed, it's a story."

"It's got nothing to do with us."

"That a fact?" Taylor said. "How can you be sure?"

"Okay, maybe I'm not all that sure. But there's no reason why I should believe it's connected to what he was doing for us."

Taylor didn't know Bierly well. When Taylor'd been a feature writer for the *American*, he'd done a piece on advertising agencies and had met Bierly as part of his research. Over the years, he'd run into him around town a few times and had used him as a source on a few stories, so while he wouldn't really call him a friend, they stayed on good terms.

"Got a favor to ask you."

"What's that?"

"I need a list of the people Wallace was checking out."

"Oh, Damon, you know I can't do that."

Taylor caught Paul Carter's eye and mimed drinking a cup of coffee. The copy boy nodded and hurried over to the coffee pot.

"Look, Ken, you're saying the murder didn't have anything to do with either you guys or what Wallace was working on. Unless I can go through that list and prove you're right, nobody's ever going to believe it. You guys are going to be all over the news."

"What for? We haven't done anything wrong."

"Not from your point of view, maybe, but what do you think the press is going to have to say about your witch hunts?"

"We're not witch hunting. We're helping to get rid of a menace to this country. It's the left wing press that doesn't get it. You should know that."

"I didn't call to debate you. Here's the fact: the newspapers are going to be all over you if you don't clean this up. It's in your best interest to get that list to me."

"I can't do that."

"You know I'm just going to get it somewhere else."

Bierly said, "You'd do that, wouldn't you?" He was quiet for a moment. Taylor could hear him breathing. Then he said, "Okay." For a moment, Bierly hesitated. "Okay. I'll messenger the list over to you."

"Thanks, Ken."

"And, Damon?"

"What?"

"Be fair, will you?"

"I'll be fair but I'm not going to roll over for you."

"Don't expect you to. Listen, what you say we get together for a drink pretty soon?"

"You got it."

7

Marsczyk tapped Taylor's copy with his fingertips. "This ain't bad, considering. I don't hate it."

He wore a square cut suit he must have had made on one of his shopping trips to Savile Row, and he topped it off with a plaid hunting cap. To Taylor he looked like the guy who played Dr. Watson in the Sherlock Holmes movies. For a man who was proud of his wardrobe and spent a lot of time and money staying up to date, Marsczyk could decide to look like a card carrying eccentric every once in a while. Today was definitely one of the odd days.

"Considering what? Considering the point that I haven't got a clean fact in there?"

"You got enough to pique people's interests," he said, "and you don't try to pass it off as fact. You're open about the speculation. When you come back with more next week, they'll be oriented to the story and ready to roll."

"And if I don't have anything next week?"

"You will."

Back during the summer, Taylor had grown disgusted with the magazine, his life—everything. He'd finished up a big story in this very office and then he quit, telling himself he'd never work at reporting again. He'd gone home, slept late for a few days, and when he felt recharged, began planning a novel. Publishers had been calling, asking if he had a book in the works, so he figured this was a good time to find out. One afternoon a few months later, he'd been pounding away at the typewriter when the doorbell rang. He opened it. Marsczyk stood in his doorway. He'd worn tan slacks and a navy blazer, as if he were on his way to the country club for drinks.

"Who buzzed you in?" Taylor said.

"I don't know. I just hit every buzzer but yours and somebody opened the door. You might want to talk to folks here about security, know what I mean?"

His blazer looked brand new and, from the fit, it was obvious that it had been made to order. When Taylor had worked for him, Marsczyk had always been after him to upgrade his clothes. He was constantly offering to take him shopping but Taylor'd never worked up any enthusiasm for a makeover.

"What can I do for you, Lou?"

"You can offer me a drink."

He walked into the kitchen area, opened the cabinet and scanned its contents. "Bourbon or Irish whiskey. Those are the choices."

"Bourbon."

"You got it."

He poured drinks for the two of them and carried them back into the living area. Marsczyk was standing beside his dining room table, looking at the typewriter and the big piles of paper, most of which were blank.

"Writing a book, are you?"

"Yeah."

He nodded, took a sip of his bourbon and inhaled. "Good stuff. Thanks." Pointing the drink at the table, he said, "I was going to write a book once. Same as you. I'd left a job and figured it was time to let everything that had been building up inside me come spewing out." He shook his head. "Problem was, turned out there was nothing inside me. How 'bout you? How's it coming?"

"Still in the planning stages."

Marsczyk grinned. "You haven't got shit, have you?"

"It's coming a little more slowly than I'd figured."

"Same thing that happened to me. I spent six months finding out I didn't have anything to say. So then I figured I'd do a comic novel and found out I wasn't funny." He finished his drink. "That what's happening with you?"

"It's a little better than that."

Marsczyk sat down on the couch. A surprised look came over his face, as if he hadn't expected it to be as comfortable as it turned out to be. He nodded approvingly. "Tell me something," he said. "What's it going to take to get you to quit screwing around like this and come back to work?"

Taylor shook his head. Gathering up their glasses, he poured them a fresh round, bourbon for Marsczyk, Jameson for himself. As he was taking them back into the living area, the doorbell rang. Putting the drinks down, he answered it. O'Bradovich stood there.

"Hey," he said. "I was just going to invite you up for a drink but I see you got company."

"Nothing much going on," Taylor said. "Come on in. Jim Beam or Jameson?"

"No contest. Jameson." He waved at Marsczyk. "Hey, Lou. How you doing?"

"Not bad."

"Trying to get our boy here to come back to work?"

"You got it."

"Good." He accepted his drink and took a swallow. "I do hate to see a man throw his life away."

"I'm hardly throwing my life away."

"Call it what you want," O'Bradovich said. "You're not doing the work you were born to do, are you? You sit up here staring at a typewriter all day and then drink yourself silly every night."

Marscyzk's eyebrows raised. "It's that bad?"

O'Bradovich nodded. "Every bit."

"Look," Marsczyk said, "the magazine needs you, you need the magazine. Why don't we all just recognize that and get on with our lives?"

"Lou, you don't know what I did."

"You mean other than making a deal with the Costello mob that let a murderer go free?"

"How'd you find out about that?"

"Till I said it and you responded, I didn't. It was a guess, based on what you wrote, the way you wrote it." He tossed off his bourbon. "I been editing you a long time. You think I can't tell when you're faking?"

"Look, I sold out everything I thought I knew. How could I keep on doing the job after I turned my back like that?"

"Taylor, I know you. There's the law and then there's what's right. You're on the side of what's right. I'm guessing what you did needed doing and that it might not have obeyed the law but you did the right thing."

"I like to think so."

"Well, then, let it go and come back to work."

"I can't feel good about it."

"You know what your problem is?"

"Right now, it's you."

"Hell, man, I'm not it. Your problem is that where most people, even informed people, are okay just knowing what's going on, you're not. You, well, you are compelled to raise the level of the conversation. That's why we need you and that's why you need us."

"Go back, Damon," O'Bradovich said. "It's where you belong."

"Only way you're ever going to be sure whether you did the right thing is to come back."

So he did it, starting working again, and he had to admit it felt better. It gave him somewhere to go, something to do, and if he didn't like what he was looking into, at least he could admit to himself he enjoyed the process.

Now, in Marsczyk's office, he said, "You're going to go with that story?"

"Like I said, it's a good start. Now go get the rest."

When he got back to his desk, Bierly's list was centered on it, held down by a brass paperweight. He sat down, picked it up and read it. Most of the names weren't familiar to him but there were a few he recognized from radio, television and the stage. Mostel was on it. So was Pete Seeger, Lee Hayes and Woody Guthrie.

Paul Carter brought over a piece of mail for him. "This just arrived, Mr. Taylor," he said.

"Thanks, Paul."

He took the envelope. The scent of an expensive perfume emerged as he opened it. Inside were two tickets to *Street Scene*, a Broadway opera by Kurt Weill and Langston Hughes. The note that accompanied the tickets invited him backstage to meet with Faye Campbell, one of the stars of the show. She'd written it was important and, with an actress's sense of the dramatic, underlined the word important three times.

He picked up the phone and called Terry Louvin. Her voice, when she answered, was strong, melodic and musical. Hearing it brightened his mood.

"Hi," he said. "It's Damon. Listen, can you get free tonight?"

"Tonight? That's short notice, but if my neighbor can babysit, sure. Why? Don't tell me you're just dying to buy me dinner?"

"Sure I am. Even better, I've got tickets to *Street Scene*. Have you been?"

"Really? I heard the dancing is wonderful in that show. I've been dying to see it."

"I'll feed you after the show."

"How about before? I can't stay out late with the baby."

"Then we'll eat beforehand. Pick you up around six, say?"

"Great."

"Oh, we'll be going backstage after the show. Faye Campbell wants to meet with me."

"Good. I haven't seen Faye in a long time."

"You know her?"

"Dance classes, a long time ago. See you at six."

8

"The grilled salmon is fantastic," Terry said. "Sure you won't have a bite?"

"No, thanks. The prime rib pretty much did me in."

Terry Louvin scanned the dining room. It was filled with people who looked like they were on their way to the theater. Tourists craned their necks to see the Al Hirschfeld caricatures on the walls. One lady studied one of Hirschfeld's pieces and muttered, "Who's that?" to her companion. She kept pulling her mink stole back into its proper position on her shoulders, as if it were going to fall any instant.

"Did you choose Broadway Joe's because Damon Runyon used to hang out here?" she asked.

"Not really." He considered the question. "Maybe. He was the first guy who brought me. Lots of newspaper guys hang out here, though. Table twenty-seven back there is pretty much reserved for Winchell."

"Walter Winchell comes in here?"

"You'd be amazed how many show biz types had their reputations created in this room."

"I didn't know it was that easy. Maybe I should have hung out here."

"You'd rather be performing than running the school?"

"Are you kidding? Getting hired to manage the dance school was the best thing that ever happened to me. I get to teach young dancers, choreograph for them, guide them into their careers. Damon, I'm even getting hired to choreograph for companies every once in a while. I couldn't be happier." She finished off her last bite of salmon and pushed her plate away.

"You don't miss dancing?"

"You saw the dancing I was doing. Are you asking me if I'd rather be working in a third rate swing dance company again, struggling to get work, fighting to get paid? No thanks. Where I am now, dance is an art again. I love my job. It's still a miracle I got it."

Not so much a miracle, Taylor thought. He was pleased for her, of course. And for himself. Now, when he lay awake at night, wondering if he'd done the right thing when he made the deal with Costello that had gotten her the studio, he'd have this moment, these words of hers to put his decision into a little perspective.

"That's terrific," he said. "How 'bout a slice of cheesecake?"

"Oh, I'm not sure...."

"Terry, you telling me you're going to come to Broadway Joe's and not try the cheesecake? That's like going to the theater and not watching the play."

Faye Campbell and Terry Louvin threw themselves into each other's arms, each screaming the other's name with the kind of enthusiasm that only people in show business can muster. It was as though they were long lost sisters, just now located and returned home. The heightened energy, the bigness of everything, the over the top enthusiasm of show people caused Taylor to recede, to draw back within himself as if protecting his body from an assault.

"And you must be Damon Taylor," Campbell said, when she'd freed herself to Louvin's embrace. "I didn't know you knew Terry! I'd heard you could be trusted but now I trust you even more."

Her dressing room was about the size of a studio apartment in the Village. A mirror with a circle of bare light bulbs framing it hung behind her dressing table, which was covered with makeup, cotton balls, brushes big enough to be used for painting a wall—all of the stuff it took to transform a pleasant looking woman into a sensational Broadway beauty. Up close, in this room, Faye Campbell looked like a child who'd broken into her mother's cosmetics kit. She was garish, overdone, with bright slashes of red on her cheeks, her eyebrows penciled in until they were twice their normal size. She looked like a circus clown, but when he'd watched from the audience, she had looked spectacular.

"Maybe we can talk while I remove this stuff?" she said and without waiting for an answer, then sat at her table and began wiping her face with cold cream. "Damon, I understand you're looking into Russell Wallace's murder."

"Word travels fast."

"In this community, yes. Woody Guthrie told Will Geer, Will told me." She began to work on her eyebrows. "Have you any suspects yet?"

"That's not what I do, Miss Campbell...."

"Please, call me Faye."

As the layers of cosmetics came off she began to look older but somehow more vital, fresher.

"I don't look for suspects, Faye. That's the cops' job. I report on the murder. I'm trying to put it in context, figure out why it happened, what it might mean."

"I understand. But still, you come into contact with actual suspects. Isn't that right?"

"I go around, talk to people, sure."

"Can I count on what I tell you now being off the record?"

"I'd rather be able to use it."

She was watching him in the mirror and she shook her head at him. "I'm going to give you background. I'm going to give you a lead you don't have, one that, when you put it together with other people's stories, is going to enrich your article. It doesn't cast me in a good light, though, so I have to give it to you in a way that won't do my reputation any damage."

"Okay. Off the record."

"I'm afraid I may be one of those people you go around and talk to."

"I know. I got a list of people Wallace was investigating. Your name was on it."

Her eyes, clean now, locked onto Taylor's reflection in her makeup mirror. "He wasn't investigating me, Mr. Taylor."

"It's Damon. And your name *is* on his list."

"I didn't say he had no interest in me. I'm saying he wasn't investigating me because I was paying him not to."

"He was blackmailing you?"

"When I was very young, Damon, when I first got to this town and was still a naive little country girl, I met the most fascinating man. He was a member of my acting class. We both studied with Stella Adler." She waited for him to be impressed with Adler's name and then went on. "His name was Paul Baker and I was fascinated by him. I wanted to share everything he did so we could be together all the time. So when I found out he was a member of the Communist Party, I joined. Have you ever heard of a worse reason to become a Communist?"

"I'm sure there are some."

Terry Louvin said, "You aren't the first woman to make a bad decision for a man, believe me."

"But, Terry, for the time, it wasn't a bad decision. The Party back then was filled with exactly the kind of people I came to New York to meet. Artists, intellectuals, bohemians, you know the type. They were all young and exciting, all filled with enthusiasm and big ideas. They loved the type of theater I wanted to do and they loved poetry and each other and we were all young and beautiful and it was a wonderful time."

"But the way it's being looked at now, it doesn't look so beautiful?"

"No, it doesn't. They're trying to make my past filthy. There are people who would destroy me because of my associations."

"And Wallace was willing to make it go away for a price?"

"That's right. I know what you're thinking. You're thinking I should have been stronger, I should have told him to go to hell, should have had the strength to tell him to do his worst."

As she spoke, Terry crossed the room and stroked her arm sympathetically, the way she would have caressed a kitten. Campbell relaxed, her face softening, the tension in her arms fading.

"I'm not judging you, Faye," he said. "It's not up to me to say what you should or shouldn't have done."

"Remember, I was young and in love," she said. "Just a stupid, naive young girl. Today, I wouldn't join the Party for anything and who do you know that doesn't have a stupid mistake in her past? But I can't afford to let that mistake ruin me. These days, I look around and all I see are beautiful and talented young girls like Terry here coming up, all of them looking to take my place. I'm at a dangerous age, Damon. Any day now, producers are going to realize that there are younger, more beautiful and more talented girls out there who can do my job and will, for a lot less money. All I've got is my reputation—if anything happens to that, I'm through."

"You were paying off Wallace to protect your reputation."

"Exactly."

"You realize this gives you a motive for murder."

"I know. He got killed around four o'clock, didn't he?"

"That's right."

She held her hands out helplessly. "Then I don't have an alibi. I was taking a nap in my apartment. You get to be my age and you're doing eight shows a week, you need to nap in the afternoons." Shaking her head, she said, "All I can do is assure you I didn't do it. You've got no reason to believe me, I know, but that's the truth."

"I believe you."

"You do?" She seemed startled.

"What are you, about five-one?"

"That's what it says in my bio, but it's really more like five feet even."

"From the way I gather he was stabbed, I think it had to be a bigger and stronger person than you."

"Will the police think so too?"

"I hope so. Remember, their big interest is in clearing the case."

"Even if they have the wrong person?"

"It's happened before."

"What do you think I should do?"

"Nothing. Don't volunteer any information to anybody. Don't give the cops anything. If they want it, make them find it. And if they do want to talk to you, don't say a word without your lawyer sitting next to you."

"But won't that make them think I'm guilty?"

"The cops are going to believe what they believe, but they can only act on what they think they can prove. You don't want to give them anything."

"I see. Thanks." She drew her hand up to her face and rubbed her cheek with her fingertips. It struck Taylor as a very theatrical gesture. "Do you think the police have any interest in me right now?"

"All I can tell you is they're looking in a different direction from what I can see." He and Terry stood up to leave. "I'll get back to you if anything comes up," Taylor said.

In the doorway, Terry turned and said, "Faye?"

"Yes?"

"Whatever happened to Paul Baker?"

Faye Campbell stared down at the cotton pad she held in her left hand. "He was killed at Okinawa," she said.

"I feel sorry for her," Terry Louvin said.

They had stopped off in a bar on her block for a drink. They didn't have any trouble finding one; New York had more bars per block than any city in the country. Terry Louvin nursed a glass of white wine while Taylor toyed with a Jameson on the rocks. The bar was almost empty. Down at the far end, a couple of neighborhood guys watched TV while they sipped drafts. The bartender was leafing through a copy of that morning's *Daily News*.

"So do I," Taylor said, "if she's telling the truth."

"You don't believe her?"

He looked into her eyes. "Terry, people lie to reporters. They lie to cops, they lie to their doctors, they lie to their bosses. I talk to people, they know what they tell me is going to wind up in a magazine and a lot of the time they don't want to see the truth published. So they lie."

"If they're going to lie, why do they talk to you at all?"

"Lots of reasons. They think if they don't, I'll go harder on them. They think they can fool me. They want to protect some image of themselves." He shrugged. "Lots of reasons. More than you can imagine."

"Is that one of the things Damon Runyon taught you?"

"Yeah, and when he brought it up, I thought it was the cruelest thing I'd ever heard. Took me two weeks to learn he was right."

"Why would Faye lie to you?"

"You mean, other than the fact that she might have killed Wallace?"

"You said she wasn't big enough."

"You go to Times Square with fifty dollars and you can find a dozen people who'll do the job for you."

"You don't believe she did that."

"Maybe she did, maybe not. Hell, probably not. I do know this, though: it's too soon to take her off the list."

She stirred her drink. The action seemed to require all of her attention. "You know, every time I start warming up to you, you remind me how cold you can be."

9

While Taylor was going over the Bierly list again, Woody Guthrie loped across the office, his guitar banging on his back with each step. Paul Carter hustled along beside him yelling, "You can't just come busting in here like this."

"Why, sure I can, son," Guthrie cried out. "I'm doing it, ain't I?"

His accent was stronger than Taylor had heard it before, his voice booming throughout the office so that reporters on the far end of the room looked up to see what was going on.

"Hey, Damon Taylor," he called out as he neared Taylor's desk. "How you doing, boy?"

"I'm fine, Woody." Turning to Carter, he said, "It's okay, Paul. And while I've got you here, want to do me a favor?"

"Sure." Carter's face showed his excitement.

"Take a look at the names on this list," he said, handing the paper to him. "See what we got in the files on them, okay?"

"When do you need it?"

"Quick as I can get it. No more than an hour?"

"You got it."

They watched the boy walk away. Guthrie said, "Enthusiastic young pup, ain't he? You ever trip over him, the way he frolics at your heels?"

"He keeps it up, he's going to be one of the good ones." Taylor spread his hands on his desk. "Sit down, Woody. Tell me what I can do for you."

"Well, son—" he curled himself into the chair on the side of Taylor's desk, his legs twisted to one side so that he looked like he'd been bodily tossed into the chair from ten feet away—"thought you might like to know I got another visit from New York's finest."

"That would be Danny Murphy?"

"That would be the man, all right."

"He didn't arrest you?"

"Nope. Told me not to leave town, though." He grinned. "Don't you just love it when the these guys have seen so many cops and robbers movies they start sounding like the ones on screen?" He laughed. "I tell you, this Murphy boy thinks he's Dick Tracy." He leaned forward. "Speakin' of which, me and Pete and Will Geer went and saw that movie the other night. You seen it?"

"Comic strip movies don't do anything for me."

"Yeah, but Boris Karloff was in this one. I'm telling you, boy, I'll go see anything that's got Boris Karloff in it. He's a friend of Will Geer. You met Will?"

"Not yet. Name's familiar but I don't know him." Faye Campbell had mentioned Will Geer and Taylor remembered his name on the Bierly list.

"He's an actor. He's on Broadway."

"He's also on the list of suspected reds that my copy boy is checking out right now."

"Well, hell, boy, everybody that's worth anything's going to be on that list. My name right at the top?"

"Not at the top, no, but it's there."

"Well, I'm surprised. If they knew I did a column for the *Daily Worker*, I reckon they'd boost me up to the top of that list."

"You a member of the Party?"

"Not that one. I'm a member of the *human* party."

"If you aren't a member of the Party, how come you do a column for the Party paper?"

"Lou Budenz saw me playing at a rally, liked my union songs and the way I got the workers all fired up so he asked me to write for him."

"But you're not a red?"

"I'm a red, I'm a blue, I'm an orange, a pink, a yellow. Hell, boy, I'm a regular rainbow. I told you, I'm a member of the human party."

"But I suppose Murphy's got you at the top of his list of suspects?"

"I reckon he does."

"And you felt you had to come tell me about it for what reason?"

"You joking? 'Cause it's a hell of a story for you."

"Is it?"

"Big time folksinger suspected of murdering a red baiter? Hell, man, tell me that won't sell some copies."

"I'll look into it."

"You oughtta."

"And the fact that if the story breaks and you get some publicity out of it, it might slow Murphy down a little, keep you out of jail a while, I guess that never occurred to you?" He tapped his blue pencil on the desktop. "Who knows? Might even get you a couple of paying gigs."

"A paying gig," Guthrie said longingly. "Now wouldn't that be worth having."

"You're working me like a PR man, aren't you?"

"Well, hell, can't fool a sharp boy like you, can I? Fact I get a little nudge out of it don't make for any less of a story."

"Why not use it in your column?"

"Don't nobody see my column 'cept the boys that are already on my side, the true believers. You reach a lot more people."

"I'll see what I can do, Woody."

Toots Shor's Restaurant was located at 51 W. 51st Street. When you walked in, the first thing you saw was the oversized circular mohagony bar that thrust out into the center of the room. Then you noticed all of the famous people. Right now, Ernest Hemingway was choking down booze at a corner table and an up and coming comic named Jackie Gleason was being treated by Shor as though he were much more famous than he was.

A skinny singer named Frank Sinatra who had just left Tommy Dorsey's band and had become catnip to young girls hung out there whenever he was in town and as often as not, you could find Orson Welles doing magic tricks by the bar. Shor especially loved baseball players; a menu signed by Babe Ruth hung on the wall. Just about every night, players from the Dodgers, Giants and Yankees would come in after their games and unwind at the bar. All of this had come about because Joe DiMaggio had dropped by there one night, discovered that Toots Shor, thinking Dimaggio was God, refused to let him pay for anything. DiMaggio, who was the cheapest man Taylor had ever met and thought of himself as way too important to have to pay for anything, was in Shor's place every night.

One of the things these men enjoyed about Shor's restaurant was that wives were discouraged from coming in. Shor said he ran a booze and broads place and that wives were definitely not broads.

"What do you think?" Ken Bierly said. "Want to get a table?"

The bar was packed three people deep. "Sure," Taylor said. He spotted Toots Shor walking by and signaled him. "How you doing, Toots?"

"Damon." Shor slapped him on the the upper arm. "Good to see you."

"Same here. Got a table?"

"For you? Always. Follow me." As he led them to the back of the room, he said, "You know, I was thinking about Runyon the other night. When he was doing sports writing he was in here every night. Got all his material here. Terrible what happened to him. Just terrible."

"I know."

"For a man that was one of the great talkers of our time, a man that could spin a yarn like nobody else on this earth, to lose his voice to cancer? Man, that's indescribable."

"I know."

He showed them their table. "I'll have another round of drinks sent over."

"Thanks."

"Any time, Damon, any time. It's on the house. Dinner, too."

"You don't have to do that."

"I know, but it feels good to be able to do it. Do me a favor, though, will you? Take good care of your waiter. Some of the boys, I comp 'em, they don't tip so good. My staff gets pissed off at me, you know what I mean? Claim I'm taking money out of their pockets."

"I'll take care of them."

"I knew you would. You got too much class to stiff a working guy."

When he was gone, Ken Bierly took off his glasses, wiped them with a handkerchief and said, "Do you know everybody?"

"When I first got into the newspaper racket, Damon Runyon took me around. He was a legend, knew everyone in the city, so I met a few people."

"I see." He took a sip of his drink. "What's on your mind, Damon? I'm glad we could get together and talk things out."

"I need some background. What do you know about Russell Wallace?"

"Not much, really. He worked for us and he's dead. Got mugged in his apartment or something. Why do you ask? What more is there to know?"

"Well, for one thing, it wasn't a random killing. Somebody sought him out. Makes sense that something he was up to got him killed. How'd you come to hire him, anyway?"

"You say this is background? We're off the record?"

This was the beginning stages of the story, when nobody wanted to be quoted, singled out by name. Right now, the people involved were hoping the story would just go away. When they realized that wasn't going to happen, they'd begin opening up to protect themselves, but not yet.

"Okay, sure. Off the record."

"Well, we hired him because he was committed to the cause. He'd worked for HUAC, you know."

"He had?"

"Sure, he was one of the foot soldiers. He gathered information for the committee."

"Hard to see him doing that. I mean, he came off as a cowardly little weasel. At least to me."

"Maybe that was why he was so good at what he did."

"Why'd he leave the committee?"

"Said he wanted to come back to New York."

"You check his references?"

"Not personally. Somebody must have."

"You might want to take a look at whether that happened."

The new round of drinks arrived. Both men were silent until the waiter left. Bierly looked worried, as if he didn't like the direction this talk was taking. He cleaned his glasses again.

"I take it you discovered something?" he said.

"Did you know your boy was blackmailing some of the people he was investigating?"

Bierly's hands froze. He was quiet for a long moment, as still as a phonograph record in its album. "He was what?"

"Blackmail, Ken. He was extorting money."

He tossed off his drink. "Oh, God. We're in so much trouble."

"So it would seem."

"This throws the whole crusade into question."

"It does, doesn't it?"

"You can't print this."

"Of course I can."

"But it'll create a bad impression. Damon, we're not blackmailers. We're patriots. We're trying to change this country for the better, keep it safe from our enemies, not extort money from people. If you print this, you could set the movement back years."

"I can't worry about movements. All I can do is print the truth."

"The truth? You want to know the truth? The truth is this country has been infiltrated by reds. What's true is that Russia will never have to invade us, they're taking over from within. And they've got their sights on the entertainment industry. If they get that, they can control the message that goes out, and before you blink your eyes, the whole country will fall. That's the truth. If you talk up this backmail thing, you're playing right into their hands."

"Then go on the record. You can get your side into the story."

"I thought you were a straight shooter."

"Go on the record."

Bierly stood, his face flushing red. "Here's what you better understand, Taylor. You can't print that story. We'll stop you."

"You going to claim I'm a Communist?"

"Let's just say we'll stop you."

"Let me see if I got this right: you're going to try to block a true story from being printed? Isn't that something the Communists would do?"

"We've got to keep the big picture in mind."

"You mean you'll let the ends justify the means."

"Kill the story, Taylor," he said as he walked away.

10

Herbert Huncke stood in front of Hubert's Museum, blocking the picture of Olga the Bearded Lady. The sign, in blistering red letters, screamed that Olga was the only woman in America with a beard thirteen inches long. For a quarter, you could go into Hubert's and check out all of his living museum exhibits. There was Olga herself, as well as Susie the elephant-skinned girl, Estelline the sword swallower, the man from World War Zero and Princess Sahloo the snake dancer. In the basement of Hubert's, live fleas attached to very thin wires raced miniature chariots around a little track.

It was all quite a sight, one that Huncke found disturbingly erotic—although the fleas didn't do a damn thing for him—and on a lot of slow afternoons, when he was high and had a quarter, he spent way too much time in there. Today, though, he watched the street. He was broke and hungry and he was going to need to score a shot, so he scanned the crowd like a detective with his eye out for a suspect. It was too early for the hookers to be out, either cats or chicks, and the sailors wouldn't be along until late, so he waited. That was one thing Huncke was good at: waiting. Somebody with a little bread would come along. Somebody always did.

Today that somebody was Damon Taylor. Huncke said, "Bingo," as he watched him approach. He'd been doing leg work in the underground for Taylor since before the war. When the reporter needed to know something about street life, he came to Huncke. So as Taylor legged it down 42nd Street, Huncke strolled over to join him, turned and began to walk in step with the reporter.

"What's up, man," Huncke said.

"You had dinner?"

"Not yet."

"How about Hector's?"

"Very cool."

Food was taken care of. Now he had to figure a way to play Taylor for a few bucks. Sometimes the reporter was generous with a dollar but other times, when he felt Huncke's information was thin, he held back. They turned up Broadway to walk the two blocks to Hector's Cafeteria, a favorite of Huncke's when he was eating on somebody else's dime. The place served huge plates of pretty good food but was mostly known for its dessert bar that was twelve feet long and three feet high. Like most junkies, Huncke sported one hell of a sweet tooth.

When they were seated, he ordered meat loaf and mashed potatoes. His teeth weren't that good, so he tended to stay away from stuff that was hard to chew. Taylor had a steak, which looked and smelled wonderful to Huncke, but that only made the meat loaf taste better.

After dinner, he ordered another beer. "What's up, Damon? You need something?"

"Take a look at these names, Herb. Tell me if you know anything about them."

That was the thing he liked about Damon Taylor: he always used your name. To most people in Times Square, he was just Huncke the Junkie. Taylor didn't diminish you like that. Huncke took the sheet of paper Taylor passed across the table and studied the names, concentrating.

A lot of guys would eat Taylor's food and just babble some kind of nonsense about the names, but not Huncke. He liked to give good service. You were more likely to build up repeat business that way. As he read the list of names, he tried to figure out how much this was going to be worth.

"Three of these cats I never heard of, but with the others, you hit the jackpot here."

"Yeah?"

"Bill Hayden's queer. Jean Carlson and Linda Grafton are junkies and Eddie Nixon, well, he's the ball game: a queer junkie."

"You sure about this?"

"You know me, Damon. I don't say it if I ain't sure. Let's just say I've had dealings with these people."

This was one of Taylor's generous days. He picked up the check and laid a twenty-dollar bill on the table. Huncke hoped the sigh he let out was inaudible.

"Stay and finish your beer, Herb. I've got the tab."

"Always good talking to you, Damon."

He waited until Taylor was out of sight before he picked up the cash.

11

When Taylor introduced himself, Bill Hayden pumped his hand firmly and said, with a wide show business smile, "Good to see you, Mr. Taylor. Thanks for dropping by."

"Please, call me Damon."

"Fine. And I'm Bill. Tell me, which of my shows are you intersted in? I direct four local kiddie shows and *Dottie's Rainbow*, which is national. That's the one most people know about. I guess...."

"I'm not here about your radio shows, Bill."

Bill Hayden was a short pudgy man who wore a white shirt with his tie loosened and a corduroy coat with leather patches on the sleeves. His hair was turning gray and he held a pipe in his left hand, though he wasn't smoking it.

"Oh," he said. "But you said you were a reporter."

"I am."

"And you're not interested in my shows?"

"No, what I want to talk about is your relationship with Russell Wallace."

"I'm afraid I can't help you. I don't know any Russell Wallace." He made a circle with his pipe in the air, as if erasing a blackboard.

"You don't know the man?"

"I've got no idea who you're talking about."

Taylor took a deep breath, exhaling slowly. He shook his head as if something his pet dog had done disappointed him. Looking over at Hayden, he took another breath and said, "Then he wasn't blackmailing you?"

Hayden almost staggered backward. He reached out with his left hand and gripped the edge of his desk, letting his pipe fall to the floor. "I have no idea what you're talking about."

"I see. So Wallace did not begin investigating you because of your left wing activities and discover you were a homosexual and begin blackmailing you?"

Hayden stared at the floor for a long time. His shoulders slumped and Taylor could see his hands begin to shake. Then the director drew himself up to his full height, nodded a few times and, indicating the chair opposite his desk, said, "Maybe you'd better sit down, Taylor."

Damon sat.

Settling behind the desk, Hayden slid open a drawer and pulled out a bottle of bourbon and two glasses. Pouring each glass halfway full, he slid one across the desk. Taylor took it and nodded thanks.

"I'm going to have to insist on going off the record," Hayden said.

"Unless you killed him, I can protect your identity."

"Killed him? Killed who?"

"Russell Wallace. You didn't know he was dead?"

Hayden shuddered, drawing so deeply into himself that it looked to Taylor as though he were shrinking. "I've been out in Chicago, meeting with the network out there, trying to sell them my other shows. I just got back this morning."

"How long were you gone?"

"A week."

"If that checks out, then you didn't kill him."

"It'll check out. I'll give you names and numbers. What happened to Wallace?"

"Somebody sliced him up like a side of bacon and then gutted him with a knife."

After taking a sip of his drink, Hayden stared at something on the far wall for a long time. Then, with a shake of his head, he said, "This is a terrible thing to say, a *horrible* thing, but I'm glad. It couldn't have happened to a better man."

"What are you talking about?"

"We *are* off the record, right?"

"Yeah, sure."

"I mean, if this gets into print, it'll ruin me."

"I told you, this is background."

"That son of a bitch ruined a lot of lives and he was about to ruin mine."

He finished off his drink and poured another one. The afternoon had faded into evening and the office was getting dark, so he turned on a lamp. His face took on an orange cast in the light.

"What do you mean?"

"What do you think I mean? The bastard comes at you for being red.... Hell, not even for being red, for having hung out with a couple of Party members. Says for a price he can clear you, so you can go on working. All you got to do is give him money and a few names. All the time, though, he's digging into your past and if he finds anything there, all bets are off. He's blackmailing the hell out of you. Why shouldn't I be glad he's dead? Who wouldn't be?"

After speaking to Jan Carlson, Linda Grafton and Eddie Nixon, Taylor agreed—who wouldn't be glad he's gone?

That was the hook he used for the followup story he turned in to Marsczyk: The Man Everybody Wanted Dead.

Kristen Eldredge was big for a woman; at least six feet tall without heels and muscular. She couldn't be described as fat or big-boned, just *big, muscular.* She wasn't by any means masculine. Quite the opposite: she was the kind of woman to inspire an Amazon. Her beauty was such that nearly every man she met would feel an instant respect if not outright attraction, certainly an admiration, a feeling she rarely reciprocated.

Not that Kristen had anything against men. In fact, she liked them, despite the depths of their failings. She felt she'd quite moved on from the disappointments of her earlier years, at least as far as the other gender was concerned. It was just that right now, she had other things on her mind. There was something else she needed to make right. Something much more recent. The next step was dealing with the man before her.

She tucked a huge napkin into her lap and checked out the feast assembled in front of her. She forked a steak, centered it on her plate and placed a breaded pork chop next to it. A pile of mashed potatoes the size of a baseball lay next to the chop. Checking her plate, she found room for a load of corn. After she poured gravy over everything, the woman, who Irish Jack Sheridan figured was a good six feet tall and might have weighed as much as he, used a hunk of bread to push loads of food onto her fork, which she placed into her mouth, sighing audibly with satisfaction.

She'd missed eating as much as she wanted. One of the many things that fit into that category. Even now she still felt the need to indulge though she knew she couldn't do it too often. She refused to gain weight.

Irish Jack sat opposite her, trying not to watch the woman eat. It was like trying not to watch an earthquake. He couldn't turn his eyes away. The woman wasn't by any means fat; her muscles rippled as she lifted a fork and the way her biceps flexed fascinated him. She was as muscular as a body builder and he would have bet she could have won one of those best build contests. And the thing that for some reason scared the hell out of him was that she was beautiful. You didn't expect a giant to be a beauty.

"Have you seen this?" Kristen slid a copy of *Crime Scene* across the table.

"No. I don't read shit like that."

As she chewed a forkful of steak, she said, "You're going to want to look at it. They got an article on Russell Wallace in there." She wiped her chin with her napkin.

"Don't mean a thing to me."

"Let's understand something: it means something to me. So as long as you're taking my money, it's going to mean something to you."

Irish Jack picked up the magazine. "Wallace. That the guy got knifed downtown?"

"That's what the article says."

"What do they know?"

Kristen signaled for him to wait while she swallowed. She was carrying on, Irish Jack thought, as though she hadn't had a meal in years, almost as if the very idea of cooked food was something new to her. He watched her cut off another hunk of beef. He was fascinated despite himself. His face reddened as he became increasingly uncomfortable at the degree of enthusiasm she brought to the task.

"They don't know much yet. The investigation's ongoing, the cops have a bunch of suspects. You know how they write it."

"Anyone worried about it?"

"Not yet. They're going to do more articles, though. They promise followups."

"Who's writing them?"

"Guy named Damon Taylor. You know him?"

"I've heard of him. He's stirred up trouble for some people I know. They say he's thorough and has a network of people that dig stuff up for him."

"Maybe he needs a little discouraging."

"According to what I hear, he don't discourage easy."

The woman pointed a chunk of steak at him. It fell off of the fork and her eyes followed it to the table, stabbing it and lifting it back to her mouth. Her lips closed around it like a python swallowing a rat.

She said, "Discourage him anyway."

"I'm telling you, I don't think that's a good idea."

Kristen Eldredge put down her silverware and slowly finished chewing. Irish Jack watched her staring eyes and wondered what was going on in there.

"Listen. You don't tell me. I tell you. I'm the boss, you're the hired muscle. I do the telling."

"I know that and I don't mean to be disrespectful but still…."

But still?

She hadn't left home when she was twelve years old to be ordered about by overbearing men. No, she'd walked out the door and left her silly mother reading her Bible and her father the reverend substituting his church for his family. It was easier to *forbid* than to *understand*, to tell rather than ask, to ignore instead of comprehend. To dictate rather than love.

But still?

Kristen had made her own way from that point. She'd found a new family for herself—well, a man anyway, a salesman with his own car. A man who'd said they could make a family, one all their own. It worked alright for a while, too, until Kristen let slip her real age. The man had always suspected something wasn't right but it had been easy to tell himself that as long as he didn't *know* anything different, nothing bad could really happen to him.

But things didn't stay the same. He began drinking. Kristen knew she'd made an error and when he began to change, talking more and more like her father, she saw how big her mistake had really been. Once the hitting and the slapping started, she'd thought briefly of returning home, throwing herself on her father's alleged mercy, but when it really came to it she couldn't imagine forgiveness coming from that man.

Already a big girl, Kristen was still growing. The actual violence didn't hurt her so much physically as show her how ugly the world was all over. She hadn't really run away so much as run to something else. It wasn't long before she grew large and strong enough to hit back. If she didn't stop the beatings, she thought, no one else would.

So she did. Her man left, unable to stay, his right arm broken, one eye swollen shut. His chest was battered and it was hard for him to breathe as he staggered out of the small house and disappeared down the street. Kristen didn't wait. She took all the money from the man's wallet and got in his car and drove away.

She didn't have much but she had more than she did the first time she ran away. Now she had more of herself. She knew no man would ever hurt her again.

But still?

She took hold of the table between herself and Irish Jack, gripped it with both of her large hands, and smiled. Kristen Eldredge had always had trouble trying to control her own impulses and she squeezed the wooden edges, knuckles whitening.

"Look," she said. "Let's not get off on the wrong foot. I don't intend to have to explain myself to a hired tool. If you think I'm going to let some reporter get in the way of my.... Well, it's not going to happen."

"So?"

"So discourage him."

Irish Jack was done with arguing. He said, "How far do you want me to go?"

"Leave him alive, but give him something to think about."

"Leave him alive? You're sure of that?" He couldn't help himself. The capacity of this woman for violence was palpable. He hadn't expected her to hold anything back.

"For now."

12

"Come on uptown with me," Woody Guthrie said. "I got to see some people."

"Sure," Taylor said.

It was four in the afternoon. After he'd left Eddie Nixon, he'd gone down to Times Square to see if Will Geer was hanging out at People's Songs, or if Guthrie could help locate him. When Taylor agreed to go uptown, Guthrie strapped his guitar across his back and led the way down to the subway.

"Most of the musicians I know carry their guitars in a case," Taylor said. "Aren't you afraid yours is going to get battered up, carrying it in the open like that?"

"Used to use a case till I figured out how much money it was costing me."

Taylor whistled for a cab. It pulled to the curb. Guthrie flashed him a grin as he climbed into the back seat.

"So we're going in style, are we?" he said.

"A cab's first class?"

"It is if you're a folksinger." Guthrie called out to the driver, "30 Rockefeller Center."

"Why we going to NBC?" Taylor asked. "You got a radio gig?"

"You kidding? These days, Norman Corwin's the only man that'll hire me to sing on the radio. Used to have my own show, but they wanted me to clear what I was going to sing before I went on. Came to me with an approved list of songs, so I sung a song that shocked the hell out of 'em and they canceled me on the spot." He grinned again, looking as though he should be chewing on a stalk of hay. "Ain't that the way it goes, though?"

Taylor wondered how many ways to commit career suicide Guthrie knew. As they rode uptown, Guthrie strummed a tune absently and said, "Back when I used to carry the guitar in a case? I'd go in a bar, scrape me up change for a beer, and sit there and wait for somebody to ask for a song. Hell, I could wait all night. Get to carrying the guitar on my back, though, and I ain't in a place five minutes before somebody asks if I can play that thing. I tell 'em yes and they ask for a song."

"And you sing for them?"

"Oh hell, no. Few minutes later, the guy's going to buy me a beer and ask for a song. I still hold back. Then he says he'll give me a quarter if I sing one that's when I pull the guitar around and give the old boy a song. Then somebody else puts his quarter down and by the time I walk out of there I'm a regular cash register." The cab pulled over and Woody said, "Hey, here we are," and hopped out.

Taylor paid the driver and joined him. They went into the RCA Building and onto the elevator. When Guthrie punched the button for the sixty-fifth floor Taylor said, "We're going to the Rainbow Room?"

"Yep. Got me an audition. Manager heard me sing at a party, liked what he heard and asked me to come up and sing a few tunes for him."

Guthrie was wearing blue jeans with a patch on the knee and a flannel shirt that had last been ironed before the war. He was going to audition for the Rainbow Room in those clothes?

One more way to commit career suicide. The Rainbow Room was one of the most exclusive clubs in the city. It featured gourmet Northern Italian cuisine, a revolving dance floor, art moderne architecture and a wonderful view of the city skyline. Big bands played the room and did radio broadcasts on national hookups from there. Duke Ellington, Artie Shaw and Tommy Dorsey played regularly on this stage. If you wanted to attend their annual New Year's Eve party, you had to not only reserve a year in advance, you had to be ready to drop close to a grand.

The manager, a man in his forties in an expensive suit and a sharp Van Dyke beard, came over with his assistant, a bright young woman of twenty-five or so who pretended not to be shocked by Guthrie's appearance. They greeted Guthrie warmly and asked him if he was ready to sing.

"Always," Woody said.

"When I heard you at the parrty," the manager said, "I thought I'd never heard anyone so genuine, so close to the real people, and I thought you might be exactly the spark of energy we need here."

Waiters and busboys were setting up the tables and two men were vacuuming the dance floor. The manager waved an arm in a distracted manner and said, "I trust it won't interfere with your performance if the staff keeps on working?"

"I'm a folksinger. I'm used to people not listening when I sing."

The manager and his assistant chuckled appreciatively. "Well, if we can just hear a couple of songs?"

"Sure."

Woody ambled out onto the stage and struck up a song about being broke, down and out in New York City, or as he called it in the song, New York town. Taylor thought it odd that you could be in the Rainbow Room, a symbol of money and prestige, singing about being down and out on the streets, but Guthrie made it work. He followed that with a song he said his friend Lead Belly wrote, "Goodnight, Irene." As he listened, Taylor found himself amazed. One man, one guitar, and not that great a voice, yet his performance was something powerful, beautiful. Taylor actually thought the crowd at the Rainbow Room would enjoy it too.

"Can we hear an uptempo piece, Mr. Guthrie?" The manager lit a big cigar.

"Sure. This here's a tune I made up that my uncle Jack put on the Hit Parade a couple of years back." He sang a song about riding his pony through the Indian Nation back in those Oklahoma Hills.

When he finished, the manager said, "That'll be fine, Mr. Guthrie." As Woody came back to the corner where Taylor waited, the manager said to his assistant, "Well?"

She nodded vigorously. "You're right. This could work. It could give us a whole new dimension. Of course, he's got to be packaged right. Nobody's going to buy that costume he's wearing now. If we put him in a cowboy outfit, though…." She tapped her pencil on her pad for a moment and said, "I see him in white, with furry chaps and a hat with gold medallions around the brim…." The girl inhaled sharply, the enthusiasm for her own idea growing. "Of course," she said, "we'll seat him on a bale of hay. It's going to be wonderful."

"That's good," the manager said, "but how about if he's a swamp rat, sitting on a tree stump in the hollow, with his rifle leaning against the stump, maybe one of those big sacks country people carry things in next to him?"

"You know what would really make it work?" The girl bubbled over. "A clown costume. Pierot, you understand. It'll highlight the whole theatricality of his show."

Taylor glanced over to see how Guthrie was responding and discovered the man was halfway to the elevator already. He hurried over to catch up with him. "You okay?" he said.

"What you say we get me out of here and back to a place where a man can breathe."

Taylor was beginning to understand; sometimes a little career suicide wasn't such a bad thing.

When they were on the street, Taylor started to flag a cab but Guthrie stopped him with a hand on his arm. Without breaking his stride, he said, "How 'bout we walk a little? Give me a chance to get my brain back on."

They walked silently for a few blocks. The offices were letting out and the people within the crowd jostled each other, hurrying for the buses and subways. Guthrie threaded his way through the mass as if it wasn't even there. His face was tight, the wrinkles around his squinted eyes prominent.

"When he first got out of prison and came to this town," Guthrie said, "They made my old buddy Lead Belly—you know Lead Belly? Huddie Ledbetter? Well, anyway, they made him perform in a convict's outfit. He hated going out on stage in those jailhouse stripes, you know, but the people that were supposed to be looking out for him told him he wasn't going to get nowhere if he didn't dress up like that." He clenched his fists. "I swore wouldn't nobody ever do a thing like that to me. And by God if I ain't about to let nobody else do it, I sure as hell ain't going to do it myself."

13

Guthrie was in a better mood by the time they reached the People's Songs office. It surprised Taylor; he'd never seen a man shake off a bad experience the way Guthrie did. After they'd walked a few blocks it was as if the objectionable event had never happened. Since he had a tendency to hold grudges himself, he admired Guthrie's ability to let things go.

When they arrived at the office, a huge bear of a man with a thick beard and long curly brown hair walked over and gripped Guthrie in a hug that appeared it would crush Guthrie's ribs. Beating him on the back with his open hands, the man let out a shout.

"Woody, how the hell are you? I ain't seen you in what, forever?"

Guthrie worked his way free from the hug and said, "Been fine, Will, fine." Turning to Taylor, he said, "Damon, this here's my running mate, Will Geer. You know who he is. He's on Broadway right now, doing *Tobacco Road*. Will, shake hands with Damon Taylor, the magazine writer."

"Good to meet you, Damon Taylor. How's it going?"

Geer was one of those guys who tried to break your hand with his grip, as if a simple greeting was a test of masculinity. Taylor endured the shake, resisting the impulse to massage his hand when it was finally free.

Geer turned his attention back to Guthrie. "I have to be at the theater in about an hour, but I got time for a beer if you want to buy me one."

"You ever known me to turn down a beer? Come on, Damon, let's take the big man across the street to Harry's."

"Now hold on," Geer said, "I'm not about to give that place any business."

"Why not?" Guthrie said. "Cheap beer, free sandwiches…."

"You seen that sign they put up in the window?"

"What sign is that?"

"One that says it's against the law to serve homosexuals. Says 'Please don't ask us to break the law.'"

"You don't mean it. When they put that up?" Guthrie said.

"I don't know but I'm not about to spend my money in a place that discriminates. Even if the law says they can. Why don't we walk up to Rector's? It's closer to the theater, anyway."

Rector's was one of the lobster palaces that had sprung up all over Times Square once the area became a tourist trap. The palaces took a look at Fifth Avenue hotels and society destinations like Delmonico's and figured if they could bring the look and some of the opulence of these places to the masses, they could make a killing. Taylor had written about the trend back in his newspaper days. Sure, places like Rector's imitated the better and more expensive places when it came to decor and the menu, but instead of serving fine food, they were content merely to serve a lot of it. He had to admit, though, that the beer was good.

When they were settled in at the bar, Guthrie spun around on his stool and said to Geer, "I just finished me an audition up at the Rainbow Room."

"How'd it go?"

"Audition went great. They offered me seventy-five bucks a week."

"That's good money."

"Woulda been."

Geer polished off his beer in a couple of swallows and called for another round. Taylor had barely started his but he figured somebody would drink his next one if he didn't get to it. These two guys enjoyed their beer.

"You turned it down?"

"Walked out on 'em."

"Damn it, Woody, you can't keep on doing stuff like that. There aren't that many seventy-five dollar a week gigs out there and every time you tell somebody to shove one of 'em up their ass, there's less of them. You can't keep on playing for nickels and dimes. You got a wife and kids to take care of, boy."

Taylor scanned Guthrie's face as if he were looking at a different person now. He hadn't had any idea that Guthrie was married. As irresponsible as the man was, he'd just assumed he was single.

"Well, hell, Will, don't you think I know about Marjorie and the kids? Do you think she'd be proud seeing her man humiliated by playing to that uptown crowd? Dressed up as some sort of fucking clown?" He said the word as if it were a curse. "You know they wanted to dress me in an actual clown suit, make me sit on a bale of hay? Hell, man, Marjorie married an artist, a fighter. She don't want no song and dance monkey."

"You know, what I think is she'd like to be married to a man that can bring home seventy-five bucks a week. You got to learn to compromise a little, man. You know I'd much rather be working in People's Theater than being on Broadway but I got responsibilities, you know? I got to pick my times to be political and my times to be in show business."

"Maybe that's the difference between us, Will. I never been real good at compromising."

Geer finished his beer and noticed Taylor's second one waiting on the counter. He grabbed it and tossed it off in a swallow. He stood to leave.

"Woody my friend, you got to be the single most frustrating man I ever met."

The problem with being a freelance goon, Irish Jack Sheridan thought, was that you wound up working for some weird creep like the big woman, a woman that thinks you can discourage a reporter without killing him. Christ, anybody with the brains of a squirrel knew that couldn't be done. It was Sheridan's business to discourage people, he'd been doing it all his life, and if there was one thing he knew, it was this: if you wanted a guy to back off, there were only two ways to do it. The first was to kill him. The other was to kill a member of his family.

That's how they'd done it when he was muscle for Joe Adonis's Broadway Mob, back during Prohibition. A nightclub wouldn't fall in line, Irish Jack—he loved that name, it fit him much better than Eric, the one he was born with—went and talked to its owner. Usually, all he had to do was point out how iffy life could become for the guy's wife or his youngest kid, how you never knew when one of them could be hit by a car or killed in a senseless robbery. Life was so touch and go, man, you had to recognize that. Every once in a while, though, you ran up against a guy who wanted to be a hero and you had to either dump him or his wife in the river. Sometimes both.

Now he was supposed to get this Taylor guy to back off but he couldn't use the best weapon he had? It didn't make a damn bit of sense. Well, he'd just have to use his second best weapon. He wished Big Bill Dwyer were still around. When Dwyer was running things, everything happened the way it was supposed to. Sheridan had grown up in Hell's Kitchen, the same neighborhood where Dwyer had been raised, and the older man was a legend; Sheridan heard stories about him the way other kids heard about the easter bunny. Dwyer had been working the waterfront when Prohibition came in and he saw that he was in a position to dominate the whiskey business. From his time on the docks, he knew how to get hold of trucks, garages, drivers, goons—the whole machine. He put together an operation that dominated all of Manhattan in just a couple of months. Picking up Owney Madden and Frank Costello as partners, he started up a smuggling operation that brought first-rate booze in from Europe.

By this time, Sheridan was working as muscle for Joe Adonis's Broadway Mob, a gang that partnered with Dwyer. Somehow Dwyer had noticed him and he'd gone to work for the man, where he learned everything he knew. For a while there, he'd been someone in the rackets, but then Dwyer had gone to jail for violating the Volstead Act and those bastards Madden and Costello had thrown him out of the gang for the great crime of being Irish.

Now he was putting together his own gang and it took capital to do that so he was taking on any job that came his way, including beating up a reporter. He looked at the five men gathered around him. Good men, the kind he liked: strong and not too smart. They'd do what they were told and—as long as they were paid—never dare make a move on him.

He'd hand chosen every one of these guys so he knew they were all capable of taking care of Taylor. If the woman didn't want him dead right now, these guys could do the next best thing, even if he didn't think it would give the woman what she wanted. Whatever. Irish Jack was going to make sure that son of a bitch reporter spent a long time in the hospital.

14

Taylor met Marsczyk at the Emerald Inn, an Irish pub that had opened last year on Columbus Avenue, between 69th and 70th, an easy stroll from his apartment. He dropped by there a lot. The Jameson was plentiful and inexpensive and the food, everyday Irish fare like shepherd's pie and bangers and mash, was delicious. It was the type of place where, if you had been there a single time before, you felt like a regular.

Marsczyk was new, had never been. He placed his hat on the bar, looked around, taking in the long bar and the few booths that lined the far wall. "Comfortable," he said. Pointing at Taylor's drink, he added, "You drinking Jameson?"

"Sure am."

"I'll have one, too." He signaled the bartender and ordered a double. "What's on your mind, Damon?"

"This story still isn't coming together. I keep feeling like I'm missing something."

"Let's hear what you got."

Taylor rested his left elbow on the bar, rubbing his jaw with his hand as he thought. After a moment, he said, "What I have is one dead guy, half a dozen of his blackmail victims, and another half dozen being investigated by him. I have a ton of suspects and a sinking feeling that none of them had anything to do with the killing."

"I don't know, blackmail's a pretty good motive."

"Yeah, but most of the victims have alibis."

"You checked out their stories?"

"Had Paul Carter check them out. They're all clean."

"You like that Carter kid, don't you?"

"He's pretty sharp. Get him the right seasoning, he'll make a good reporter."

Marsczyk's drink arrived. He took a swallow and sighed. "Good stuff. I'm thinking another couple of months, I'll move the Carter kid up to rewrite, see how he does."

"Makes sense."

"So, let's get back to your problem. If your blackmail people don't pan out, it's got to be one of the reds."

"Look, Lou, if a guy was looking into your past, finds out you went to a few meetings back before the war, maybe even joined the Party, would you go so far as to kill him? I mean, none of it's against the law. It might be kind of embarrassing but it's not a motive for murder."

"It is if what he knows can ruin your career."

"You sure you're not giving these guys more power than they've got?"

"Your friend Mostel got fired from his show today."

"Oh." Taylor took a drink from his own glass. "I hadn't heard."

"Came over the radio this afternoon."

A man and a woman walked into the bar. In their thirties, they looked prosperous, dressed to the nines, the woman wearing a full length mink coat. Her makeup was overdone. Maybe she thought she looked stylish but to Taylor, she looked like a Victorian china doll with bright red cheeks and garish, painted lips. They sat at the bar a couple of seats down from him and Marsczyk. The woman looked familiar but he couldn't place her.

"If these guys get their way, a lot of people in show business ain't going to be in show business anymore. The House Committee on Un-American Activities is calling Hollywood actors and directors to testify. You got Senator McCarthy claiming that Hollywood is riddled with Communists, everybody's running scared. A lot of careers are going to come to a screeching halt."

"Joe McCarthy's an out of control drunk."

"Sure, he is," Marsczyk said. He was staring at the woman. "But he's also the most powerful man in Washington right now."

"Maybe. I just have this feeling that Wallace's murder has nothing to do with all this red-baiting crap."

"Could be you're right. You're overlooking something."

At the bar, the man ordered bourbon and water for himself and a glass of white wine for the woman. When he saw Marsczyk staring at his date, he said, "Something on your mind, buddy?" He sounded as if he thought he was a tough guy.

"Not really. I was just wondering when your friend there got out of prison."

"What?"

The woman looked straight ahead as if she were trying to use her mental powers to make them all disappear. Her hair was way too blonde to be natural and Taylor realized that was why he hadn't been able to recognize her. During her trial she'd been a brunette.

"You don't know who you're with?" Marsczyk said. "This is Barbara

Heller."

"What the hell you talking about? Her name's Wanda Cooper. Tell them, Wanda."

The woman swallowed a couple of times, blinking quickly. She turned toward Marsczyk, her eyes pleading, and opened her mouth to say something. She twisted the hem of her coat in her fingers.

Before she could speak, Marsczyk said, "Wanda Cooper? You're not Barbara Heller? Damn, I'm sorry, ma'am. That Heller woman looks a little like you but now that I see you real good, I can tell I'm mistaken. I apologize."

"That's all right." Her voice was shaky.

"Who's this Heller woman you're talking about?" the man demanded.

"Nobody. Forget it."

The man stood, came around the stool the woman sat on and stopped in front of Marsczyk, his fists clenched.

"I said who's this Heller woman?" His voice was as tight and clenched as his fists.

Marsczyk stood, closing the space between them. "I said forget it. The lady's satisfied. I recommend you be satisfied, too."

"You threatening me?"

"Seems to me you're the one doing the threatening. I'll tell you this, though: you throw a fist at me and I'll break your arm. And that's not a threat. That's just how it's going to be."

The man's face reddened. He raised his clenched hands, but hesitated, then lowered them. Waving an arm dismissively toward Marsczyk, he said, "Hell, you aren't worth it." Turning to the woman, he said, "Let's get out of here, Wanda."

As she slid off of the stool, the woman threw a quick, grateful smile at Marsczyk. Then she followed the man out the door.

"You going to drive off all my customers?" the bartender said.

"Not me," said Marsczyk. He looked at Taylor. "I shouldn't have done that."

"You know damn well that was Barbara Heller."

"Yeah, I also know she served her time. She deserves to be let alone."

"You know that's not going to happen. As soon as the papers find out she's back in town...."

"Yeah, but it won't be me that blows her privacy. Doing the crime is a story. Getting out of jail after paying the price, well, that's something that doesn't mean a damn thing to any of us. You ready?"

He signaled for another round. "Look, about the Wallace thing. You ever consider maybe you're going in the wrong direction?"

"What do you mean?"

"I mean that six months you took off dulled you like a used-up razor blade. You're trying to figure out why a guy got killed but you don't know a damn thing about him."

Taylor caught sight of his own face in the mirror behind the bar. He needed a haircut. Tomorrow morning, on the way in to the office, he'd stop off at Louie Dee's and get it done. He studied himself for a moment; his eyes looked tired. God damn it, Marsczyk was right: he was losing it. He was losing his grip on the basics, ignoring the fundamentals.

"Okay," he said. "I had Carter do a background check and when he didn't turn up anything, I figured there was nothing there."

"I know you like that Carter kid. I do, too. But let's keep in mind he's a kid."

"You're right." The new drinks arrived. He tossed off the rest of his old one. "I've been looking too much at the suspects and not enough at the victim. Back to square one."

Marsczyk raised his drink in a mock salute. "Makes sense to me."

"Our parents were Communists," Fred Wallace said, "but I don't suppose Russell told you about that."

"No, he didn't," Taylor said.

"Oh, yeah, my dad was big in the Party. He was an old union organizer. Took part in the coal mining wars down in West Virginia in the thirties. Said when he saw sheriffs and deputies, even the National Guard, shooting down unarmed union workers, he knew democracy wasn't going to help these guys. So he joined the Party, tried to take the unions red."

Fred Wallace looked like a man satisfied with his life. A plump man in his forties, he wore wool slacks and a starched white shirt, open at the collar. His tie and sport coat lay draped over one of the two matching easy chairs in his living room. A smoked mirror rose from floor to ceiling, centered over his fireplace. The brass fire tools, neatly racked on the left side of the hearth, looked expensive.

"I take it you didn't follow your father into Party work?" Taylor said.

"I went to a few things with him when I was younger but, I'll tell you, those guys were too intense for me. I like a sense of humor myself. I kind of like to take things easy, you know? These guys, their measure of everything is whether it fits the party line." He flashed Taylor a grin. "You know a lot of reds won't drink anything but vodka?"

"How'd Russell feel about his father's affiliations?"

"Hated it. One time when we were kids, he told me the Communists had taken our father away from us."

"That's a little over the top, isn't it?"

"That's what I thought. Couldn't do anything about it, though. Soon as he got a chance, he quit the bank to start looking under people's beds for Commies."

"He worked at City Bank?"

"I'm a branch manager for City Bank. I got him a job. He didn't like dealing with the public, though."

"I didn't know that. I understood that before he came here, he worked for HUAC."

"Who told you that?"

"The guys who hired him as an investigator."

"Russell never worked for HUAC. Hell, best of my knowledge, he's never even been to Washington. Except for a couple of years when he lived down in Baltimore, he spent every minute of his life here in the city."

"What'd he do in Baltimore?"

"He never talked about that very much. All I know's he came back up here and I got him a job."

Fred Wallace must have been doing pretty good at the bank. He lived in a nice brownstone on Jane Street that seemed to have been professionally decorated. It had that remote and abstract look that said everything had been put together by someone who did not live there. Taylor found it as sterile as an operating room but Fred Wallace appeared to like it.

"Where did your brother live?"

"Next door. I own that house, too. It's divided into apartments."

"I'd like to see where he lived. Would you mind?"

"Sure."

He walked over to the kitchen with a fat man's waddle, even though he was not overweight. Digging in a drawer, he came up with a ring of keys. Taking two off, he said, "It's 4D."

Taylor went to the apartment and began climbing the stairs. He couldn't help wondering why Fred Wallace didn't seem more broken up by his brother's death.

15

The brother didn't put the same amount of care into his rental property that he did his own house. The paint on the door was chipping and once Taylor got inside the building, he found the hallway was dark and musty. It reeked of garlic, along with some other cooking odors that Taylor couldn't identify.

Russell Wallace's apartment was stuffy, the air thick and hot, uncomfortable to breathe. It hadn't been cleaned up after the killer had taken it apart, searching it. It looked like it could have been tossed an hour ago. Drawers had been emptied onto the floor, and the cushions from the chairs and sofa had been slashed open, the stuffing ripped out, dumped onto the floor. Taylor opened a window and stood for a moment, letting the breeze flow over him. Then he checked the bedroom. He didn't think whoever had searched the place had found what they were after. If they had, Taylor assumed, the search would have ended there, but there was no sign that the searcher had stopped before the whole place had been tossed.

He wondered if whatever the searcher had been after was actually in the apartment or not. Shrugging, he told himself there was only one way to find out and began to methodically go over the apartment. The haste it had been searched with made him wonder if it was possible that whoever had done this had overlooked what he was after. There might be a chance. Not a very good one, but still.

He started in the kitchen, ignoring the impulse to wash the dirty dishes piled up in the sink, if only to diminish the nascent smell. The drawers yielded no treasures, the cabinets were mostly empty, containing only a couple of boxes of cereal, which when he looked inside contained nothing.

Taylor was willing to bet that he was searching either for a pile of money or a key to a locker or safe deposit box where money was stored. Wallace had been a blackmailer. That meant he'd be receiving piles of cash—blackmail victims don't write checks—and cash wasn't all that easy to hide. If Wallace had just stuck it in the bank, all kinds of questions would have been raised: a guy who made next to nothing as a red-baiter depositing thousands of dollars? It didn't fit. It would bring too much attention to him.

When Taylor was satisfied there was nothing in the kitchen, he headed for the bedroom. Most people hid their treasures there, in the most intimate room in the house. He followed the destruction, going through everything that was left. Nothing. He was moving the bed back into place when he realized a section of the floor sagged under his weight. If someone else hadn't torn up the apartment before he got there, he'd never have found it. Normally he wouldn't have thought anything about it but in this case Taylor didn't want to take anything for granted. If something was wrong with the floor, he wanted to know it wasn't simply a sign of the house's age.

Stepping back a couple of feet, Taylor walked across the area, verifying the problem area. He paced back and forth until he was certain he had it, then pulled back the carpet and got down on his knees, tapping different places on the floor with his knuckles. A section gave a hollow sound and he felt around the surface, found a purchase for his fingertips and pulled upward. A panel of floor rose. Beneath it, he found a shoe box.

He replaced the floorboard and the carpet, took the box out to the kitchen, sat at the table and opened it. It was filled with money. He counted it: seventy-two thousand dollars.

"Looks like the red hunting business pays pretty good," he told Marsczyk.

"Where's the money now?"

He slid a deposit slip across the desk. "It's in the bank."

"You stole seventy-two thousand dollars and put it in your account?"

Taylor leaned back, folded his arms across his waist. "It's not in my account. It's in a safety deposit box, in the magazine's name."

"Oh, that's much better. You've made us all thieves."

"I made us caretakers. For the rightful owners of the money."

"You figure that's blackmail money?"

"Yeah. I called Bierly. They were paying Wallace fifty bucks a week. No bonuses, no big clumps of money. He couldn't have earned it on the job."

"Okay. We hold it. What's next?"

Across the street, a drunk banged on a tambourine while holding his hat out for donations. The people passing by ignored him, so he broke into a pitiful shuffle. He danced until he lost his balance and had to grab onto a light pole to keep from falling.

"Before he came back here, Wallace was down in Baltimore. His brother said he didn't talk about that time in his life."

"You're thinking maybe a field trip is in order?"

"Why not?"

"Why not indeed?" Marsczyk picked up his phone and barked into it. "Get Paul Carter in here. You know, the copy boy."

Seconds later, Carter burst ointo the office as though he'd been flung by a slingshot. "You want to see me, sir?"

"Find out everything you can about Russell Wallace's time in Baltimore. Search the newspaper files there, the city records, everything you can find. If Wallace was doing it in Baltimore, we want to know what it was."

"Yes, sir. When do you need it?"

"Yesterday."

"Yes, sir. Is that all?"

"That's it."

"I'm on it."

Taylor took a company car down to Baltimore, a manila folder stuffed with Carter's research on the seat next to him. As he drove south, he could sense a relaxation coming over him; it was good to get out of the city. By the time he got to Baltimore, he felt as if he could stay here. If it was good enough for H. L. Mencken, it ought to be good enough for him.

He'd come down to Baltimore to interview Mencken a couple of times, once in his house on Hollins Street and the other time in his office at the *Baltimore Sun*. Even though by that time he'd retired from the paper and was working on the third volume of his memoirs, he still held onto an office at the paper where he'd spent just about his whole career. His work and his talk made Baltimore sound like heaven.

As he drove through it, the place looked idyllic to Taylor. Losing himself permanently in another town was one of his fantasies; every time he went into a place he had not been before, he imagined himself living there. In his mind, whatever place he was fantasizing about was infinitely superior to New York. He saw peaceful, calm people as friendly as southern politicians, with no crowds, no maddening traffic noise, no garbage trucks clammering down the streets banging metal cans around at four in the morning. He longed for that kind of idealized peace.

Until he was in the middle of it. His second night in a different place, he always found his nerves screaming to get back to the city, where things were *real*. He didn't trust the calm. It was, to him, the placid and undisturbed aura of the eye of the hurricane; it gave you a false feeling of safety, masking the dangers that lurked in every direction.

He found a parking place on North Charles Street and took a moment to check out the neighborhood. Johns Hopkins University was two blocks west of here, so students filled the streets, walking quickly with arms filled with books and slide rules hanging from their belts. A coffee shop had set up outdoor tables across the street and a couple of girls sat at one, drinking coffee and reading.

He wondered what it would be like to go to college. It hadn't been in the cards for him. By the time he'd turned fifteen, he was already working on a daily paper and though he loved the work and always had, he couldn't help but wonder what he'd missed by not getting an education. Taylor didn't regret the lack of a diploma. No, what he missed was the lack of formal learning. No matter how hard he worked at educating himself, he couldn't shake the notion that the gaps in his knowledge lacked the right context, that he may have had all the pieces but only an incomplete picture of how they fit. It was possible he'd go someday, he thought, but most of the time he was pretty sure it was never going to happen.

He checked the address in his file and then walked down to number 144, which was a row home with a plain concrete stoop decorated with a stone lion. Like all of the row homes on North Charles, this one had been divided into apartments and the one he wanted was on the third floor. He walked up and knocked on the door.

The woman who answered the door looked as though the daily grind had done her in. She wasn't old—the research said she was thirty—but had he seen her on the street, Taylor would have guessed that she was firmly in her forties. Her hair reminded him of stalks of wheat in a field, her face pale, with wrinkles around her mouth and at the corners of her eyes. She appeared remote and withdrawn. Her housedress was as gray as her personality. She looked at him without curiousity.

"Mrs. Wallace?"

"I haven't been Mrs. Wallace for two years. I took my maiden name back. It's Bloch. Amanda Bloch."

"I'm Damon Taylor, Mrs. Bloch. I'm a reporter for a magazine in New York."

"A reporter?" Although she said it as a question, she did not seem to be all that interested. Taylor's occupation was simply one more piece of information for her to have to process. "What's a reporter want with me?"

"It's about your ex-husband, Mrs. Bloch."

"He's gone and gotten himself in trouble again, hasn't he?"

"Again?"

"It's not the first time, believe me."

"Listen, standing in the doorway talking is a little uncomfortable. I noticed a coffee shop right cross the street. How about I buy you some lunch and we can talk there?"

Her eyes flared and her demeanor came to life for the first time. "I can buy my own lunch."

"Well, I know that. I didn't mean to imply anything. It's just I'm on an expense account so it only makes sense for me to pay."

"An expense account? Your magazine pays for the food?"

"That's right."

She considered that piece of information for a moment. "I'll need to get changed. Wait for me downstairs."

The two students had left so Taylor led Amanda Bloch to their table. She had changed into a flower print dress. It's brightness brought out whatever color was in her complexion. She looked more sprightly now. Her hair was brushed, held back with barrettes, and even though she wore no makeup she appeared younger than she had in her doorway.

"You say this is about Russell? What's he done now? How much trouble is he in?"

"You don't know?"

"Don't know what?" she said.

"Wallace is dead. He was murdered a week ago."

She stopped with her coffee halfway to her mouth. "Murdered?"

The waiter brought their sandwiches. Taylor waited until he left before speaking.

When he did his voice was low, as if saying the words softly would lesson the impact. "He was stabbed to death in New York City."

"Russell was in New York? I thought he was still down in Miami."

"What was he doing down there?"

"I don't know. He went down there after we broke up. If you want to know what he was doing, you'll have to ask Henry Fadden. He's the guy Russ went down there with."

"Got an address for Fadden?"

"Oh, he's back in town now. He called me about a month ago. The bastard actually had the gall to ask me out. What happened to Russ? Was it just one of those freak things?"

"No. Somebody went after him deliberately. Mrs. Bloch, your ex-husband was a blackmailer. It looks like somebody he was targeting did him in."

She nodded thoughtfully. "I'm not surprised. It was bound to happen sooner or later. Russell always thought of himself as some sort of master criminal. Always had some kind of angle working."

"Russell Wallace a master criminal?"

"It does strain credibility, doesn't it? I mean, a tiny little mouse of a man like that? He always said the way he looked was an advantage, though. No one would suspect him until it was too late."

"What kind of crime was he involved with?"

"I don't know. He never told me anything. Said if I didn't know, I couldn't turn him in. He had a hard time trusting me or anybody else."

"Do you have an address for Henry Fadden?"

"He's living in a boarding house down on St. Paul Street. I'll get you the address."

Taylor watched as she took her address book out of her pocketbook, found the entry she was looking for, copied it out on a slip of paper and handed it to him. She was organized, a woman who looked and moved straight ahead, with hardly any use for peripheral vision at all. No need to worry about her—she'd be all right.

"Thanks," he said, as he finished off his sandwich. "Mind if I ask how you've been taking care of yourself since the divorce?"

"I've got the best job I've ever had," she said. "I'm the secretary to the Dean of Humanities at Hopkins." She finished off her coffee. Standing, she said, "I've got to get back. I wish I could say it was pleasant to meet you, but considering the news you brought...."

"You certainly seem to be handling it well."

"Mr. Taylor, if a dog won't stop chasing cars, it's inevitable he's going to get hit by one. My husband got what he was headed for his whole life."

16

"You're looking for Henry Fadden?" the woman said.

She was small, with a hunched over posture that made her appear shorter than she was. The apron she wore had once been white but had faded to an indeterminate color and she darkened it a little more by wiping her hands on it. She looked as if she'd been baking when he came to the door—flecks of white flour decorated the top of her dress.

"Yes, ma'am," Taylor said.

"Well, then, I'd recommend you go look in the graveyard. Henry Fadden went and got himself killed."

"He's dead?"

"Ain't most people that get themselves killed? Of course, he's dead. Murdered. Right out there on the street. Heard the screaming myself."

"What happened?"

The house smelled of cinnamon. Taylor would lay odds she was a fine baker.

"Don't know. I heard a car pull up, heard it hit its brakes, you understand? So I went and peeked outside—I wasn't about to open that door wide that time of night. Anyway, I peeked out and saw somebody pushing him out of the car. He fell in the gutter, rolled over and just lay there, dead as hell. There was blood on the sidewalk for a week."

"You know the names of the cops that worked the case?"

"Why should I know that?"

"Can I use your phone to call the precinct?"

"Get back. You think I'm going to let a stranger in here? For all I know you might be the killer, back to get me. There's a drug store on the corner, got a pay phone in it."

"You Taylor?" the man said. "Ron Byrnes. I caught the Henry Fadden case. You got something I need to know?"

"Maybe. I'm not sure. I know a friend of his got killed in New York last week. I'm wondering if there's any connection."

Byrnes wore a wrinkled brown Robert Hall suit with black shoes and white socks. Lou Marsczyk ought to get a look at him, Taylor thought; if he did, he'd stop giving Taylor a hard time about the way he dressed.

"What's your interest in this, Taylor?"

When he'd called the precinct and located Byrnes, the detective had suggested that they meet at a bar down in Fells Point, which was a working class neighborhood down by the harbor. They were in a boilermaker or a shot and a beer joint, filled with longshoremen who had finished their shift and weren't quite ready to go home yet. It was strangely quiet in there; people gathered and drank but they didn't look to be all that excited about it.

"I work for *Crime Scene*. I'm covering the story."

"*Crime Scene*, huh. Can't tell you how popular your magazine is around the precinct. We all read it and laugh our asses off."

"Sometimes I do, too." Taylor sipped his whiskey and felt lucky that it turned out to really be Jameson. He'd known places like this that would substitute rotgut Irish whiskey for the good stuff. "Look," he said. "What I'm trying to figure out is whether the same person killed both men. Your guy killed by a knife? Maybe get himself gutted?"

"Doc says he was tortured and then slashed from his belly to his ribs, if that's what you mean. Your guy, too?"

"Yeah."

"Who is your guy? He got a Baltimore connection?"

"His name's Russell Wallace. His wife lives up in Charles Village."

"But he was killed in New York."

"Right."

"So my killer's probably in the city."

"He was a week ago."

"I'll get in touch with the New York cops. Who's working the case?"

"Guy named Danny Murphy. At the twelfth precinct."

"Be straight with me. This Murphy guy any good?"

Taylor hesitated. "He closes a lot of cases."

"But he isn't too careful how he does it? I got you. I'll give him a call."

While he wrote up his story Taylor had to put up with Woody Guthrie, who sat with his feet propped on the edge of the desk, softly picking out tunes on his guitar. Other writers drifted over to hear Guthrie, who didn't acknowledge them; he wasn't playing for an audience, just for his own pleasure. If you looked at his face, you couldn't be sure whether he was even aware whether they were in the same room or not.

When he turned in his copy, Marsczyk said, "Got yourself a strolling musician now?"

"Sometimes I wish I could get rid of him."

"Must make the work day go more quickly. Maybe I'll get myself a string quartet to follow me around."

"Thought jazz was more your style."

He shook his head. "Wouldn't get any work done with a jazz band playing."

When he left Marsczyk's office, Guthrie stood up and said, "Tell you what, son. Buy me a beer and a sandwich and I got a story for you."

They went to Big John's's, a cop bar in the neighborhood. As they walked inside, Guthrie absorbed the atmosphere and said, "Nice. I could make me some money in here." He pointed to the back of the room, where the lunch table was set up. "Is that roast beef I see back there? How 'bout you get the beer, I'll make the sandwiches."

After he'd eaten, Guthrie appeared ready for a nap. He yawned and sipped his beer, elbows resting on the bar, face propped on his left hand. He was almost always in motion, nervous energy causing him to rush here and there, talking incessantly, and when he sat, he wasn't still. His right leg would vibrate like a piston engine. Now, though, he looked like he was almost asleep with his eyes open.

"You seem tired."

"Never could get a night's sleep in a jail cell."

"You been in jail?"

"That guy Murphy tossed Will Geer and me in the jug. Said he was booking us for killing that Wallace guy. It was strange, man." His voice drifted off. "I mean, I been in the can before, but this? This was something different."

He'd been working a hootenanny with the Almanac Singers out in Brooklyn—he and Pete Seeger, Lee Hayes, Sonny Terry and Brownie McGhee—and the night was going fine, he said. The crowd liked them, beating on the tables and cheering while they sang and it was a good night, despite the fact that Pete was unhappy because the union guys in the room liked everything they did except the union songs.

"I keep telling Pete that singing those union rally songs is a big giant Mother–May–I step into yesterday, but he keeps on insisting the battle ain't over and we got to keep it up till we've won. So I tell him maybe the battle ain't won yet, but it sure as hell done reached the point where it bores the hell out of everybody."

"Pete won't listen, huh?"

"I'm telling you, Damon, it's like the Hundred Years' War: at first everybody was all puffed up, all full of it, excited about the battles and ready to march through the bogs and win one for whoever the hell the was king that year. After year eighty-six or so, you got to expect the enthusiasm to wane just a touch."

"I know what you mean."

They'd been arguing the point when Murphy and his two goons had barreled into the hall, ordered them off the stage and placed Guthrie under arrest. Pete had been about to whack one of the goons in the head with his banjo but Guthrie signaled him not to. When Will Geer, who'd come along to help out with the show, demanded to know why Murphy was taking Guthrie in, Murphy arrested him, too.

As the cops dragged the duo out, Guthrie called out, "Pete, keep the show going."

Seeger climbed back onto the rickety stage and sang "Solidarity Forever" as the cops took them through the front door.

Once they'd got over to Murphy's Manhattan precinct, the detective shoved Guthrie into an examination room, complete with a one way mirror on the wall and began throwing questions at him as fast as the Dodgers' starting pitchers. All Guthrie would say is, "I want a lawyer." Every time he said it, he'd wave at the people behind the one-way mirror.

"Why? You guilty?"

"I'm just a country boy. I can't keep up with you big city cops. I need me a lawyer to help me out." He waved at the mirror again.

"Cut that out. What the hell you waving at the mirror for?"

"I ain't waving at the mirror. I'm saying hello to the people on the other side of the damn thing."

"Look, Guthrie, we both know you killed Wallace. It's time you told the truth. You cooperate with me and we'll go easy on you. You don't want to die over this thing, do you?"

"What's the matter with you?" Guthrie said. "You don't like my songs or something? Maybe the way I sing? You know damn well I didn't kill nobody."

"Your buddy Will Geer's over in the other room talking his head off.

He says you did it."

"Will Geer was on Broadway doing a matinee when it happened. He saw anything, it's the biggest miracle since Jesus Christ."

It went on like that for another two hours. Then Murphy got frustrated and threw Guthrie in a cell for forty-eight hours. As the uniformed cops led him out of the examination room to the holding cell, Murphy said, "Don't forget, Guthrie, I can throw you in the tank without charging you any time I want to."

"You know," Guthrie said, "there's been times I was praying for somebody to lock me up for two nights, just so I could get myself some indoor sleep."

They had let him out this morning, telling him he was still a suspect and to stay available.

"At least they didn't say don't leave town," Guthrie said.

"So, you just got out of jail and came straight here?"

Guthrie flashed him what was supposed to be an innocent boyish grin. "Yep. Had to see my old friend Damon Taylor."

"What's really on your mind, Woody? What is it you need?"

"Can't fool you, Damon. I need two things: breakfast—can't tell you how hungry I am—and I need you to go out to Coney Island with me."

"What for?"

"How 'bout I tell you over breakfast?"

17

Kristen Eldredge was walking Broadway to 14th Street. When she hit 14th, she turned right, walked halfway down the block to a house on the south side of the street, trotted up the stairs to the boxes and pushed buzzers until someone let her in.

Some security, she thought. No matter how expensive the building, no matter how much stealable stuff was inside, someone always buzzed you in without making you identify yourself.

Roy Warren lived on the third floor. The tall woman climbed quickly up the steps and knocked on his door. She supposed she might feel bad about what she was going to do, and at one time she would have, but these days it was way too late for any kind of feelings. It was too late for her soul now; all the killing had driven it out of her. When she'd shot the first armored car guy, she'd felt whatever was still good and decent in her fly away, leaving her empty. At first she'd mourned what she lost but three years in prison had finished emptying her out. Now she realized that it didn't make any difference any more what she did; she could kill a man or burn down a city. Her preachy father would have said it was too late to save her immortal soul so if that were true, why worry about it?

When he opened the door, Warren was smiling but when he saw Kristen standing in his doorway, she could see the recognition flare in his eyes and his face contort in fear. As he backed up a step, he licked his lips and blinked uncontrollably.

"Roy, you act like you weren't expecting me."

"Kristen, I didn't have anything to do with it. Really. It was Wallace and the rest."

She walked into the apartment as if it were her own. Warren backed away from her as she approached. The apartment was small, a studio. The bed was a convertible couch and though it was four in the afternoon, it hadn't been made up and closed.

"Who did what doesn't make any difference."

"It doesn't?"

"We all go too far back together to worry about stuff like that, don't we?"

"It's good you feel that way, Kristen."

"The money, though, that makes a difference." She closed the door behind her. "Where is it, Roy?"

"I swear to God, I don't know."

The apartment was very quiet. Since his unit was in the back of the building, she couldn't even hear traffic noises. That was good. She swore to God, with all the non-stop noise, how could anybody live in this cesspool of a city? Jesus, she just wanted to finish this crap up and get out of here.

"You really don't know?"

"No. I swear it."

"You know, I can't tell you how much I hate hearing you say that."

"Kristen...."

Before he could continue she cut him off. "I hate to hear you say it because both

Fadden and Wallace told me that you had it."

"I did. I did have it, Kristen, all of it. I was holding it just like we said, but somebody stole it from me. That's the truth, I swear."

"That's the truth, huh?"

"Yeah. Really."

"You're telling me the solid truth. No lies?"

"I wouldn't lie to you."

"That wouldn't be very smart, would it?"

"Lord no, Kristen. I swear, I'd never lie to you."

Oh, God, she couldn't help but smile. Seeing him squirm was so delicious. What was even better was seeing him relax as he misinterpreted her smile.

She pulled out the knife. "Since you'd never lie to me, you won't mind if I verify what you're telling me."

Taylor sipped coffee as Guthrie polished off half a grapefruit, a double order of bacon, both scrambled and fried eggs, a side of sausage and half a dozen biscuits. When he was finished, he piled up his plates, sat back and lit a cigarette.

"Ain't nothing like a couple of nights in the jug to build up an appetite."

The automat was quiet. The breakfast crowd was gone and the lunch customers wouldn't be in for another hour or so. Right now, a room as big as a union hall had maybe a dozen people scattered throughout. Most of them looked as though they had nowhere else to be. Three tables over a man who badly needed to have his suit pressed circled want ads in the *Times*.

"You said you'd tell me why you need me to go out to Coney Island with you."

"It's real important, Damon. You're the only one that can save me."

"How am I going to do that? Hold you in on the roller coaster?"

"We ain't going to the park. I live out there. Got me a house on Mermaid Avenue. That's where we're headed."

"You got a house?"

"Yep. And you know what's waiting for me in it? A really pissed-off wife."

"You're just one surprise after another, aren't you? I heard you were married but it didn't fit. You're the last person I can picture with a wife."

"Well, I got me one. Hell, man, I been married to more girls than most people have dated. This time it's the real thing, though. Marjorie's the sweetest girl you ever saw. Smartest, too. She's a dancer. Ballet. A good one. Had a good career going. Now she teaches, so she can stay close to home with the kids." He stubbed out his cigarette, looked around and refusing to meet Taylor's eyes, finished his coffee. "I'm telling you, Damon, that woman deserves so much more than I'm giving her…."

"Give her the rest, then. Give her what she deserves."

"Well, I try. But it ain't that easy. I'm a musician, man, a folksinger, for Christ's sake. Ain't a whole lot of money there to begin with and I got to scramble to bring in what little I can."

"Woody, I watched you throw away seventy-five dollars a week."

"I know that, but I got to think about my integrity, too. If I ain't true to my beliefs, I can't be true to nothing."

"Like you're true to your wife?"

He hesitated, tapping his coffee cup with his fingertips. He rolled another cigarette, lit it up and blew smoke toward the ceiling. His eyes still on the ceiling, he took a deep breath.

"Reckon that depends on what you mean by 'true.' Maybe I ain't always been what you'd call faithful but I never been nothing but true. Here's the way it is: I'm always true in my heart." Now he looked at Taylor, his eyes pleading. "What you got to understand, Damon, is I always go home. Sometimes it might be six in the morning, but I do go home. Marjorie knows she can depend on that. If I'm in town, I go home. Now I been gone two nights without even telling her where I am. That woman's going to kill me, Damon. You got to go with me, tell her I been in jail and couldn't get word to her. She'll believe you, considering you're covering the case for that magazine of yours."

"Woody, if you're always true to her and you always go home, then you two have a way of understanding each other. You don't need me." Taylor almost wanted to laugh at his friend's discomfort.

"She'll think I'm making it up. You have to tell her the truth."

"Why me? Why's she going to believe me?"

Guthrie shook his head and banged his fist on the table. "Because you're respectable, damn it. Hell, you're the only respectable person I know. I ran through the entire list of my friends and I couldn't find a one that Marjorie wouldn't think was lying to her to protect me. Damn it, Damon, you're the only person I know that's even got a job. You're the only one that anybody'd look up to, you know what I mean?"

Taylor felt helpless; there was no way he could turn Guthrie down: the man was just too pathetic. "All right," he said, smiling. "Let's get it done."

"Thanks, Damon. Can't tell you how much I appreciate it."

As they headed for the subway, neither of them noticed the two men, one on either side of the street, following along behind them.

Guthrie's wife sat on the front porch of their Mermaid Avenue house, nursing a baby. She was a striking woman, with a strong face and hard-wrapped curly hair, wearing a peasant skirt and a fringed top. She looked ready to take the stage in a gypsy-themed ballet. She watched them approach the house and, as she studied Woody, an expression that Taylor found hard to label came over her face. It looked to him like resigned affection, as though she had been angry with Guthrie so many times over the years that she no longer felt the need to get worked up about it. Now she could work her way straight through to forgiveness, even though she still carried her own sadness.

"Two whole days, Woody," she said. "Don't you think that's pushing it a little?"

Guthrie took off his cap, held it in front of his chest. "Well now, Marjorie, I know you're going to find this a touch hard to believe, but this time it ain't my fault."

She removed the baby from her breast, laid it over her shoulder and patted his back. "You got that right. I *do* find it hard to believe."

"Damon here'll tell you. Tell her, Damon."

"Now you're bringing home strangers to back up your stories?"

The baby burped, so she took him down and held him in her lap. To Taylor the infant looked to be about six months old. As he lay in his mother's lap, he played with her fingers. Taylor watched and an odd sensation spread through him, a feeling he couldn't quite identify.

"How's little Arlo?" Woody said.

"He's fine. Now, how come you're bringing home strangers to get you out of trouble?"

"'Cause I knew you weren't going to believe me. If I was you and somebody come home and told you what this guy's going to tell you, I'd have a hard time taking it serious, too. And he ain't a stranger. This here's Damon Taylor. You've heard me talk about him."

"The reporter."

"That's right. Damon here, he'll tell you what happened to me. Tell her, Damon."

"He's been in jail, Mrs. Guthrie, and not for anything he did. The detective on the Russell Wallace case sees your husband as his prime suspect, so he pulled him in, grilled him and kept him for forty-eight hours."

"That's the truth, darlin'."

Marjorie Guthrie shook her head as though this story was exactly what she had expected. Then she stood. "Come on in. I'll put on some coffee."

As he sat at the rickety kitchen table sipping a cup of coffee, Taylor thought about what a strange couple Woody and Marjorie made: the Oklahoma drifter and the city-bred ballet dancer. He asked her how they met.

"How'd I meet this guy?" Marjorie said. "I was dancing with Martha Graham's troupe when I heard Woody's album *Dust Bowl Ballads*, and I figured the songs would make a great modern dance routine. So I began adapting them and as a part of that process, I met the guy that wrote and sung them—back then he had a radio show that he hadn't walked away from yet. I guess by now you've figured out that every time he gets close to being successful, he has to find a way to screw it up." She said it without emotion, as if it were just one more fact about Guthrie, like his birthday. "Anyway, I really messed up by going and falling in love with this cowboy and as soon as he got his first furlough from the Army, we got married."

Taylor turned to Guthrie. "You were in the Army?"

"That's the United States Army," Guthrie said in his deadpan voice. "I was on our side."

"Funny, I just can't picture you in uniform."

"Neither could the Army. I'll tell you, when it started going crazy over in Europe, the Almanac Singers, well, we were great followers of Henry Wallace, the peace candidate, and we were determined to do everything we could to keep the country out of the war. We made us an album of anti-war songs and went all over the country playing and singing 'em and then the Japs went and bombed Pearl Harbor. I remember walking into the office and saying to Pete, 'Well, I reckon we won't be singing any more anti-war songs for a while.' Then me and Cisco Houston—you know Cisco? No? Well, you should. He's a great guy. Anyway, me and Cisco went down and joined the Merchant Marine and started us a career of having ships shot out from under us by German submarines. After a while they read my enlistment papers and discovered I leaned a little too much to the left for 'em and threw me out. Well, evidently, the Army didn't care as much about my left-wing ways as the Merchant Marine did 'cause they drafted the hell out of me and like Marjorie says, we got ourselves married up when I was home on leave."

After Marjorie put the baby down for a nap, she went over and sat on Guthrie's lap. Taylor felt a pang shoot through him when he saw the affection they shared. As they leaned into each other, he felt as though he were disappearing, as if he wasn't even in the house anymore. Since there was no real demand for his presence he let himself out and headed back to the city.

18

Taylor got back to Manhattan at dusk. Instead of transferring to an uptown train to go home, he got off at the 42nd Street and Fifth Avenue station and strolled over to Broadway, figuring he'd grab a little dinner while he thought through the story. It was getting complicated, turning out not to be the story he'd anticipated. That was fine—he really loved it when a story grew and changed while he was in the middle of it—but he was still in that place when nothing about the story made sense. He had to find the handle, something he could use to pry this thing open, and see what was really inside.

Jack Dempsey's Restaurant was across the street and they served a great steak dinner, but he wasn't in the mood for a huge hunk of meat. Next to Dempsey's was the Turf, another steak house. He rejected it also. Longchamps was a couple of blocks up. He decided to go there. Since the owner of Longchamps, a nine restaurant chain, had gone to prison last year for siphoning off profits and not paying the ten million dollars of taxes that was due on them, the guys who owned the Exchange Buffet had bought the place and now it was even better.

Hungry now, he walked a little more quickly, but came to a sudden stop when he saw three men approaching him. They could not have been more obvious if they'd been wearing saddle signs that read HERE TO BEAT UP DAMON TAYLOR. One of them was even pounding his fist into his palm. Turning, he saw two more behind him. He had only two choices: fight or run.

Breaking for the curb, he began to move, but one of the thugs, a big guy with slicked back black hair, jumped in front of him and threw a punch at his face. Taylor slid the punch, which grazed his jaw, and slammed one of his own into the thug's belly. It was like hitting a concrete wall.

"Get off the Wallace case, Taylor," the gangster said and hit him hard in the stomach. As Taylor folded, the man landed a right on his eye. Taylor's head grew fuzzy, his vision blurry.

Then the others were on him. He swung wildly, trying to connect with whatever flesh and bone was in front of him until someone pinned his arms and the big guy began hitting Taylor in the face, alternating rights and lefts. After the third punch, it didn't hurt anymore. He felt himself fading.

As his attacker drew back to hit him again, Taylor saw a hand close around the big man's forearm, jerk him to and a fist slam into his ribs and again into his face. The man staggered backward and fell to the ground. The other hoods let go of Taylor, who sagged to his knees, and went after the new guy, who, methodically and systematically, with a big smile on his face, beat them all senseless.

Two of the thugs ran and made it away but the other three were collapsed on the sidewalk. Using an outstretched hand for support, Taylor pulled himself to his feet.

"You all right?" Zero Mostel said to him. Mostel's eyes were huge, bulging much more than usual.

"You did this?" Taylor indicated the mass of bodies at his feet.

"Oh, hell, no," Mostel said. "I was coming out of Dempsey's place and saw those guys jump you, so I ran back inside and got Jack. He's the one that helped you."

Jack Dempsey stepped forward. He was a stocky man with a shock of black hair and muscles the size of Cadillacs. He grinned. "Hey, Damon, you all right?"

"I think so. Hurts like hell but I don't think anything's broken."

The cops arrived. Dempsey did the talking, signed autographs for each of them and came back over to Taylor. The cops saw the thugs loaded into the the ambulance they'd called and drove off, the convoy headed to the hospital.

"You're bleeding, Damon, come on over to the restaurant and we'll get you fixed up."

"That will be one hell of a black eye in the morning but nothing's broken," Dempsey said. He applied a bandage to the right side of Taylor's forehead and rubbed the ridge of Taylor's right eye lightly. "Man, I got to tell you, I haven't had that much fun in years."

"Glad I could help you out," Taylor said.

Turning to Mostel, Dempsey said, "Zee, go out and get Taylor a drink. You want anything in particular, Damon?"

"Jameson. On the rocks."

"Sounds good. Get three of them, Zee. Doubles." As Mostel left the office, he said, "Never could drink when I was fighting. Now I like a taste very once in a while."

The pain was coming in strong now. Taylor inhaled sharply as a wave of agony shot through his ribs. Dempsey had checked them, assured him that none were broken and wrapped them. "You're okay there," he said. "I know about bruised ribs from the old days. I know when one's broken, too."

"I guess you do. You broke enough of them."

Mostel came back with the drinks. He spread them around and Dempsey said, "Pour that down, Damon. That'll do it."

Dempsey grinned. It reminded Taylor of a little kid who'd just gotten a present. "Oh, lord, Damon, that was so much fun. Man, I can't tell you how long it's been since I've been able to mix it up like that. Wow. We did a job on those boys, didn't we?"

"Well, you and Zee did. Me, I just got the hell beat out of me." He took a sip of his drink, felt the burning liquor ease down his throat. It struck him as just the medicine he needed, and he took another big sip. "No telling how far those guys would have gone. Thanks for helping me."

"For a friend of Damon Runyon's, anything. I ever tell you, Zee? Damon turned me into a contender. First time I ever came to this town, back in 1915, nobody had any idea who I was. I'd been knocking around out west, fighting people for nickels, you know? Finally got a fight here in town and Damon wrote the first big story on me, made me look like a champ. People looked at me different after Runyon wrote about me. That guy was the best sports writer I ever saw and not just because he wrote about me."

"I know. He was."

"So if Damon Runyon's old friend is in trouble, I'm going to be there. You can count on that."

"Fact is, Jack, since you put those guys in the hospital, I don't think they'll be giving me any more trouble."

"Anybody does, you just pick up the phone, buddy. I'll be there."

The doorman at Dempsey's flagged down a cab for him and Taylor climbed into the back seat and gave the driver his address. As he settled into the cushion, the pain in his face and ribs swelled, rising like a temperature. He was having trouble breathing and for a moment he thought he was going to pass out. Taylor felt a sadness the size of the Bronx sweep over him: he'd been beaten senseless and was on his way home, by himself, to an empty apartment. That wouldn't do. When he felt under control again, Taylor placed a hand on the driver's shoulder.

"Never mind that 93rd Street address. Head downtown. 356 Fifth

Avenue."

As they cruised downtown he breathed shallowly, rhythmically, in order to relax, maybe keep the pain under control. When they arrived, he paid the driver, got out and staggered up to the door, ringing Terry Louvin's bell.

When she asked who was there, he said, "Damon Taylor. Sorry it's so late. Can I come up?"

"You sound strange, Damon. Are you all right?"

"Not really, no. Can I come up?"

She buzzed him in. He walked down the hall past the studio to the stairs and slowly climbed up to the third floor and knocked on Terry's door. She stood in the doorway, blocking his entrance, her expression suspicious and quizzical. When she saw his face, she inhaled sharply.

"My God, Damon, what happened to you?"

"It's all right," he said, but a fresh wave of pain racked him and he continued, "No, no, it's not all right. Can I come in?"

"Sure," she said, stepping back, giving him room.

She gripped him by the elbow, supporting him as she half-led him to the couch, where he collapsed as he was trying to sit down. His face tightened and he gasped as fresh pain shot through his ribcage. Terry Louvin hovered over him, hands out, and she appeared helpless, wanting to help but unable to figure out what she should do. Finally, the tension drained out of his face and she exhaled slowly.

"What happened, Damon?"

"A bunch of guys jumped me. God knows what would have happened if Jack Dempsey hadn't come along."

"Jack Dempsey? The boxer? He helped you?"

"Yeah."

"Too bad he couldn't show up five minutes earlier," she said. "Let me get you some aspirin."

"And some whiskey."

"I've got some of that Jameson left you brought over."

He nodded.

When she came back, he wolfed down the aspirin and took a long sip of the whiskey. Being here, seeing her before him, he began to relax. The pain by now had stopped stabbing, becoming simply a dull throbbing. He leaned his head against the back of the couch, his head nodding. Now that he was off the streets, he was suddenly very tired.

"I didn't know where else to go," he said. "I started to go home but I couldn't. I didn't want to be alone. I hope you don't mind."

She patted the back of his hand. "It's fine. You'll sleep here tonight."

"What about—"

"Oh, he's in his bed. We won't wake him."

"Thanks."

The last thing he was aware of before he dozed off was her hand on his.

19

"I'm close to arresting your friend Guthrie," Danny Murphy said. "For real, this time."

"He didn't kill Wallace, you know that."

"All I know is he's got motive and opportunity. Means, too. It ain't hard to lose a knife on 42nd Street, you know. Add to that the fact that two dozen people saw them arguing in the street right before the murder, well, that makes it pretty solid to me."

Taylor's ribs ached. He shifted in the chair, trying to find a position that eased the pain, but it was impossible. It was dark here in the precinct house; Murphy's desk was over in a corner, thirty feet from the nearest overhead light. There was a lamp on his desk but it wasn't lit. Evidently, Taylor thought, he prefered the dark, like a bat.

Murphy had called Taylor at the office and told him to drop by, said he had a couple of questions for him. At this point, Taylor had a few of his own, so he hopped a cab over to the precinct.

"You and me, we've had a few arguments in public," Taylor said, "but neither of us ever tried to kill the other."

"I maybe thought about it from time to time," Murphy said. "Look, I'm building a case against your guy and he's beginning to look as bad as your eye."

"What have you got?" Taylor took his pad and pen out.

"Never mind what I got. All I'm going to say is it's looking good. I'll have your guy before he can get over last night's hangover." He leaned back in his chair, tapping his fingertips on the blotter on his desktop as he studied Taylor's face. "I don't know how you can defend him. Look what he did to you."

"What are you talking about?"

"Last night you got the hell beat out of you after dropping Guthrie off at his house. You ever stop and wonder how those guys knew where you were going to be?"

"You getting at what I think you are?"

"Your buddy set you up, Taylor. He gets you to venture out where his boys can pick you up, they follow you back to the city and beat the living hell out of you."

The pain in his ribs grew more intense; it seemed to come in waves. He needed some aspirin. If he ever got out of here he'd stop at a drug store, pick up a pack. In the meantime, he tried to look as though everything was fine; some weird pride made him not want to show Murphy how badly he was hurting.

"It doesn't make sense, Murphy. If they picked me up in Coney Island, why would they follow me all the way back to Midtown Manhattan before they made a move?"

"'Cause if they hit you out there, it'd be real obvious who set you up for the beating. No, your boy did it, all right. That pain in your ribs you trying so hard to cover up. Well, that's a gift from your new best friend, Guthrie. Why don't you get wise and tell me what you know about him? Help me out a little."

"You think there's a chance I'm going to help you build a case against an innocent man?"

"I want to know what you've got. I want to know if he gave you anything that relates to motive and I want to know where that knife is."

"Okay, I'll give you something. A guy named Henry Fadden was sliced and diced just like Wallace down in Baltimore a while back. He and Wallace were doing crime down in Miami together. Guthrie's never been to Baltimore."

"Never been to Baltimore? A wandering folksinger's never been to a major city just down the road from where he lives? You fucking amaze me, Taylor. You're supposed to be the big time crime reporter and you let him take you in like that?"

"He didn't do it, Murphy. This case is bigger than you think it is. It's more complicated and people aren't dying for the reasons you think they are. Guthrie wouldn't kill anybody to keep the fact that he's a red secret. He's proud of it. Just ask him, he'll tell you he's a Communist. He's pissed off because the Communist Party won't let him join up."

"Then he did it in a fit of rage."

Taylor stood. "Are we done here?"

Murphy waved him off as though he were a fly hovering over a stack of pancakes. "Yeah, we're done. Get the hell out of here, Taylor."

Taylor walked down 42nd Street. He crossed to the other side, walking all the way to Hector's Cafeteria. It was early afternoon and the street was relatively quiet; the tourists wouldn't be along till evening. As he'd hoped, Herbert Huncke was already out on the street, leaning against the wall of Hector's watching the street traffic, looking for a score. He was ready to move.

He saw Taylor coming and smiled. Huncke's smile was not a pretty sight; his face was pitted with acne scars and when his lips curled upward into a grin, the scars were accented, thrown into sharper relief.

"Damon, how you doin', man?" Huncke said.

"Not bad."

"For a guy that ain't doing bad, you look terrible." He studied Taylor's face. "You look like somebody's been tap dancing on your face."

"I had a run-in with some guys," Taylor said.

"So I see."

"I need a favor, Herb."

"Name it."

"I need a pistol."

"Any type in particular?"

"I like a .45 caliber automatic. It's what I used in the Army."

"You the only guy in the Army that didn't bring home a souvenir?"

"Had a little incident last summer. Cops confiscated it."

"Ain't that the way it goes?" Huncke nodded sympathetically. "Seventy-five dollars ought to get what you need."

"Remember, Herb, for seventy-five bucks, I'm looking for first rate. The gun's got to be in good shape, with at least a box of ammo, maybe three extra mags."

"I'll get you the best that's out there, Damon, you know that."

He passed Huncke four twenties, which Huncke slid into his front pocket without counting.

"I mean it, Herb. I'm not paying for junk."

Huncke looked down at the sidewalk, shaking his head slowly from side to side. "Damon," he said in a soft voice, "have I ever let you down? Have I ever once brought you shoddy goods?"

"This is important, Herb."

"I know it's important. I can tell that from your face. Meet me here tonight, around ten. And Damon?"

"Yeah?"

"Don't do anything stupid, man."

20

"So, let me see how this works out," the tall woman said. "I ask you to discourage a man and the guys you send wind up getting the shit beat out of them by Jack Dempsey? Three of them go to the hospital? Good thing I didn't send you after two guys. We'd wind up with a severe shortage of thugs in this city, wouldn't we?"

Sheridan squirmed in his chair. If the woman hadn't been eating a plate full of pork chops, he would have been able to stand up under whatever bitching she was going to do. He understood that if somebody bought a job, they had a right to bitch if it didn't turn out the way it was supposed to. But if the customer who was doing the complaining was dripping grease all over her chin and onto the white cloth napkin she had tucked into her collar, well, that was something different altogether. He'd never thought of eating as an act of aggression against another person, but that's exactly what was going on here. He swallowed, licked his lips nervously.

"Okay, so it didn't work out. Listen, my boys messed him up pretty good. At least he won't be in such a hurry to press on with this thing."

They were in Leon and Eddie's, a nightclub Sheridan knew from Prohibition days, on West 52nd Street. He normally enjoyed it here; the place jumped, with four floor shows a night, starting at eight o'-clock—about an hour from now—and with dancing between shows. The liquor wasn't expensive, the food was good and plentiful, and the rowdy crowd was out for a good time. Right now, though, being in here with this woman made him really nervous.

"You haven't done a damn thing to discourage him. I know how guys like Taylor think. All you've done is piss him off. Look, there's a lot of money at stake here and as far as you're concerned, it's even more than that. Your reputation is on the line. So what I want to know from you is this: what do you intend to do next?"

"I intend to finish the job."

The woman brushed him aside the same way she would a fly. "Then go do it."

After he saw Huncke, Taylor headed back to the office. Sitting at his desk with a cup of coffee, he made a few notes and then wrote a draft of his second Russell Wallace story. His slant was the obvious one for the magazine: the police were about as likely to solve this murder as an elephant was to float in the air like a helium balloon. While they were chasing the wrong suspect because they were working from an incorrect narrative of the crime, the real murderer was walking free and was likely to strike again.

He covered Wallace's activities in Miami and Baltimore and pointed to the fact that one of his partners in crime had been murdered in exactly the same way Wallace himself was killed. Maybe, he wrote, Wallace's death was related to the fact that he'd had a falling out with his gang. Then he crossed out the word 'maybe' and substituted 'most likely.' After describing the condition Wallace's apartment had been in when he'd gone there, torn apart during a search, he speculated that Wallace had possession of something that at least one of his old partners wanted.

He stopped there and re-read what he'd written. It was pretty solid but needed cutting. As usual, when he didn't know quite where he was going with a piece, he'd overwritten it, becoming repetitious, making the same point two or three times. He picked up a blue pencil then put it down, refilled his coffee and reached for the telephone. Before he could pick it up, it rang.

"*Crime Scene*," he said.

"Damon, is that you?"

"Terry," he said. "I was just going to call you."

"You were?"

"I wanted to thank you for taking care of me last night. I appreciate what you did for me."

"Don't worry yourself about it. I was glad to help out. How are you feeling?"

"Much better."

"Good. Listen, the reason I called is the most amazing thing just happened."

"What's that?"

"The people who own the dance studio? Their lawyer called, asked if I wanted to buy it. They're moving to Europe and want to sell."

He smiled. "Well, now, you're right. That is amazing."

"You know, the studio is doing amazingly well. It's making money like you wouldn't believe. And what's even better, they own the whole house and want to sell everything." The excitement caused her voice to break. "I'll own the school, my apartment and the two apartments upstairs. I've been working the figures and I think between what the school's making and the rent on the apartments, I can make this happen. It'll be mine, Damon! I won't just be managing the place for some absentee owners. I'll really have a future." She appeared to run out of breath and stopped talking for a second.

"You're right. That is amazing. I'm really happy for you."

"I never dreamed something like this would happen. It's all too much, you know what I mean?"

"You deserve it, Terry. You've worked hard for you and your little boy."

"Thanks. The only problem is I'll have to come up with a down payment. I don't know how much. I'm going to meet with the lawyer and he'll tell me, but I'm not sure if I can raise it."

"Don't worry about it. I'll lend it to you."

"I couldn't borrow money from you again. It took me forever to pay you back last time."

"It was only three months."

She laughed. "Well, it felt like forever."

"And the crucial thing is you *did* pay it back. I don't have any hesitation about lending to you again."

"Look, last time I was desperate. That's the only reason I took it. This isn't desperation, this is a business opportunity. I'll talk to the lawyer. Who knows, maybe I've got enough."

"Who's the lawyer? What's his name?"

"Let me see. I've got it written down. Oh, here it is. He name is Leo Salmon. Do you know him?"

Despite himself, a grin spread over Taylor's face. It hurt a little. "I've heard the name."

After he finished the conversation with Terry, he called Leo Salmon. When Salmon picked up, he said, "Leo? It's Damon Taylor."

"Well, now, I expected you'd be calling. How are you?"

"I'm good. And you?"

"Damon, I detest talking over the phone. Are you in your office?" When Taylor told him he was, Salmon continued, "I'm going to come over and pick you up, all right? Wait right there. Fifteen minutes."

"Good enough."

When Taylor climbed into the back seat of the 1948 Cadillac next to Salmon, the lawyer reached out to shake hands with him. As he gripped Taylor's hand, he scanned him quickly and frowned as if he weren't quite happy with what he saw.

"You look like hell, Damon. With that eye, you look like a Dalmatian."

"Somebody doesn't want me working the story I'm doing."

"And they think beating you up will stop you? Some people never learn, do they?"

"It just means I'm getting somewhere."

"Samuel," he called out to the driver, "head uptown to Roger Basile's place, will you?"

"Yes, sir."

"I don't know Samuel," Taylor said. "What happened to Joe Levinson?"

"I promoted him. He's got a head with figures, so he's looking after my money now. Speaking of which, you made me a bundle on that *Finian's Rainbow* investment you recommended. It paid off big time. Thanks."

"You're welcome."

"Got any more Broadway tips?"

"*Guys and Dolls.* It's a musical, based on a couple of Damon Runyon's stories."

"I haven't heard of it."

"It's in the script stage right now. Jo Swerling wrote a script but they threw it out. Abe Burrows is doing the rewrite. Frank Loesser is doing the songs."

"Throwing out the script and starting from scratch doesn't sound very promising."

"I've seen both of the scripts. Swerling didn't have a feel for Runyon's work. They were right to toss it. Burrows has got a handle on it. It's going to be big."

"I'll look into it. How far away is it from opening?"

"At least a year. They're looking for up front money. Get in now, you can get a great deal. Look, tell me about Terry Louvin."

As they car pulled to a stop in front of a shop on Columbus Avenue, Salmon said, "Damon, you and me, we made a deal about the Louvin woman. You've got to admit that so far I've lived up to our agreement. Now, I'm finishing it off, like I said I would. Come on in here a minute."

Taylor followed him into the building. Inside, in the dim light, he saw rolls of fabric, a dressmaker's dummy and a large work table covered with scraps of fabric, scissors and tape measures. A large sewing machine sat at one end of the table. A short, energetic man with a bushy mustache came around the table, his hand out.

"Mr. Salmon," he said, pumping the man's hand, "good to see you again."

"Thanks, Roger. Good to see you, too. This is my friend, Damon Taylor. I want you to take care of him."

"For a friend of yours," Roger Basile said, "anything. Anything at all." He fingered Taylor's suit gingerly, as if he were handling an explosive. "We'll fix him up. You want to move him up in quality, I assume?"

"What's going on?" Taylor said. "Leo, what are you up to?"

Salmon smiled. "Damon, you're an embarrassment. I can't stand to look at you, wearing those crappy suits. They're worn out, they bag in the knees. Hell, man, they never fit you to begin with, even when they were new. I owe you and I'm paying you back by making you look like a human being." He turned to Roger Basile. "Measure him, Roger."

"I can't let you do this."

"You can't stop me," he said with a smile that really wasn't all that friendly. "I'm a man that's used to getting his way, Damon."

"So am I."

Salmon softened. "Okay, look, I know how you feel but this is important to me. You have to let me do this for you."

The whole time they were talking, Basile had been measuring away, calling out numbers to his assistant who wrote them down. When he had everything he needed, he backed off, studying Taylor's build. He walked around him, checking him out from the back also.

When he'd first made a deal with Salmon, Taylor had known he was stepping over a line but had thought he could negotiate it. Now Salmon had begun referring to him as a friend and that bothered Taylor; a reporter shouldn't be friends with the people he was covering, especially when the people he was covering were gangsters.

"You can't make me wear the suit."

Salmon laughed.

"What's so funny?"

"When you see the suit, you can't help but wear it. This man is a master."

Roger Basile beamed.

"When did you become a mortage banker?" Taylor asked.

They were back in the car, heading downtown again. Salmon leaned forward and said, "Samuel, drop us off at P. J. Clarke's, will you?" Then he turned to Taylor. "It's the simplest way to handle the transaction with the Louvin girl. Incidently, you were right about her. Just from talking to her on the phone, I can tell she's the real thing. It feels good to be able to help her."

"Good."

"What's the story with you and her?"

"She's a friend, that's all."

"You take care of all your friends this way?"

"You know what was happening to her. She was on the verge of going down hard and it wasn't her fault. I saw a way to help her and a way to keep Costello's niece away from the gas chamber at the same time and both of those things needed doing. Given the situation, what did you expect me to do?"

"Take it easy, Damon. No need to get defensive." The car pulled up in front of P. J. Clarke's. As they climbed out, Salmon said to the driver, "We'll be about an hour."

They walked into the bar. Clarke's had been here on 55th Street since 1854 and the interior looked it. No one had tried to modernize the place; the owners were proud of its history and let it wave like a flag. It was small and crowded, with a bar proudly scarred by age. The bar stools were uneven; no two were exactly the same height. Every time he stepped in here, Taylor felt that if he ignored the jukebox, he could be back in the nineteenth century.

"How's Terry going to get the down payment?" Taylor asked.

"Second mortgage. She'll make enough to pay it off in five years."

"Remember, the deal was she owns the school, not she goes into debt up to her ass."

"Have I ever gone back on a deal, Damon?"

"You've been straight with me, I'll give you that, but Terry's a little more vulnerable than I am. I don't want her hurt."

"What's going on? You in love with the girl?"

"Lord, no. Like I said, she's a friend. But I went to the wall for her. I want to see it pay off."

"It will. You drinking Jameson?"

"Yeah."

He ordered two of them, then turned to Taylor and said, "Look, the easiest way to handle this thing is for me to hold the mortgage. I got a company that does that kind of stuff, so it'll wash pretty good. She gets the property, we keep on feeding her students, boosting her rep, she gets a couple of choreography assignments and from what my people are telling me, it won't be long at all till she won't need the help. The girl's a born choreographer. So she pulls in big enough to pay off the mortgage in a reasonable amount of time. My people keep an eye on her money, make sure she has enough. It's as simple as that. Believe me, Damon, Terry Louvin gets every thing we agreed on."

"And she never knows where it comes from?"

"Never."

"Sounds good."

The drinks arrived. Salmon handed him one and said, "Let's drink to it."

Taylor did not feel good about the fact that he was so comfortable having a drink with Frank Costello's second in command.

The fact that Taylor obviously had some pretty strong feelings for the girl shouldn't have bothered Salmon but it did. He was developing some feelings for her himself. It was odd, she wasn't the type of girl he normally had anything to do with and maybe that was why he couldn't figure out what was going on with her. For sure, nothing should have been. As he sipped his whiskey, he thought about what he'd been doing just that morning, how he'd been in Brooklyn, down on the docks where the abandoned Navy ships were tied up, an area that nobody entered without his permission. As he waited by his car, a 1947 Pontiac drove slowly into view and came to a stop in front of him. The back door opened and a man spilled out, hitting the ground and rolling. His hands were tied behind his back and he was gagged. Two men got out of the car and dragged him to his feet.

"Take his gag off," Salmon said. He held a hand out and one of his men put a .38 in it. "You know what I want," he said to the bound man.

"Mr. Salmon, I didn't take it."

"Don't confuse me for a fool," Salmon said. "Don't you think I'd've made sure it was you before I went to all this trouble? Don't you think I'd've checked it out?"

"It wasn't me."

"Eighty thousand dollars, Cosetti. I put you in a position of responsibility and you steal eighty thousand dollars from me. Now, here's the deal. You've got about one minute to tell me where it is and then things get painful."

"Mr. Salmon, sir...."

"Thirty seconds."

Cosetti sputtered, suddenly unable to speak. He shook his head. His eyes swelled with fear and he began sweating, even though it was cold down here on the dock.

Salmon aimed and shot him in the left knee. He screamed and fell, trying to grip his wound but unable to because of his tied hands. He whimpered as he lay there on the ground, his eyes pleading with Salmon.

"One minute and I shoot the other knee." He cocked the gun. "You'll never walk again. Right now, you can stumble out of here alive. I shoot your other knee, you're in a wheelchair the rest of your days. You don't tell me then, you'll never use your arms again."

"All right," Cosetti said. "I've got the money. It's right over there, in the trunk of my car."

The man who had driven the car down here opened the trunk. A leather bag rested against the spare tire. He opened it and nodded to Salmon, who uncocked his gun and tossed it back to the other man.

"Good work, Cosetti." He transfered the bag to the trunk of his car. Turning to one of his men, he said, "Take him out of here. I don't ever want his body found. You know the drill."

"Yes, sir," his man said.

Now, as he swirled his whiskey in his glass, Salmon wondered if who he was and what he'd done would make a difference to Terry Louvin.

Down at the end of the bar, Irish Jack Sheridan took a sip of his Pabst Blue Ribbon and wondered what Taylor was doing palling around with Leo Salmon. Taylor had a rep as a straight arrow guy and Salmon, who was second in command in the Frank Costello family, was the most dangerous man in New York. On the surface, they sure as hell didn't seem like two guys that would hang out together, but here they were, having a drink like they just got off work and stopped in for a quick one before going home.

Were these two guys really friends? If he went ahead with the assignment to discourage Taylor, would he bring the Costello mob down on himself before he was ready to face them? And what about when he went ahead with the bigger plans he was making, because, God damn it, it didn't make any difference who hung out with who, he was going through with his intentions. Costello and his mob had to fall. Still, though, was there something he didn't know about that he'd have to look out for?

Maybe before he made any moves, he'd better get hold of a little more information.

21

When he got back to the office, Taylor read over his messages then picked up the phone and dialed a number.

"Detective Rebbenack," a voice announced when the phone was answered.

"Detective, this is Damon Taylor at *Crime Scene* magazine. I'm returning your call."

"Right. Look, I saw your story on the Russell Wallace murder. He get knifed the way you said? You weren't exaggerating or faking it?"

He was used to this kind of mistrust from the police. With this magazine, it happened all the time. "That's exactly how it happened. Call Danny Murphy. He'll verify it."

"Murphy," Rebbenack snorted. "I'd as soon take a pass, you know what I mean?"

"Think I do. Anyway, that's how it happened. Why?"

"'Cause I caught one down here just like it. Can you come downtown?"

"Sure. Meet you at the precinct?"

"Let's meet at the Gryphon. It's right down the street from here. Best strombolies in town."

"I can appreciate a good stromboli. Give me half an hour."

"*Crime Scene* give you an expense account?"

"A very good one."

"Dinner's on you."

The Gryphon was an Italian restaurant on the Lower East Side, a neighborhood joint that could more properly be called a pizza place than a restaurant. A storefront establishment, it was brightly lit. A few rickety tables were covered by red-checked tablecloths with Chianti bottles holding melted candles in their necks for centerpieces. The beer came by the pitcher and the food might have been basic but it was magnificent. Taylor tried to get there for lunch when he was in the neighborhood.

Since it was past dinner time but not yet late enough for the evening drinkers, the Gryphon was almost empty. The waitresses gathered at a back table, chatttering among themselves. When Taylor walked in, one of them broke from the herd and came over to him.

"You here to meet Charlie Rebbenack?"

"Yeah," Taylor said.

"He called, said he's running a little late. How 'bout a beer while you wait?"

"Make it an Irish whiskey. You got Jameson?"

"Not much call for Irish in here."

"That's fine. Beer's good."

He sat at a table by the window, watching the foot traffic go by as he waited. When his glass was half empty, Charlie Rebbenack walked in. He was a short, stocky guy with a receding hairline, a set jaw and a cop's tendency to scan everything in his line of sight continually. He carried a file folder in one hand.

"Taylor?"

Taylor nodded and shook hands with the smaller man. "Good to meet you, Detective." When Rebbenack sat down and had a beer in front of him, Taylor said, "Any chance you know the guy sitting in the stoop across the street? He's been checking me out since I been here."

Rebbenack glanced quickly out the window, a movement so quick that most people wouldn't have noticed it. "Julie?" he called out.

One of the waitresses got up and came over to the table.

"Charlie, this isn't my station," she said.

"You know Tony's been sitting across the street all night? Just watching the place?"

"Oh, no. Not again."

"Again. He's over there now."

Turning to Taylor, Rebbenack said, "Tony's her ex-boyfriend. They broke up a while back and he hasn't quite accepted it yet." Then he looked up at Julie again. "You want to tell Brenda we'll be having a couple of strombolies? That okay with you, Taylor?"

"Perfect."

Julie said, "Tony bothering you? You want I should go have a few words with him?"

"If he's still there when I leave, I'll take care of it." When she had gone back to her friends, Rebbenack said, "Wait till you taste the stromboli here. It's fucking beautiful."

"You mentioned something about a murder?"

With the tip of his finger, Rebbenack slid the file folder across the table. "There's the case file. Guy named Roy Warren, a luggage salesman, got himself slashed from his balls to his sternum, just like your Wallace guy."

"And just like a guy named Henry Fadden down in Baltimore."

"There's three victims?"

"So it would seem."

"Then I'm looking for a multiple murderer, huh?"

"Had this Warren guy been tortured?"

Rebbenack nodded. "Dozens of little cuts. Looks like the killer was after information and when he got it, he finished it by gutting him."

"Or when he didn't get it."

"Also a possibility. Then I guess what I need to know is what do these guys have in common?"

"We've got a bank clerk, a luggage salesman and a blackmailing commie hunter. I was thinking Wallace got it from one of his blackmail victims but now I'm not that sure."

"Can we put these guys together?"

"I don't know how."

The strombolies arrived, so they took a break to eat. Rebbenack had been right, Taylor decided; this was the best stromboli he'd ever eaten. In fact, he thought, if this was a stromboli, then what were those things he'd been eating all this time? Because they were nothing like this....

As he ate, he also thought, his mind roiling like dust in a windstorm, until a possible connection hit him. He played with it a few moments, letting it turn over in his mind until he decided it was maybe worth pursuing.

"You know," he said, after a swallow of beer, "Wallace and Fadden spent some time in Miami. They were there at the same time and knew each other. What if the other guy, what's his name?"

"Warren. Roy Warren."

"What if Warren was there, too?"

Rebbenack shook his head. "Unless he did a crime down in Florida, I can't track him there."

"I can," Taylor said.

When he left Rebbenack, Taylor headed up to Times Square. He wandered down 42nd Street until he spotted Huncke, who stood next to the ticket booth at a movie theater, talking to a couple of guys who didn't have the look of reputable citizens. Huncke reached into his pocket, quickly and carefully slid a couple of bills into one of the men's hands, while the other guy dropped a small envelope into Huncke's pocket. If you hadn't been watching carefully, if you hadn't in fact been looking for the transaction, you'd never have noticed it at all.

The group broke up, the two men walking toward Broadway and Huncke heading toward Sixth Avenue. Taylor moved a little faster till he caught up wth Huncke and fell into step with him.

"How you doing, Damon?" Huncke said.

"Not bad. How 'bout you?"

"I been better. Can't shake this cold. Got something for you, though. Come on down here with me, okay?"

They walked down 42nd Street till they came to an alley. Stepping into the shadows beyond the opening, Huncke checked the street traffic. Raising his jacket, he reached into his waistband and came up with a package carefully wrapped in a cheap yellow dish towel. Opening it up, he handed Taylor a .45, blued and shiny and smelling of oil. As Taylor checked out the gun, Huncke slid two boxes of shells and a few empty magazines into his pocket.

Taylor was satisfied with the action. "Looks good," he said.

"You don't have to go by looks. Take it out to Jersey, try it out. If it ain't perfect, bring it back, we'll get you one that is."

"I'm taking a little road trip tomorrow," Taylor said. "I'll check it out on the way."

He went back to the office, wrote up his story for the week and checked out a company car. He would have flown to Miami but there was a stop in Baltimore he wanted to make on the way.

22

Miami was hot and wet, the humidity so great that every afternoon a crashing thunderstorm brought cars to a stop at the side of the road. It would rain like hell for half an hour, then stop. The sun would come out again and burn off the standing water and an hour after the storm you could no longer tell it had even rained. The storm, though, wouldn't do a thing to break the humidity. It was like eternally being in New York City in August.

He had stopped in South Carolina on the way down to test out the .45. It had been a good buy: nice action, well-maintained and as soon as he got it sighted in, an accurate weapon. He hoped to hell he wouldn't have to use it. Right now it was in his suitcase in the hotel and he hoped it could stay there.

There was no way he could be sure it would, though. He was following the trail of a madman, one with a sharp knife who liked slicing people to pieces, and if his trip were successful, there was a good chance the two of them could end up facing each other.

The fan in Jeremy Benson's office didn't do a thing to break the heat. It just blew heavy, moist air throughout the room. Taylor could have sworn that it left a film of damp on his skin. Benson's office was on the fifth floor of a nondescript office building in Coconut Grove, one of the few higher than one story. In South Florida, Taylor had read, they built things close to the ground because of the hurricanes and he felt a litle uncomfortable with the idea that heavy wind could turn this structure into a pile of rubble.

"So," Jeremy Benson said, "let me see if I have this right. What you have is three murders, all done by the same person, one in Baltimore and two in New York. What these murdered guys have in common is they were all living in Miami a few years back and one of them had seventy thousand dollars buried under his floorboard. And you want me to find the Miami connection."

Benson was a burly guy. He looked like a former football player who hadn't taken care of himself. He still had the muscle, still looked as if he could get the job done when it came to the physical stuff, but he also looked like he didn't move nearly as fast as he once had.

"That's right." Taylor wiped sweat from his forehead with the back of his hand. "Two of them were in Baltimore not long ago. I checked, couldn't find any evidence that the third man had ever been there."

"What that means is the connection's probably here." Benson placed his feet on his desk and leaning back in his chair folded his hands over his belly. "You think these three and the killer are all there is? You got any more potential victims?"

"No idea. That's why I came to you. Can't do it myself. I don't know the city."

"Lots of PIs in Miami. Why'd you pick me?"

"You did some stuff for the magazine before. Lou Marsczyk used you. He says you're good."

"You know Marsczyk?"

"He's my editor."

"You know, if I'd known you were connected to that guy I might have thrown you out of this office. Swear to God, I never worked for anybody as mean as that son of a bitch in my life."

"I know exactly what you're talking about."

"The guy's a real hardass. He's never satisfied."

"That's the truth. You know what's even worse?"

"What's that?"

"I'm exactly like him."

Benson started where he always started: in the morgue of the *Miami Herald*. He didn't know what he was looking for but that was all right; when you started these things, you *never* knew what you were after. The trick was to recognize it when you saw it.

"I need to look at the crime sections from three years ago," he said.

The morgue attendant was an old man. He was hunched over and pale, his wispy hair falling in his face, his cheeks sunken. Benson guessed he was sick.

"What you looking for?" the smaller man asked.

"I'm looking for the crime sections from three years ago, buddy."

"You know, if you're a little more specific, I won't have to haul as many papers up here."

"Well, we'll just have to live with things the way they are because I can't be any more specific."

The old man muttered under his breath as he walked back to get the papers. Benson couldn't hear what he said, but that was all right.

He really didn't give a damn.

After a few laps in the pool Taylor stretched out in a reclining beach chair, thinking how odd it was that the hotel built a huge and elaborate pool between the building and the beach. To get to the ocean, you had to walk past the pool, teasing you between saltwater and fresh. As he watched a couple of kids frolic in the shallow end he reflected that the intense sun didn't seem quite so harsh when you were soaking wet. He'd oiled himself up pretty good and felt pleasantly sleepy. Since he had nothing to do until he heard from Benson, he thought maybe a nap wouldn't be such a bad thing. He let his eyes drift shut.

"Excuse me, do you think I could use some of your sun tan oil?"

He opened his eyes. Standing in front of him was one of the tallest woman he'd ever seen. She stood a good six feet, maybe a little more, and, as he gazed at her in her swim suit, he felt that to call her statuesque was to understate. She was well-defined, with a body whose muscles made it look like she was ready for the Olympics in weightlifting. The overall image was decidedly feminine.

He wondered if he were panting.

"Oh, sure. Here it is."

"Thanks." She sat on the lounge chair next to his and flashed a quick smile.

As she oiled herself up carefully and thoroughly, she said, "My name's Karla. Karla Byrnes."

"Damon Taylor."

She wrinkled her forehead. "Damon Taylor. I believe I know that name. Where would I know you from?"

"Well, I'm a reporter for *Crime Scene* magazine. Maybe you saw my byline there."

Karla Byrnes stretched her left leg as she smoothed on the oil. Taylor watched her long muscles contract and relax as she drew her leg back and extended the right one. He thought about Terry Louvin then, considering how tiny she would appear next to this Amazon.

"*Crime Scene.* Is that that magazine with those garish covers? Half-clothed women in jeopardy every month?"

"Every Tuesday. We're a weekly."

"I've read it. It's one of those magazines you feel like you shouldn't be enjoying but you always do. What are you working on now, Mr. Taylor?"

"Nothing, really. I'm just down here enjoying the sun."

He lied because that was the way he always answered that question. For one thing, it was too easy to talk a story away, to lose it in the chatting. He was still trying to get hold of this one in the actual research and writing of it. The second reason was that he had no idea who this Karla Byrnes was; for all he knew she was a rival. He didn't want his story running in another magazine before he was ready to go to press.

"Would you mind putting some of this on my back?" She held out the lotion.

"Not at all."

The muscles in her back were firm and strong, responsive to the pressure of of his hands. He couldn't tell if there was the possibility of something happening here and, even though he knew there was no reason for it, he felt he would be betraying Terry Louvin if he let it happen. All this time he'd been thinking of Terry as a friend, now he wondered if he had romantic feelings for her. Could it be he wanted more than just friendship? Something he'd have to think about when he got back to New York.

"Thank you," Karla Byrne said.

"That's okay. What do you do, Karla? For a living, I mean?"

"I'm an investment counselor. If you've got a load of money you want to turn into a huge pile of money, I handle the investing for you. For a percentage, of course."

"Interesting. Not many women in that field."

"Not many women in *any* field. I started out as a bank teller and this was a goal I'd set for myself."

"Your own business?"

"That's right."

"Is it hard for a woman to get clients?"

"Actually, in the beginning being a woman made it easy to get appointments. Now all my clients come from recommendations." She smiled at him. "Do your conversations always become interviews? Is that a reporter thing?"

He laughed. "Probably."

She slapped him lightly on the thigh. "Sun's too hot out here. Come on, Damon Taylor, boy reporter, I'll buy you a drink."

He hesitated.

She looked at him, her eyes dancing with some private delight. "Just one drink, though. I've got a date I have to get ready for."

"Why not?"

They were standing up to go into the bar when the pool attendant walked up to them. He was older than Taylor and his graying hair needed trimming. His eyes were bloodshot and the hand he held out quivered just a little.

"Are you Damon Taylor? There's a phone call for you. You want I should bring a phone out here or will you come into the lobby?"

"I'll come inside. Karla, looks like I'll have to take a raincheck on that drink."

Her expression changed as she looked at him. The playfulness faded as she grew thoughtful, curious. "I'm looking forward to it later on, then."

When Taylor got to the phone, Benson said, "I'm over at the *Miami Herald*. How fast can you get here?"

"Half an hour."

"Come to the cafeteria. There's a chance we can blow your whole story open right now."

23

As she drove up A1A to Fort Lauderdale, Kristen Eldredge wondered what Damon Taylor was really doing in Miami. It stretched the boundaries of coincidence to think that the guy looking into the murder of Russell Wallace could be here for any other reason. What did he know? Worse yet, what did he suspect? Was he coming after her? When she'd spoken to him by the pool, he hadn't given any indication that he'd known who she was.

Was he that far behind the story or was he that good an actor?

She hated to think that twerp Irish Jack Sheridan may have been right but she didn't want to make a permanent move on Taylor until she figured out what he knew. It was just possible Taylor could lead her to the money but it was a fine line following him while he kept up his investiagion. His coming to Miami was cause for concern.

She had checked out Taylor's room before making contact with him at the pool. Aside from the handgun, she didn't find anything out of the ordinary; still, she wondered why a reporter needed one. Was it the beating he took from Irish Jack's guys? Or was there another reason?

If anything, that attack on Taylor had spurred on his investigation, which might still prove useful. Killing him would have been a mistake, at least at the time. One thing for sure, she was going to have to be more careful from here on out.

And if she did have to take out Damon Taylor? That would be a shame. The thing of it was nobody was going to miss any of the men she'd killed so far but you mess with someone that people know about, someone like Damon Taylor, well, that could cause complications.

Still, if it had to be, she wasn't going to lose sleep over it. And when the time came she certainly wouldn't hesitate.

Benson was sitting at a table with another man, a short guy with rounded shoulders and a deep tan. As Taylor entered the room, Benson stood and waved him over. Taylor joined them.

"What have you got?"

"Maybe nothing, maybe the key to the whole thing. This is Chris

Block. He writes for the *Herald*."

Chris Block stood and held his hand out. His face was so tanned that it looked like a tree trunk. His hair was bleached blond and Taylor wondered if that was a result of the sun or a bottle of chemicals. They shook hands and the *Herald* reporter sat back down.

"How you doing, Taylor?"

Block's voice was soft, lacking in energy, as if he were sick. Taylor almost expected him to break into a series of coughs. He studied the man's face, looking for signs of illness.

"I'm doing fine. How 'bout you?"

Block nodded. "Pretty good. Cup of coffee?"

"Sure."

"Be right back," Block said.

As he watched the reporter walk slowly, as if he doubted his balance, over to the coffee pot, Taylor said, "What's this about?"

"I'll let Block tell it. I think you're going to enjoy it, though," Benson said with a grin.

When Block returned with the coffee, he slid a file folder across the table and said, "I think I got something for you here. A few years back I covered a story that might explain what you're dealing with. Here's copies of my stories, police reports, all that."

"What's the story?" The coffee was vile.

"A few years back, five people knocked off an armored car delivering a payroll. Big gunfight with the guys on the truck. They were killed and the thieves got away with a hundred grand."

"How does that connect to Russell Wallace?"

"A couple of ways. Before Wallace went into the securities business, he worked for the bank the armored car was delivering the cash to."

"It's getting more interesting."

"It gets more so. One of the robbers was shot in the gunfight. The others left her behind, took off with the money, leaving her for dead."

"Her? A woman?"

"Yeah. Her name was Kristen Eldredge. She took three bullets but she didn't die. At her trial, she claimed she was just the driver, said she was only a poor, dumb kid who fell for the wrong guy and wound up running with bad company. The jury was buying it so the prosecutor offered her a deal. She wound up getting five years and serving three. She was released on parole about four months ago."

"So she's tracking down the people who left her for dead, got her sent to prison?"

"And searching for the money, probably. It's still out there."

"You know, Wallace had seventy thousand dollars hidden away."

"Sure. He tells the others they have to wait till it cools down before they divide up the money, he'll just hide it away till it's safe, and then he takes off with it. Spends thirty thousand over three years. Makes sense."

"Maybe he paid the thirty grand to get the rest laundered. Thirty percent isn't out of the question." Taylor nodded. "So the question becomes who found him, the girl or one of the other bandits?"

"I'd put my money on Eldredge," Block said. "She was probably tracking the money. That would explain three murders, all done the same way." He slid the file folder across to Taylor. "There's pictures of Eldredge in here."

Taylor turned to the pictures. There was a mug shot, photos of her entering and leaving court, and an eight by ten that looked like a portrait that could have been taken from her apartment. He studied them, his head cocked, and he inhaled sharply.

"You look like you recognize her," Benson said.

"I should. An hour ago I was rubbing her back."

Shortly after dark, Kristen Eldredge pulled up in front of a concrete block and stucco house on Northeast 16th Street a couple of blocks east of US 1 in Fort Lauderdale. She watched the house for a little while. A light was on in what she took for the kitchen. After a couple of minutes, another came on toward the front. She waited a few more minutes and then got out of her car, shutting the door carefully so it wouldn't slam, then she walked around to the rear of the house.

The back door was unlocked. She smiled—Harold Goodman had never been very bright. Carefully, silently, she entered the kitchen and made her way toward the lit room she'd seen from the street. Stopping in the shadows, she smiled again, although anyone seeing her facial expression would not be made happy by it. Harold Goodman sat on the couch, a can of beer in his hand, listening to George Burns and Gracie Allen on the radio. Gracie was telling a story about her brother and Kristen stood silently, listening to it—she loved Burns and Allen. All Gracie had to do was say George's name with those crazy inflections of hers and Eldredge would break up. In fact, standing here in the darkness, listening to the radio in the other room, she had a hard time not laughing out loud.

She waited until George said, "Say 'Goodnight,' Gracie,'" and Gracie said, "Goodnight, Gracie." Then she stepped into the room. Before Harold Goodman could see her, she spoke.

"They're very funny, aren't they, Harold?"

Goodman jumped, startled. Standing quickly, he turned and caught sight of her. Then he glanced toward the door.

"You'd never make it to the kitchen," Eldredge said.

"I thought you were in jail," he said.

"I was. Three years. And you know something? Somebody's going to pay for that."

"Kristen, it wasn't me. I told the others we had to go back for you. They wouldn't listen to me."

"And you just climbed in the car with them and left me to die."

"What else could I do?"

"You could have helped me."

"I tried, Kristen, I swear to God I tried."

After the announcer read the headlines, a dance band began playng over the radio. Both of them ignored the music.

"Thanks for nothing, Harold. Where's the money?"

"What?"

"The money, Harold. The hundred thousand dollars."

"I don't know. Wallace had it. I figured he just ran out on all of us."

"Harold, Harold, you're disappointing me." She shook her head sadly. "I got to tell you something. I spent three years in hell because of what you guys did. And for three years, I thought about what I was going to do to all of you when I got out. But then, Harold, I found out the money was still out there, I just didn't know which one of you had it. Everybody said somebody else had it. People died swearing somebody else had the money. That's my money, Harold. I paid for it with three years of my life and I want it back. You understand me?"

Goodman nodded. "I hear you, Kristen. I'll tell you the truth. Wallace kept the money. Said it was too hot to spend it, he was going to launder it and then we'd split it. But he disappeared. I haven't seen a penny."

"Wallace told me someone stole it from him. Said it had to be one of you."

"If he told you I had it, he was lying."

"You know, the conditions when we talked, I don't think he'd lie to me."

Goodman shivered. "If somebody stole it, it wasn't me."

"You're sure about that."

"I swear it."

"I wish I could take your word for it, Harold, I really do."

He backed up a step, then another one, trying to escape the look in her eyes. It was like looking into hell. "I'm telling you the truth, Kristen. Look, I found God a while back. I'm a Christian now. I don't even care about the money. All it does is remind me of the sinner I used to be. You find the money, take my share. Take it all, as far as I'm concerned."

"You're a Christian now."

"I am."

"So you would't lie."

"No."

She took out her knife. "Then it ought to be that much easier to get the truth out of you."

24

Taylor was back in New York, finishing up a draft of his story, when the phone rang. He hated these interruptions and figured maybe he ought to just let it go, but that was impossible for him. He could no more pass up a phone call than he could let a day go by without food. No reporter could ignore a ringing phone.

"Hello?" he said.

"Mr. Taylor, this is Pete Seeger. You know, Woody Guthrie's friend?"

"Right. You're the banjo player."

"That's me. Listen, I know you and Woody were getting pretty close, and when this thing happened, I didn't know who else to call...."

"What thing, Pete? What happened?"

"They just arrested Woody. Claim he murdered that guy. They gotta be wrong. Lordy, I know Woody better'n just about anybody on this earth and I know he's no killer."

"You're right on that. He isn't."

"Can you help? We got to get him out of there," Seeger said. "Woody, well, he ain't made for jail. I mean, he talks about his days hoboing, riding the rails and stealing food to stay alive, but, when you get right down to it, truth of the matter is all he wants to do is be out there in Coney Island with Marjorie and the kids. Down deep, he's a regular guy." He paused and then said, "Can you see about getting him bail or something?"

"I'll see what I can do, Pete."

He took his draft into Lou Marsczyk's office, placed it on his editor's desk and said, "I'll be out for a while. That fool Murphy just arrested Woody Guthrie."

"For making that caterwauling noise he calls folk music?"

"For doing in Wallace. Actually, you listen closely to his songs, he's pretty good."

"I'll take your word for it." He slammed a fist on his desk and said, "You know, I'm getting a little fed up with the way Danny Murphy operates and the way the department lets him get away with it. I think I'm beginning to feel the need for a good crusade. Don't you think it's about time we take a look at what we can do about Danny Murphy? You know, see if we can't bring that son of a bitch down a peg or two?" He went to the door and shouted, "Haynes, get your ass in here." To Taylor he said, "That's what's been missing around here: a good crusade."

His secretary had quit a month or so ago and Marsczyk hadn't gotten around to replacing her yet. Taylor thought he preferred to stand in the doorway screaming for people; it probably struck him as colorful. Sometimes Taylor thought that Marsczyk cultivated eccentricity the way some people did a vegetable garden.

When Haynes showed at the office door, Marsczyk didn't even give him time to sit down. "Tell you what I want out of you, Haynes. I want you to go through all the cases Danny Murphy has closed, all the convictions he's gotten. I want you to find me an innocent man. I need a guy he sent up that didn't do the crime. A whole bunch of them would be better but we got to have at least one."

"You want me to prove Murphy's dirty?"

"Not dirty, necessarily, but definitely careless, which is just as bad, don't you think? If he's deliberately closed a case by sending an innocent man to jail, I want us to be able to prove it. If there's a pattern, well, I really want to know about that."

"Big job, Lou."

"Choose somebody to work with you. Just get it done."

"What if he's clean?"

"Walter, we're talking about Danny Murphy."

"Have you thought this out, Lou? You bring down a cop, the NYPD isn't going to be all that happy with us."

"Oh, and I do so live my life trying to win and keep the good will of the NYPD. Get on it, Haynes."

"What's my deadline?"

"Five minutes ago."

Walter Haynes was a tall, skinny guy. He wore glasses and claimed they were the reason he'd survived the war. They'd kept him off of night patrols. Statistically, he said, more people bought it on night patrols than day patrols and there was no arguing with him when it came to statistics. That was the kind of guy Haynes was, Taylor thought: if there was a figure attached to it, if it could be numbered, he'd have the results at his disposal. He was the best researcher Taylor had ever seen. A lousy writer, but a great researcher.

"You," Marsczyk said to Taylor, "go see what's up with Guthrie. I'll read this crap"—he tapped Taylor's story with his fingertips—"while you're gone."

Taylor stopped off at the People's Songs offices first. Seeger and Will Geer were standing on stage while about a dozen other people gathered restlessly on the floor in front of them. They were all talking at once, quickly, nervously. There was an energy in the air but it was disturbed, as if too many people were running in too many directions.

"Everybody quiet down and pay some mind," Seeger said.

Nobody paid any attention to him. They just kept chatttering. If anything, their voices were growing louder. One man kept shouting that this was the first great step forward in the revolution.

Will Geer stepped forward, watched the crowd for a moment, then shouted in his loudest stage voice, "Shut the fuck up!"

Silence fell over the room. Seeger appeared startled, looking at Geer and then taking a step away from him.

"We got to take up money for his bail," Seeger was saying.

"Pete," a balding black man said, "there's no bail for murder. It's a capital crime."

"He hasn't been arraigned yet, Josh," a woman said. She pushed her curly hair back from her face. "If he draws a charge lesser than first degree murder, there could be bail."

"We'll put together some benefit concerts," Seeger said. "Who's in?"

Hands shot up. Taylor thought if there was anything this crowd would volunteer for, it was performing.

"Beth," Seeger said. "You want to get on the phone, line up some shows? All over the city."

A serious looking young woman with rich brown hair pulled back in a tight bun nodded her head. She took a small pad from her purse and made a couple of notes.

"We'll need character witnesses," Will Geer said. "People to get up in court and speak for Woody."

"I'll do it," a young man said.

"Fred, the first thing they're going to ask you is if you've ever been arrested. What are you going to say?"

"Never for a crime. It was just political."

"What were you doing? Supporting left wing causes?"

"I sure was," the young man said proudly.

"Great. You go into court, the district attorney's man says you've got a history of breaking the law because you're a Communist."

"But I only support good causes."

"To the law, that doesn't make any difference," Will Geer said. "Let's see what we're dealing with. How many of you guys have been arrested before?"

"Demonstrations count?"

"Of course, they do."

Almost every hand went up. "Well," Geer said, "none of you can be character witnesses."

"I've never been arrested," one young man said.

"You're a homosexual. Don't you think in the name of the law that's going to disqualify you?"

"Why should it?"

"Because what you do is against the law."

"Well, it shouldn't be."

"Of course it shouldn't," a woman with streaks of gray in her hair said. She was wearing a gingham dress and an apron as if she'd just arrived from Appalachia but she spoke with a Brooklyn accent. "But what do you think's going to happen when we send a queer in to speak for Woody?"

"Now wait a minute...."

"I don't like the word any more than you do," Will Geer said, "but you have to admit, she's got a point."

"I've never been arrested and I'm not a homosexual," a middle-aged man with thick black hair and a deep voice said.

"No, Cisco, but you *are* a Communist."

"I don't believe it," Pete Seeger said. "In this whole room, we don't have a single acceptable character witness?"

"That seems to be the way it is," Will Geer said. "If it was left up to us, the poor boy'd be hanging from a tree by morning."

25

"What happened?" Pete Seeger said. "Well, all I can tell you is we were here in the office…."

"Who was here?"

"Me, Woody, of course, Josh White, Burl Ives and Cisco Houston."

"I wasn't here," Will Geer said. "I was still on stage."

"Anyway, we were hanging around, just sharing a jug and passing a guitar back and forth, swapping songs, you know, just like we'd done a thousand other nights, when the door went flying in and suddenly there were more cops in here than you could count. You'd'a thought there was some kind of cop convention going on around here. I swear, you never saw anything like it."

When Seeger spoke, he tried to sound down home, as if he were fresh out of the mountains, but Taylor had checked him out and knew he came from a family of music scholars and professors and had himself put in two years at Harvard. Taylor figured sounding like an Appalchian hillbilly must be good for folk music, like wearing blue jeans and a denim work shirt the way they all did, as if it were the folk singer's official uniform.

"Murphy say anything?"

"You mean the guy in charge? Yeah, he said 'grab the bastard' and they threw the cuffs on Woody and he was out the door before any of us could blink."

"How'd Woody handle it?"

"He just told me to take care of his guitar and tell Marjorie he'd see her later."

"Murphy didn't tell him what they were charging him with?"

"They never even told him he was under arrest. In the movies, they always say, 'You're under arrest for the murder of so and so.' Can they just haul a person away without telling them anything?"

"They're the New York City Police Department," Will Geer said. "They can do pretty much whatever the hell they want to."

"Figured you'd be dropping by before too long," Danny Murphy said.

"I need to see Woody Guthrie."

Murphy had gained a little weight. As he sat behind his desk, his belly stuck out as if he had a basketball hidden under his shirt. He smiled, enjoying the moment. "You didn't think I could make a case against that cowboy fuckup, did you? Well, I got him nailed, Mr. Reporter. Your next story's going to be all about how I solved the Wallace case."

"You want to share your big moment with me? How'd you pin him to the crime, Murphy?"

"Two things. First off, I found the murder weapon. A big ass hunting knife, six-inch blade, hidden under the stage in that theater of theirs."

"You found a knife? In a theater, where they cut canvas to make backdrops for sets, you found a knife? That's your big evidence?"

"First off, the knife belonged to Guthrie. He said he lost it a couple of months ago. Convenient, ain't it?"

"And you can prove it's the murder weapon?"

"Look, it's a knife, the victim was sliced with a knife, what's to prove? Besides, I got more."

"What's that?"

"Blood on a shirt. Same size the victim wore. It's B-positive. Just so happens the victim's got B-positive blood."

"Let me see if I understand this: Guthrie went over to Wallace's apartment, slashed him to pieces, then took off his shirt and brought it back to the theater?"

"That's exactly what he did, Taylor. He did it and that's all that counts."

"What's Guthrie's blood type? It could be his blood, you know."

"What the fuck, Taylor, I ain't arguing my case with you. What I do know is that the stuff I got's good enough to get the fucking arrest warrant, it's good enough to send his ass to the chair."

"I want to see him."

"What for?"

"For one thing, he's a friend of mine."

"And that makes a difference to me for what reason?"

"Come on, Murphy. I need to see him."

"If it'll shut you up and get you out of here, why not? He's down at the Tombs." He picked up the phone. "I'll call ahead, clear you."

When he'd been a daily newspaper reporter, Taylor had spent a lot of time at the Tombs. In fact, he'd once done a feature on the place. The building was originally called the Halls of Justice but from the beginning everyone called it the Tombs. The city had built the structure on top of Collect Pond, using hemlock logs to fill in the marshland but in less than five months the building had begun to sink, causing the foundation to crack. Crews were constantly patching and repairing the foundation, trying to keep the water out, but they couldn't. Dampness permeated the Tombs to such an extent that the grand jury condemned it, saying it was unfit for human habitation. The city, though, kept on using it for years anyway, until a new building was put up, a hideous gray structure with no personality at all. This also became known as the Tombs. Few people saw the new building—it had been the "new building" for close to fifty years now—as an improvement and from the beginning, there had been talk of replacing it. So far nothing had been done.

At least this one didn't leak, Taylor thought as he waited in the visitor's room for Guthrie. A cop led Guthrie in. Woody flashed him a grin as he sat down on the other side of the wire-lined window.

"Well if it ain't Damon Taylor. How you been, boy?"

"Fine, Woody. Better than you, I imagine."

Woody took in the surroundings with a wave of his arm. "Oh, this? Aw, hell, boy, we're having us a big time in here. You think you know folk songs? Put a little time in a place like this, you'll hear you some folk songs."

"Woody…."

"Me and the boys, we just trade songs all day. I'm tellin' you, son…."

"Woody, get serious, will you? You're charged with murder. You get convicted, you get executed."

"Well, I know that. But what makes you think I'm going to get convicted? You know I didn't kill that fellow. People don't get the chair for stuff they didn't do."

"Jesus Christ, man, how naive are you?"

"What you talking about?"

"It happens. Innocent people have been executed. More often than you'd think."

"Maybe it happens, but it ain't going to happen to me. Good folks like you won't let it."

"Tell me about the bloody shirt."

Woody looked bored, as if he'd told the story a thousand times. He took a deep breath, exhaled slowly and said, "Don't know a damn thing about it. Never noticed no bloody shirt till that Murphy guy started waving it in my face."

"You think the cops planted the shirt?"

"Maybe. Then again, it might have just grown there like those beanstalk seeds Jack planted."

"Was it your shirt?"

Guthrie shrugged. "It's a white undershirt. How the hell do I know if it's mine or not? Those undershirts ain't exactly rare treasures, you know."

"Woody, you got a lawyer?"

"Lawyers cost money, son. Where the hell am I going to get the cash to hire myself a lawyer?"

"You been arraigned yet?"

"Nope."

"I'm sending a lawyer over to see you, okay?"

"That's fine with me. Send me one of the good ones, will you?"

"Look, you don't talk to anybody, you don't sign anything, you don't do a thing till the lawyer gets here, you hear me?"

"If you say so."

He wished he could be confident Guthrie would actually follow his instructions but Woody was his own man—hell, he was his own universe—and Taylor couldn't be sure what he was liable to do from moment to moment.

26

He arrived at Terry Louvin's studio with a bag of sandwiches and coffee in paper cups. She waved to him from the studio floor where she was working with a group of little kids, some of whom looked barely old enough to walk much less dance. A curly-haired little girl on the end held her left arm out and kept doing slow turns no matter what Louvin was coaching her to do. The kid was off in her own little dance world and nothing a teacher said was going to bring her back to this one. Another little girl kept staring at herself in the mirror that covered the back wall. She appeared to like what she saw.

Whenn class was over Louvin dismissed the kids with a lot of hugs and kisses and then walked over to Taylor. She looked fantastic in her leotard. Since he'd been back from Miami he'd been thinking that this whole idea of being friends with women you could easily have deeper feelings for just wasn't working. He figured maybe it was time to do something about this pattern of behavior.

She hugged him and said, "It's so good to see you. Come on in the office and let me have some of that lunch you brought."

He'd called her, suggesting he take her out to lunch but she'd said she couldn't get free, she was too busy. He'd suggested a quick meeting here at the studio instead. A quick half-hour between appointments.

"I'll bring the food," he'd said.

"Good," she told him. "I'm glad we're doing this. I've got something I want to talk over with you."

Now, as they ate, he asked, "What's on your mind? You said you had something you wanted to tell me."

She signaled for him to wait until she'd finished chewing the bite of Reuben she was working on. When she'd swallowed, she took a sip of coffee and said, "Great sandwich. You go to the Carnegie Deli?"

"You recognize the deli from the sandwich?"

"The Carnegie, sure." She grinned and then looked serious. "Listen, how well do you know Leo Salmon?"

How did he answer that? Exactly how much information about Salmon should he be giving out? Until he knew where this conversation was going it would probably be best to hold back. "Not all that well. I've met him a few times. Why?"

"Funny, I'd think you'd know him better. He speaks very highly of you."

He stirred sugar into his coffee. "I helped him make a bunch of money. Recommended he invest in *Finian's Rainbow*."

She nodded. "Nice. Look, he's been very helpful to me. He put together a package that's going to allow me to own this place and getting it's going to be pretty painless. But he's pretty much a stranger to me and he talks such a big game, I get confused. He tells me to leave everything to him, and it sounds sort of like one of those don't-worry-your-pretty-little-head-about-it things. I'd resent that if I had any idea what I'm doing here, but this big time real estate is way beyond me. Is he an honest man? Can he be trusted?"

Taylor smiled inwardly. Honesty and Leo Salmon were phrases that didn't fit naturally together. He was probably more honest than most big time Mafia members but what was that saying? How much could he tell Terry about the man? He thought about it a moment and when he spoke his voice sounded sure.

"It's been my experience that Leo Salmon will do exactly what he says he will."

"Good." She smiled and drank more coffee. "He's asked me out to dinner."

"A date?"

"Well, yes, I suppose so."

"And you said?"

"Actually, I thought it was about the house at first, so I said yes. By the time I realized we were talking a social evening, it was too late. I'd already agreed."

"Well, then, enjoy the evening."

"I think I will. Leo's kind of an intriguing guy. I don't think I've ever met anybody like him."

I can guarantee you haven't, Taylor thought. He felt he should tell her that the man she found intriguing was the second in command of the Costello crime family, that he'd ordered the deaths of dozens of people and had probably taken on a few himself, that the fact that he laundered mob money through legitimate businesses, including hers probably, didn't classify him as an honest businessman.

"Damon, do you know how long it's been since I've been on a date?"

There was a lilt in her voice that he hadn't ever heard before and figured that he had his answer. No, he shouldn't tell her any of those things. She felt happy about the possibilities and it wasn't right to step on her happiness. You just didn't do things like that.

He said, "About as long as it's been for me, I suppose."

She wiped her chin with a paper napkin. "You ought to do something about that, Damon." Sensing she'd missed a spot of mustard, she rubbed the napkin over her chin again. "I don't like to think of you alone like you are."

"Funny," he said. "Everybody I'm interested in is interested in somebody else."

"That's too bad," she said. "So you don't know any reason why I shouldn't just relax and go out with Leo and see what develops?"

He hesitated but the look in her eyes told him everything he needed to know. "Can't think of anything. Just make sure he's good enough for you. You deserve the best, Terry."

She paused, her eyes tearing for a second until she blinked rapidly. "Nobody's ever said anything like that to me, Damon."

The next class was shuffling in. It was another group of little kids and, as they dropped their bags against the wall, they saw their teacher with a man and huddled together, whispering and giggling.

"Better let you get back to work," he said.

"I'll call you, let you know how it goes with Leo."

"Good. Do that. When are you going out?"

"Friday night."

"Got a sitter?"

"You believe this? Leo arranged for one. What a thoughtful man."

Right. Leo Salmon was nothing if not thoughtful. He was going to have to talk to Salmon about this whole thing and he wasn't happy about that. As friendly as Salmon was to him, he was still a man used to having his own way, a man who didn't like anyone telling him no.

Kristen Eldredge towered over Irish Jack Sheridan the way the Empire State Building towered over Manhattan. He couldn't get comfortable in her presence. When he was with her, he was always aware she could take his head between her fingertips and crush it like a grape. Not only could she do that, he felt like she was always thinking about what a pleasant thing it would be to do, how much she'd enjoy it. He was a bad guy himself; he'd done some stuff that scared the hell out people but compared to her, he felt an altar boy.

When she called him, told him to meet her here in Central Park, he felt a strong need to take the train over to Jersey. But he knew that if he did she'd track him down and it wouldn't go well for him. He headed into the park like a man marching to the electric chair.

She was sitting on a bench inside the East 65th Street entrance. When she saw him she stood, wrapped her jacket closely around herself and waited for him to walk over. God knows she wouldn't meet him halfway. No, that would show she had a human bone in her body.

"There you are," she said, as he neared her. "Come on, walk with me."

She turned and headed into the park. Irish Jack hurried to catch up. When he fell in beside her, she turned south, toward the pond, and walked with a swift pace, her legs as long as tree trunks, striding so that he had to almost run to keep up with her. It was like walking with a cheetah.

"Isn't the park beautiful today?" she said.

"I suppose it is. I hadn't really noticed."

"All this beauty in the middle of the city and you don't notice? It's the most wonderful thing in this town. For my money, it's the only reason anybody'd ever want to live here."

"For me it's the bars. We got the best bars in the country."

"Haven't you got any appreciation for the outdoors at all? The city has tried to preserve a big patch of nature right in the middle of all this concrete and you don't even notice it? What's wrong with you, anyway?"

"You know how it is. You live some place, you take what it's got for granted. Now the Staten Island Ferry, that's something I can appreciate."

He had taken the ferry over to Staten Island once to see a broad and the ride had been all right. He liked the fact that you could drink beer right there on the boat. But the thing with the woman hadn't worked out, so he'd never ridden the ferry again. If she had lived in Manhattan he thought they might have had a shot but Staten Island was just too far away, too much trouble to get to.

"It *is* something to see the Statue of Liberty from the ferry," she said. "But Central Park's got it all beat. If I lived in the city, I'd be here all the time."

"You don't live here?" he said. "Where do you live?"

"What difference does it make?"

"Well, none. I was just curious."

She stopped suddenly, turned to him and said, "Oh, Jack, don't you know it's not a good idea for you to get curious about me? You understand?" Her voice was soft, without any threatening inflections at all, and that made her words even more frightening.

"Yes, ma'am. I get you."

"Good."

She waited until there was no one else around and then reached into the pocket of her coat. He inhaled sharply and tried to pull away and when her hand came out, he sighed with relief because there was money in it. He hated himself for letting his fear show as powerfully as it had, hated her for smiling as if the fact that he was terrified of her amused her.

"I don't need you any more," she said. "I'm paying you off."

"You don't want me to discourage that Taylor guy?"

"He's not a threat to me."

He took the money she held out, shoving it in his pocket without looking at it. There was no way he was going to risk pissing her off by counting the money in front of her. He hoped the count was right because that money was going to get him back in the mob. He'd been thinking it out for a long time now and he'd made up his mind.

"You look kind of weird," she said.

"I'm fine," Irish Jack said. "Never been better."

27

When he got back to the office, Taylor wrote a new draft of the next week's story. Sure, he could have gone to press with what he already had, but he wasn't satisfied; the story had sprawled in too many directions and he needed to know where it was going. Whenever that happened, the only thing he knew to do was to sit down and write it out, letting the story go in whatever direction it wanted to. Then he'd edit it down into a unified, coherent tale.

This time, he went beyond the killing and wrote about the bigger picture. He traced Wallace back to Baltimore and to Miami, quoting his ex-wife on his tendency to refer to himself as a master criminal. He detailed the possibility that he had masterminded the armored car robbery down in Florida. He didn't feel good about all the speculation; all he could prove was that Wallace was in Miami when the truck was hit and that he'd had a bunch of money in his apartment. Since he was essentially thinking on paper, though, he left it. He brought in Kristen Eldredge, without naming her, suggesting that she was now searching for the missing money and might be killing off the people who had left her for dead. When he got though with it, he yanked the final sheet out of the roller of his typewriter and re-read the whole thing.

As a story, it stank out loud. Even if he'd wanted to, he couldn't possibly go to press with this piece. As a working outline, it suggested ways to proceed, though, so he was happy with that. He stood, walked over to Lou Marsczyk's office and tossed the sheets of paper on his desk.

"Read this over, will you?"

"Problems with it?"

"Not if you're a fan of abstract speculation offered without a shred of proof."

Marsczyk nodded. "You had that yesterday."

"Yeah, well, today I got even more of it."

"I'll get back to you."

While he waited, Taylor made a new pot of coffee and poured himself a cup, wishing he had some brandy to lace it with. As he was sugaring his coffee, Haynes came up, poured himself a cup.

"This is fresh, isn't it? Didn't I see you making it?"

"It's fresh. Rotten but fresh."

Haynes took a sip. "It's not that bad. Listen, I think I'm onto something with that Murphy thing."

"You are?"

"Nothing I can prove yet, but I'm looking at a murder case he handled and I found references to a whole bunch of witnesses who were ready to testify that Murphy's guy didn't do it. They were never called. Seems the DA never heard of them."

"Murphy erased them from the case file?"

"Looks that way." He sipped his coffee. "I got a long way to go on it, but it's looking good."

Taylor noticed Marsczyk standing in his doorway, the story dangling from his left hand. Marsczyk made eye contact with him and waved him over.

"Talk to you later, Haynes."

"Right."

When he got back to Marzsczyk's office the editor sat down, propped his feet on the desk and said, "You're right. This is crap."

"Seems like that's what I told you."

"You got the story but you don't have it nailed. I read this, I'm thinking he's onto something but what he's got doesn't doesn't pass the why should I believe you test. You've even got your encounter with the Miami woman in here, which would make a dynamite story if you could prove she's the one slicing and dicing these people like carrots for a stew in New York."

"That's where I intend to take it. I'll get back to work."

"How'd it feel?"

"How'd what feel?"

"When you saw her mug shot and realized you'd been with her earlier in the day."

"Scary as hell. I kept wondering if she had any idea who I was."

"If she does, you're in trouble. You think about wanting off the story?"

"What for?"

"It's not worth getting killed for."

"I'm not quitting now. You know that."

Marsczyk looked at his TV screen for a long moment, as if the set were turned on. Taylor could see the editor's reflection in the screen. "You got to see it through, don't you? Even if your life's on the line, you've got to push on to the truth."

"That's what people keep telling me."

"Well, maybe if we keep on doing it, you'll see it's true. Maybe you'll also see it's a character flaw. You know what's wrong with you?"

"I'd love to hear you tell me."

Marsczyk lit a cigar. He didn't just light it, he went through the whole cigar ritual: biting off the end, licking enough to dampen it and only then using the lighter, rotating the cigar to get the fire even and puffing away until it was going well. When he was satisfied, he smiled. He had a habit of going from one smoking product to another. Some days it was cigarettes, sometimes it was a pipe, and then like today, the occasional cigar. Taylor wouldn't be surprised to see him chewing tobacco one day.

"You want to hear me tell you? Well, I'm going to tell you, son. You still believe all the shit. You still think this is the world you learned about in high school, the world of rules and order. You think crime disturbs the natural order of the universe and by finding and printing the truth about it, you can restore order to everything." He flipped the ash off his cigar. "Jesus Christ, man, didn't the war teach you anything?"

"I'm not that bad, Lou."

"You're every bit that bad. The fact is, Damon, crime *is* the order of the universe. We live in a corrupt world that's growing more corrupt by the day. It's more than we can do to keep a lid on it."

"But we keep on trying."

"I wonder about that. Think about it all the time. Only thing that occurs to me is we all got these self-defeating things we do, like me and smoking. Trying to keep a lid on the shit. All we're doing is trying to keep the stench covered so it doesn't get any worse."

"What exactly are you telling me, Lou? To let it go?"

"Nope. I think what I'm saying is lighten up on the obsession. Don't let it eat you alive. Do what you can and have fun spending the money."

28

Kristen Eldredge had learned a long time ago that there was no way she could hide herself. No matter what she did to make herself less conspicuous, she stuck out in a crowd. When you were six feet tall and had a body with everything as muscular and firm as a Michelangelo statue, you were going to draw attention. That was all there was to it.

Even in the middle of winter, when she put on a fur coat before going out, men stared at her breasts. Not that she blamed them; they *were* spectacular but still, you'd hope for a little discretion. The least the men could do was peek, not gape with their tongues hanging out like Loony Tunes cartoon wolves.

She felt a little relieved when she went into Taylor's building. At least on the stairs going up to the second floor, where Taylor's apartment was, no men were checking her out. No, she was alone here. It was the middle of the afternoon and she'd learned that this was the best time to toss somebody's apartment, while they and their neighbors were at work. Sure, every once in a while a housewife was home in a neighboring apartment but they usually stayed inside, ironing or cooking or doing whatever the hell housewives did while they listened to soaps on the radio.

The second pick she tried opened his door as smoothly and easily as an elevator door. She walked inside, stopped in the foyer and looked around. Pretty neat and straightened up for a man's apartment; he must have a woman who comes in and cleans. Men didn't even notice dirt until it became intolerable. Even after they did, most of them didn't do a damn thing about it. It was as though they expected the house to clean itself. Or maybe they just figured if they waited long enough, some woman would come along and do it for them.

She worked carefully, slowly, without trying to cover the fact that someone had tossed the apartment but also without making too much of a mess. Starting in the living room, she worked her way to the kitchen, then to the bedroom, searching it thoroughly before she moved on to the second bedroom. She thought he probably referred to this one as his office since there was a typewriter in it. It was a long shot to assume he had the money here—that is, if he had the money at all—but she had to check.

Besides, there was a distinct possibility that she was going to have it out with Taylor and she liked to know something about the people she might have to kill. If he had any hidden strengths that could cause trouble for her, she wanted to know about them.

The apartment was hot and she wanted to turn off the heat. Since she didn't really give a damn if Taylor came home and wondered why his apartment wasn't as warm as it usually was, she went ahead and turned down the radiator. She finished searching the office. No money, no safe deposit keys—nothing but a .45 automatic, wrapped in a towel on the shelf in the closet. A gun cleaning kit sat next to it. A war souvenir, she figured. The guy was a reporter, why else would he have a gun? With a pair of pliers she'd seen in the kitchen, she broke off the firing pin. Then she rewrapped the gun and put it back in the closet.

Back in the kitchen, she spotted a whiskey bottle and poured herself a drink. It had an interesting, unusual taste to it, and she checked the label: Jameson Irish Whiskey. She'd have to pick herself up a bottle. She leaned against the counter, scanning the apartment, wondering if she'd missed anything, then determined she'd better check out the bathroom.

Only people with no imagination hid things inside the toilet tank, so she knew it would be clean. Still, she had to check. She lifted the lid and looked inside. As she'd suspected, nothing. Going back to the kitchen, she poured herself another shot and drank it while she scanned the apartment once more.

In order to make sure Taylor knew she'd been here, she placed her empty glass in the middle of the sink, as if marking her territory. Knowing how easily somebody could get to him would throw him off balance and it would be good to keep him off center.

As she went down the stairs, Kristen Eldredge realized she was left with the same question that had brought her here: if Damon Taylor didn't have the money, where was it?

O'Bradovich had just enough time to pick up the makeup case he'd left at home before he had to rush back to the studio. He kept a duplicate case at NBC so he wouldn't have to haul his back and forth but somebody had used his stuff for a drama last night and the fool must have layered everybody like a spackled wall. He'd left O'Bradovich with an almost empty case of used up containers of pancake. He was thankful he had more at home. He unlocked the front door of the building, let himself in and as he rushed up the stairs, he had to get out of the way of the tallest woman he'd ever seen, a woman with striking red hair who didn't bother to nod to him as she passed by. The scent of her perfume hung in the air like dew.

She was down the stairs and gone before he even had time to question her presence. Odd, he thought later while he was telling Taylor about her, she passed in and out of his life so quickly that he wasn't even certain what she looked like. Still, she'd been so striking he knew he'd never forget her.

The moment Taylor walked into his apartment he knew someone had been there. There was a disturbance in the energy; his living room somehow felt different, and in some odd way he couldn't really identify, agitated. A scent hung lightly in the air—perfume, expensive perfume, he'd guess—not that he knew anything about fragrances. But this one was so subtle, so *ethereal*, he knew it had to cost a lot of money.

If you simply glanced around, you'd have seen that the presence of a stranger in the apartment was obvious, inescapable. The pillows Linda had gotten him for his couch were out of place and the telephone had been moved. The place wasn't a mess, but whoever had tossed it hadn't bothered to hide the fact they'd been there.

He went through the rooms, examining them, trying to discover what had been taken, but he couldn't determine that anything was missing. Even the gun was still where he'd left it on the closet shelf. The towel had been unwrapped, though; the .45 was now covered much more neatly than he'd left it. Taylor was a little confused. It was as if a really curious dinner date, someone who wanted to know all about him, had looked around while he was finishing getting dressed. Nothing appeared to have been taken. His checkbook was in the desk drawer where he kept it. He knew check kiters were fond of taking a few checks from the back of the book where the owners rarely looked—he flipped through the blanks: all accounted for. An envelope with three hundred dollars in it that he'd stuck in the desk until he could get to the bank was still there.

He discovered the only thing missing when he saw the empty whiskey glass in the sink and checked his bottle of Jameson—a shot or two had been poured. He lifted the glass out of the sink, careful to grip it by the inside. It had been sitting in the sink long enough to dry. After coating the glass with talcum powder, he carefully wrapped clear tape around it. Then he undid the tape and spread it out carefully on a sheet of white paper. No clean fingerprints. Only smudges.

Two things were obvious to him. One, whoever had done this—and the perfume in the air indicated it had been a woman—hadn't just broken in to get a drink. And two, she'd left the glass out deliberately: she wanted him to know she'd been there.

The real question caused a mild tingling situation: what had Kristen Eldredge been looking for?

29

When he got down to the NBC offices at 30 Rockefeller Plaza, he took one of the dozen elevators up to the seventh floor and wandered down to O'Bradovich's office. Bob was in there, sitting behind his desk, watching a monitor. He looked up and grinned when he saw Taylor.

"Damon, how you doing?"

"A little confused, Bob." He sat down opposite him. "Somebody broke into my apartment this afternoon, tossed it pretty good."

"You were burglarized?"

"Don't know if I would call it that, not quite. Nothing was taken. Everything's right where it's supposed to be but the person who tossed the place made it really obvious she'd been there. She wanted me to know."

"She? It was a woman?"

"Oh, yeah, it was a woman, all right. There was perfume in the air."

"Really nice perfume? Had kind of a citrusy fragrance?"

"Something like that, yeah. How'd you know?"

"I think I saw her. I had to go home this afternoon, pick up some supplies. She was coming down the stairs as I was going up. Stunningly beautiful, the sort of woman you don't forget."

"Six feet tall? Statuesque? Red hair?"

"That's her. How'd you know?"

"I met her down in Florida. If I'm right, she's murdered four or five men."

"Oh, my God. She went right past me. She knows I saw her. Is she going to come after me?"

"No. She wouldn't mind being seen. Whatever's going on, she wants me to know she was there. She made it pretty obvious that she'd been through my stuff."

"She can't be that hard to find. You don't see women like that everyday." O'Bradovich stood and began dropping makeup containers into his bag. "I've got to get to work, Damon. How 'bout a drink after I get off? Maybe some dinner?"

"Sounds good. Where and when?"

"How 'bout Costello's?"

"Good enough. Meet you there around nine?"

"Great."

Taylor left and took a bus downtown to his office. Marsczyk was gone for the day but that was all right. Taylor needed to think, not to talk. Sitting at his desk, he rolled a sheet of yellow paper into his typewriter and began typing some notes. Nothing he hadn't already thought of and written came out on the page, though.

He thought quietly for a few minutes, then picked up the phone asked for long distance. Then he put in a call to Chris Block at the *Miami Herald*. When the reporter answered, Taylor smiled. "Hey, Chris, it's Damon Taylor."

"Up in New York?"

"Right. Got a little job for you."

"I've got a little job."

"Yeah, but this one might break a story for you."

"Now I'm intrigued. Tell me about it."

"Let me give you four names: Russell Wallace, Harold Goodman, Roy Warren and Kristen Eldredge. I think they're the folks who did that armored car job. And I think Russell Wallace ran off with the money, and Kristen Eldredge is running around killing her fomer partners."

"Looking for the money?"

"That, and revenge. Remember, she got shot, was left for dead and did three years for the crime."

"So what do you need out of me?"

"I can't prove they're connected. Right now all they've got in common is that all the men have been murdered the same way. That's all I can prove."

"And you think the connection is down here in sunny Miami."

"That's a fact."

"I'll get on it, but remember, it's my story first."

"It's your story in Miami. Up here it's mine."

"I get a byline in your magazine?"

"Additional reporting by Chris Block. Good enough?"

"That works. I'll get back to you."

They hung up and Taylor finished typing a few more notes before heading uptown to join O'Bradovich. Something was bound to happen.

O'Bradovich and Taylor were on their second drink when Zero Mostel walked in. He approached slowly, bent forward like an old man, shaking his head slowly back and forth. He looked like Oedipus right after the blinding, before he'd regained his regal nature.

"What's wrong, Zee?" O'Bradovich said.

Mostel tossed a copy of *Counterattack* onto the table. "Take a look at this."

O'Bradovich scanned the paper, his forefinger tracking down the page. When his finger came to a stop, he took a deep breath. "Oh, Christ, Zee," he said.

"Yeah. They got me."

"Let me see that," Taylor said.

He found the item halfway down the page and read it:

> *Comedian and actor Zero Mostel might be a funny man but his history of associating with reds isn't so funny. We wonder if he's all that funny at the Communist meetings he goes to all the time.*
>
> *He has a history of attending red events going back more than ten years, and has never repudiated his pro-red stance. If he's so welcome at Commie gatherings, why is he welcome in our nightclubs and on our television sets?*

"Mean bunch of bastards," Taylor said.

"Look, Zee," O'Bradovich said. "Nobody takes this shit seriously. Relax."

"My sponsors are already bailing. If I can't land some more, I'm going to be canceled."

"Sit down. Have a drink and relax. We'll take care of this."

"Have a drink?" Mostel said, sliding into the booth. "Damn right I'll have a drink. Matter of fact, I'm going to get drunk as hell. Anybody wants to join me, that'll be fine. If you aren't up for getting drunk as hell, you might as well leave now."

"Take it easy, Zee."

"Take it easy? My career's over and you're telling me to take it easy!"

"It isn't over," Taylor said.

"Oh yeah? Who's going to hire me now? Don't you understand? I've been publicly exposed as a Communist. Damn it, I worked with Earl Browder to separate the American Party from the Russian one. I've always said that communism and capitalism can coexist."

"These guys don't give a damn about nuances," O'Bradovich said.

"At least try to relax," Taylor said. "I'll make some calls in the morning."

30

Leo Salmon held the car door open for Terry Louvin. Climbing into the back seat next to her, he signaled his driver with a wave of his hand. "We're headed to the Waldorf, Samuel."

"Yes, sir."

"The Waldorf?" Terry said, her eyebrows raised in surprise. There was a catch in her voice.

"A little pretentious, but it's nice. The Bull and Bear has great steaks."

"Oh, I've never been there. Am I dressed all right?"

"You look wonderful."

Terry couldn't help but glance down at her outfit. Sure, it was her best dress—in fact, she thought of it as her only good dress—but was it good enough for the Waldorf? That place was big time. Sometimes when she walked past the hotel and saw the women, all over-dressed and self-satisfied, wearing their wealth like a shield, coming out and going in, she wanted to cross the street.

"Thank you," she said.

As they drove they chatted about everyday things, the usual stuff you use to get to know each other, until Samuel pulled up in front of the Waldorf. Salmon stepped out of the car and then held her forearm as Louvin climbed out. She felt a little high as they walked into the lobby, as if she'd had a couple glasses of wine. Leo Salmon was a step up from the men she was used to; he was tall and handsome, well-dressed in a tailored suit and his haircut was both expensive and perfect.

None of that made a big difference to her, though; it was all just window-dressing. What counted was that he appeared to care about other people. So many good looking men were only interested in themselves. Leo, though, had worried about her interests during the negotiations for the studio and had gone out of his way to make sure she got a good deal.

The *maître d'* greeted Leo by name and led them past several waiting groups to their reserved table. As she sat down, Terry thought she'd never been in a place this luxurious in her life. She'd thought she was beyond being impressed by big time surroundings but evidently she'd been wrong.

The waiter who hovered behind the *maître d'* was older than she would have thought a waiter could be. His hair was gray and you'd have to be a woman to notice—maybe a particularly observant woman—but he was wearing makeup under his eyes to minimize the lines. He could not diminish the bagginess, though. "Would you like a cocktail, Mr. Salmon?"

Salmon smiled at Terry. "How about a drink?"

"White wine," she said. "They really know you here."

His dismissive wave said it was no big deal. "I come in every once in a while." He placed the drink order and watched the waiter walk away. "So, Terry, tell me about yourself. You a native New Yorker?"

"Oh, no. I come from Georgia. Moved up here when I was nineteen." She shrugged. "There's not a lot of opportunity for dancers in Atlanta."

"You don't sound southern."

She laughed. "You should have heard me when I went on my first audition here. I had to tell them my name three times before they could understand me. The choreogapher told me to go learn to talk and then come back. Before I even had a job, I had to hire a voice coach."

"What do you sound like if you wake up suddenly at three in the monring?"

She let all the southernness she still had in her surface and said, "Why, sugar, you plain wouldn't believe what I sound like. I'd be just as southern as Scarlett O'Hara." Her accent made the words sound like molasses from an overturned bottle.

"Wow, that's strong. Sure you aren't exaggerating?"

"If anything I'm holding back."

"Amazing."

The waiter brought the drinks and hovered beside Salmon, who waited until Terry had taken a sip of her wine. He asked, "Is it all right?"

"Wonderful."

Salmon nodded to the waiter, who left the table. Taking a sip of his bourbon and water, Salmon said, "How long have you been in the city?"

"Long enough to feel like a native. Ten years."

"So that would make you twenty-nine."

"Every bit of it. And you?"

"Forty-two. Too old for you."

"Oh, I don't know. Thirteen years isn't that long. Not when you're talking about men and women."

"That right?"

"You know how women mature faster than men. Men my age are still little boys. Most men don't even start maturing before they turn thirty-five."

"Is that a fact?"

"I don't know about facts. I just know my experience."

"And you've had a lot of exerience with men?"

She knew from his grin that he was kidding her, poking harmless fun. Had his tone been just a little different, though, his remarks would have been creepy, objectionable. That bothered her. Truth be told, he was one of the nicest men she'd met in a long time and she could see from his expression that he wished he hadn't said what he had. He recognized how it sounded, that it created an impression that he didn't intend and she felt a little bit sorry for him. Damn it, there she went again, playing out the same old game. Again.

"I'm sorry," he said. "That didn't come out right."

"Forget it. No harm done."

Why was it that she was always looking for a man to take care of her? Why did she constantly, every time she met some guy she had even a touch of attraction for, begin wondering what kind of husband and father he'd make, begin asking herself if he was the man to make life a little safer and more secure?

Logically, she knew that it was up to her to make things safe and good for herself and her boy, but when you came right down to it, logic didn't do a thing. It was like the smoke from a cigarette; it made itself visible for a moment and then floated away into the sky and was never seen again.

"Have I had much experience with men?" she said. "No, probably not that much. But a lot of what I've had hasn't been all that pleasant."

"I'm sorry about that," he said. "Believe me, I have no intention of being an unpleasant experience."

"That's good to know." She smiled. "If I seem a little withdrawn, well, I've got to be honest with you, I'm a little out of my league here. In the circles I move in, you don't come to places like the Waldorf. I'm telling you, I've lived in this city for ten years and the only time I ever saw the Waldorf was in that Ginger Rogers movie."

"If you're uncomfortable, we don't have to stay. It's not like New York doesn't have a couple of restaurants to choose from."

"It's fine. I can get used to a little luxury for a night."

"It's funny. I chose this place thinking it would impress you." He toyed with his fork, not meeting her eyes. "I'd like to say I picked it because I knew you'd enjoy it but the truth is I wanted to dazzle you."

"Dazzle me? Why?"

"Well, I think you're kind of special, Terry."

Oh God, he called her special and he sounded sincere when he said it. As the waiter returned to take their order, she thought most girls would be in heaven tonight. Being here in the Walfdorf, getting set for a wonderful meal with a handsome and successful man who had good manners and was obviously stricken with her? Most girls would think this was the fulfillment of a fantasy going back to their childhood. Terry Louvin, though, was worried. She'd spent most of the past year by herself, taking care of her child and her business and just as she'd begun to enjoy her independence, had begun to see the possibility of a life that didn't depend on a man to take care of her, here came Leo Salmon throwing a brick through her window.

What was going to happen next?

31

Taylor was pouring a cup of coffee when the phone on his desk rang. Carrying his mug as carefully as he could, he hurried across the bullpen area, spilling over all the way. When he picked up the phone with his free hand, he glanced into his cup and saw that half of the coffee was gone.

"Hello?"

"Damon Taylor?"

"Yeah," he said.

"This is Chris Block, from the *Miami....*"

"From the *Herald*, I know. Got something for me?"

As he spoke, Paul the copy boy lifted Taylor's mug out from his hand and took it away. Taylor watched him stroll across to the coffee pot, carefully avoiding the spilled stuff on the floor. He refilled Taylor's mug, added sugar and brought it back to him, placing it on his desk. Then he saluted Taylor and walked away. Taylor returned the salute.

"Fact is, those guys are all connected. Wallace, Goodman and Warren all worked for the same investment house in Miami. They sold securities."

"What about the woman?"

"Kristen Eldredge was a client of the house. She worked at a battery plant here in town. Secretary. Guess what department."

"My bet would be payroll."

"Bingo."

"You're sure she was in a position to know the payroll money was coming in?"

"I've seen her employment records. She worked for the head of the department. Everything important wound up on her desk."

"So she finds out when the payroll is coming in and gathers these three guys together to hit the armored car."

"Which was delivering payroll cash to the battery plant. A hundred thousand in cash. The bills came from a branch of Wallace's bank over on the west coast. In Naples. To get here, they had to bring it across the Tamiami Trail. You know the road?"

"No."

"It's about a hundred and fifty miles of nothing but swamp. No traffic at all. It's the Everglades, you know? There's a thousand places where they could have hit that truck."

"So can we say these guys did it?"

"We know Eldredge was there. She got hit in the shootout—it was bloody as hell, these guys killed both guards on the truck. Here's the funny thing: all three men left their jobs a week before the robbery and all three of them left Florida about that time. Seems to paint a pretty clear picture. Eldredge claimed from the beginning she didn't know who any of them were, at least not their real names. Said the only one she could identify was her fiancé and the name she had for him turned out to be phony. She played quite the victim."

"Somebody bought it."

"Must be a hell of an actress. I'm figuring she was planning on going after her partners even before she went to jail."

Taylor finished off his coffee. "Fact is, she did get them. All of them. The only thing left is the money. She didn't get that."

"Well, the irony is the money's no good to her. The serial numbers are sequential and recorded. Somebody starts spending it, the feds will be all over the place."

"You said a hundred thousand was taken?"

"That's right."

"I only found seventy. Thirty percent fee to launder it sound about right?"

"About that, yeah. You've got the money?"

"Found it in Wallace's apartment."

"You want some advice?" Without waiting for an answer, he continued. "Make really sure the Eldredge woman doesn't find out you've got it. She does, she'll slice you to pieces, too."

He spent another twenty minutes getting details and source names from Block and then wrote a new verison of the story. Placing his draft on Marsczyk's desk, he went down to Dixie's for a sandwich and a drink. The restaurant and bar was a favorite of his. Aside from the small bar in the front the rest of the place looked like a tearoom. He'd discovered it during his newspaper days and went there because it had been a full tilt-cauldron of craziness and he loved the atmosphere. Dixie herself was an woman of indeteminate age—she could have been anywhere from fifty to eighty—and was as goofy as a Max Fleischer cartoon. She was gray-haired and wore a swirling red skirt, a peasant blouse and a black beret.

When he walked in, she cried out, "Where the hell you been lately, flyboy?"

Dixie liked to think or pretend that all her male customers were pilots and when they first came in, she'd quiz them about their flights. Most of the people who came in learned to go along with her and made up great fantasies about around the world adventures. How seriously she took all of this was anybody's guess but everyone had a good time.

"How about a roast beef sandwich and a Jameson on the rocks, Dixie?"

"Got a big flight tonight?"

"Going to Paris."

"I was there once. It stinks."

She placed his drink on the bar and walked off to make his sandwich. Scanning the rest of the place, he saw Hilda sitting at a table back in the restaurant section, dealing out tarot cards. Hilda was also timeless. She looked as though she could be anywhere from thirty to seventy and fell a little on the pudgy side, her round face accented by the turban she wore tightly coiled on top of her head.

Taylor carried his drink over and sat down opposite her. "How you doing, Hilda?"

"How many times I got to tell you," she said, without looking up from the cards, "don't call me that in here."

"Okay, Madame Sophia. My apologies. Everything all right?"

"Excellent, excellent. The cards are in my favor."

Back during his newspaper days before the war, he'd discovered that she'd been sitting at this table in Ernie's for ten years, doing readings. She was a nurse who spent all of her off-duty time in here. He'd done a feature on her and she'd turned out to be one of the great characters of Manhattan, so when he'd discovered after the war that she was still around, he'd made sure he checked in with her every once in a while. Sometimes a story resulted but even if it didn't, he always walked away refreshed.

"I'm going to read you, Damon," she said.

"That's not necessary."

"You're going to tell Madame Sophia, who knows everything, what's necessary?" She shook her head. "Damon, you need to be read. There are forces around you that need to be articulated."

"Oh, well, if there's forces around me, go ahead."

"You can make jokes about it, but the fact is the forces swirling about are unsettled. They might be dangerous. You need to be read."

Madame Sophia shuffled the cards, dealt them and studied for a long time, tapping her fingers on the table. She hummed tunelessly as she concentrated on the cards. During their first interview, when she'd gone off the record to tell him her real name, he'd asked why she was calling herself Madame Sophia. She'd shaken her head the same way she had a moment ago and said, "Would you get a reading from Hilda? Hilda's about as exotic as a fish bowl."

"Well?" he said.

"Shhh." She studied the layout a little longer and then said, "Right now, I wouldn't want to be you. What do you want, Damon? You want to be amused and go out of here happy or do you want the truth?"

"As long as we're doing this, let's do it right. Give me the truth."

"Dixie," she called out. "Bring Damon another drink. He's going to need it."

"I am?"

"For sure. Damon, you've got trouble coming from every direction. You've got some choices you're going to have to make. One of them," she paused, then started over. "Remember, you wanted the truth. Well, here it comes. One of your choices concerns what you're willing to do to protect the people you love. You're going to have to make a decision in that area and it's a hard one that might not work out the way you want it to. You also are going to have to fight to keep yourself alive. The possibility of death comes at you from several directions."

"Can you be more specific?"

She shook her head, her jowls continuing to quiver after she stopped. "It's not clear. I can't see it clearly. If it was just one person, maybe I could get a fix on it, but there's a bunch of them. Right now, a man is preparing your doom."

"A man?"

"This one is a man, yes, but there's a woman, too."

"What do the cards suggest?"

"The cards," she scoffed. "The cards. You know what the cards are? They're something for the tourists to be impressed by. There's no magic in the cards. It's in me. I see the dimensions, Damon, not the cards. Me. And this time I'm not seeing it clearly. It's like watching a television set through a sheet of wax paper."

"I know one person who might want to kill me. A woman."

"A very unusual woman, very powerful. Don't underestimate her, Damon."

"I won't. You've got nothing on any other source?"

"Sorry, no. I've told you everything I'm seeing."

Did he believe any of this? Did he really think Hilda could tap into the future? Not necessarily. At one time he would have dismissed the whole thing as bullshit but now? These days, he found themselves open to the possibilities. What she had to say might turn out to be true and it might not. Since he couldn't know which, he'd walk a little more carefully after hearing from her. Taylor pulled out a ten dollar bill.

"You know the rules, Damon," Linda said. "I don't take money for using my gifts. Dessert, yes, money, no. You want to buy me dessert, Dixie's got a great chocolate cake up there."

"Dixie," he called out. "Cake for the lady."

32

"Polish it and let's go to press," Marsczyk said.

"I haven't got it nailed yet." Taylor waved the sheaf of pages at Marsczyk.

The editor leaned back in his chair, propped his feet on the desk and smiled at something on his TV screen. Taylor glanced over at it. A bosomy blonde lady in an evening gown was singing a song—if you could call what she was doing singing.

"My God," Taylor said. "She's terrible."

"Does it matter?" Marsczyk said. "Look at that chest."

"You got a point there."

"Look, I wanted to tell you I don't feel comfortable going to press with this draft."

"That's why I want a polish."

"A polish isn't going to help. The story's got holes in it."

"Look, Damon, you keep complaining that you're stuck. We have to do something to break this thing open. Printing what you've got will stir up the hornet's nest. Who knows what'll come out of that?"

"I see what you mean. That could work. There's a problem with your thinking, though."

"What's that?"

"It definitely puts me front and center. We run with this, I become a target."

"That's probably the case. You want to hold off?"

He thought about it for a moment. "No, Lou, let's get it done."

"Go do the rewrite, then. Just finesse the parts you haven't got nailed down. You know how to do it. Imply without stating."

"I'll give it a shot."

"Great. And listen, be here in an hour. We got something going on you're going to want to see."

An hour later, he was at his desk finishing up his copy when Danny Murphy walked past him without speaking, heading toward Marsczyk's office. The detective was scowling, looking as though he wanted nothing more than to beat somebody up in an interrogation room. His eyes looked cold. He was breathing heavily, as if the walk up the stairs had taken a toll on him.

Taylor watched him walk into Marsczyk's office. In a moment, his editor appeared in the doorway and waved Taylor over. He pulled the sheet of newsprint out of his typewriter, placed it with the rest of the story on his desk and walked over to the office. Murphy and Warren Haynes sat in front of Marsczyk's desk while the editor sat behind it like a king perched on his throne. Whatever was going on in here, Lou Marsczyk was prepared to enjoy it.

"Sit down, Damon, you're going to like this." Turning to Murphy, he said, "How close are you to retirement?"

"What the hell you talking about?"

Marsczyk grinned. "I'm wondering how close you are to retirement because it's time for you to leave the police force and I want to know if you're going to have a little money coming in."

Murphy looked confused. His eyes furrowed and his mouth went slack. "Come off it, Marsczyk. I don't need to put up with any shit from you. You start giving me a hard time I'll haul you downtown and you'll disappear."

"Tell him what you've got, Haynes."

"We'll start with the Robert Morgenson case. Convicted of armed robbery, sentenced to fifteen years. Three witnesses placed him in Jersey the night of the robbery, only their names and their stories disappeared from the case file and they were never called to the trial."

"You're suggesting I had something to do with that?"

"We'd never *suggest* a thing like that. We've got enough to prove it," Marsczyk said.

"Look, Morgenson was a bad guy. I got him off the streets. What's wrong with that?"

"Where do I start? A, you framed him. B, the guy who actually did the robbery is still on the streets. C, you broke the law. D, you violated your oath. How far you want me to go?"

"You can't prove none of this."

"We got affidavits from the witnesses. And not just them. We can prove you doctored at least a dozen cases. We can show a pattern. Think about it, Murphy. We've got a dozen cases where we can demonstrate you ignored or destroyed evidence and sent guys innocent men to prison. And you know as well as I do that as soon as we run the story, a whole bunch of other people are going to come forward. And then Internal Affairs is going to get involved and you're done. Here's what's for sure, Murphy: we're going to destroy you."

"What do you want?"

"First, we want the charges dropped against Guthrie."

"What else?"

"We want you off the force."

"You're going too far."

"You don't understand, Murphy. We're doing you a favor. We're going to run the story…."

"You can't do that."

"What else can we do? That's what we live for, a story like this. It'd be downright irresponsible not to run it."

"You can't…."

"Here's what we can do: we can hold off long enough for you to get off the force and leave town. That is, if Guthrie gets out of jail today."

Murphy sat quietly, his hands clasped in his lap. He nodded his head as if listening to music in his mind. After a few long moments, he mumbled, "All right. Guthrie gets out today."

After he turned in his copy, Taylor left the building and walked aimlessly until he found himself in front of Terry Louvin's studio and realized he'd been coming here the whole time. Glancing through the window into studio A, he saw that Terry was wrapping up a class, so he stood in the lobby and waited. In a few minutes, the door opened and the dance students came flocking out, chatting at each other, grouping up for the subway ride home. They were all beautiful young girls in their early teens and he felt as if he were being healed by simply being in their company. When they were gone, he walked into the studio where Terry, wearing black tights, a gray sweatshirt and leg warmers, was putting away records.

"Hi," he said.

She looked up and smiled. "Damon, good to see you. I wasn't expecting you."

"I was just in the neighborhood. Can I buy you a cup of coffee?"

"I've got a free hour. Let me put this stuff away."

She slid a record into its sleeve and put the album on the table next to the phonograph. Then, looking into his eyes, she frowned. Coming closer, she studied his face.

"What's the matter, Damon?"

"How 'bout I tell you about it over coffee?"

"Okay. Come on."

"Where do you want to go? That shop on the corner any good?"

"I'll take you to the best coffee in the city."

She took his hand and led the way to the back of the studio, where she opened the door and led him into her office. An odd, off-center feeling came over him as he followed her. He felt as if he were being led by a beautiful young woman to her bedroom. When they got into her office, she pointed to the table she used as a desk and told him, "Sit down."

"You've got a kitchen in here?"

"Isn't that great?" She grinned at him.

Walking over to the counter, she filled the pot and began to brew the coffee. "Fresh pot in a few minutes," she said. "By the way, I really want to thank you for finding me Leo Salmon. He's a treasure."

Taylor sat down. He focused his eyes on the spoon that sat next to the sugar bowl. He felt a tightening in his chest and took deep breaths until he relaxed again.

"You went out with him?"

"Last Friday night. He took me to the Waldorf, to the Bull and Bear. It was wonderful."

"The Bull and Bear's a great place, all right."

"Well, that's true, but who cares about that? I would have been happy if we'd gone to the automat. He's such a nice guy."

He wondered how long it had been since anyone had called Leo Salmon a nice guy. Most people thought of him as a man without mercy, a guy who'd order the trigger pulled as quickly as you could snap your fingers. He had to tell her who Leo Salmon really was. As he went to speak, he saw the happiness in her face and hesitated. Maybe there was really no need to say anything. Maybe this would all pass like a summer thunderstorm.

He also considered the question of what would happen to the real estate deal if he told her about Salmon. Could he take a chance on her losing the studio, going back to hustling bad dancing gigs to keep the baby fed? He didn't want to be responsible for that.

"Are you getting serious about Leo?"

"Oh, I don't know." She brought the coffee to the table. "I mean, we've only been out once. Still, I think it could happen."

"You be careful, Terry."

She patted the back of his hand. "You're a good friend, Damon."

She slid into the chair opposite his and looked across at him. Taylor rested his hands on the tabletop and tried for a smile. The effort felt strained, even to him.

"Something wrong, Damon?"

"Tell you the truth, I don't know. Can I tell you what happened?"

"Of course."

"Down at the magazine, we just pulled the rug out from under a shady cop."

"Was he crooked?"

"In the way you mean, I don't know. I mean, I'm not sure. I don't think he took money under the table or anything. In a way, I wish he had been on the take. What makes it stink is that in his own mind he was clean. What we do know is he was a little too quick to close cases, he wasn't above framing a guy. He rationalized what he was doing by saying the guys he framed were dirty anyway. If they hadn't done that particular crime, they'd still done a lot of others. Problem was this time he arrested an innocent man, a guy who'd never done anything at all. We brought him down. He's going to have to leave the force now."

"Good."

"Terry, I wrecked a man's life. His career's over, his reputation's shattered. He's got nothing and it's on account of me."

"He's got the memory of all the people he hurt. That's enough. He's got everything he deserves."

"I hope so."

33

Danny Murphy walked into his apartment and switched the overhead light on.

As he always did, he stopped in the doorway, hesitating before he entered. The place was so damn dark and depressing. It brought him down just to be here. Hell, coming home was supposed to be a good thing, you were supposed to be able to relax and get comfortable and loose in your own apartment. It wasn't supposed to depress you.

But then most people's apartments weren't filled with ghosts. Abbie and the kids had been gone for more than a year but he still saw them everywhere he looked, still smelled the pot roast she made, its aroma wafting from the kitchen. He still heard the kids bickering while they listened to *The Lone Ranger* and *Superman* on the radio. The apartment was never still, never quiet. When he was away he didn't miss them, but the moment he came home, they filled his mind and heart again. If he could only find Abbie, he'd tell her how sorry he was, how he'd never meant to hurt her, and he knew he'd beg her to come back. But he couldn't find her and the whole damn New York Police Department couldn't find her, so she must not be in the city anymore.

Sighing, he went into the kitchen and opened a beer. If tonight was typical, it'd be the first of many and if those didn't quiet his brain, he'd go down to Big Eddie's and drink himself into oblivion. Except he couldn't go down to Big Eddie's anymore because by morning, all the other cops who hung out there would know about his disgrace and he'd never be able to face any of them again.

God damn that Damon Taylor to hell anyway. This was his fault. The son of a bitch had no idea what it was like out there, what the life of a cop in this city was. Every time he went to work, he put his life on the line to protect scum like Taylor. Was it worth it? Tell you what, let that bastard Taylor risk his fucking life every day, face the possibility of some piece of shit putting a couple of bullets in him every time he went out into the streets. See how much he worries about how the bastards get put away then.

If Taylor had seen that son of a bitch Guthrie smirk when Murphy had told him the charges were dropped and he was now a free man, he'd have wanted to kill the bastard just like Murphy had. Here's

Taylor complaining about him locking up innocent men. Had Taylor even seen the rap sheet on Guthrie? Beating up private cops in the California labor strikes, assault and battery on police, assault with a deadly weapon when he'd hit a man with his guitar at a union rally. The red bastard had a prison term coming to him and Taylor had gotten him off free.

And now there was't a damn thing Murphy could do about it.

No, he was done. The bastards at that magazine had all that stuff and they'd write it up so that he looked like a crooked cop, whether he quit the force or not. Like he really had a choice. Once that stuff got out, Internal Affairs would come poking around and he knew how that would end: he'd be sent up himself.

No, he couldn't have that and he'd be damned if he could just quit the force. What was he supposed to do? Become a private eye and rig divorce evidence like all the others?

There was only one thing he could do. Sitting at his kitchen table, he took out his gun, unloaded and polished it, oiling it really good before he reloaded it. When it was clean, loaded and ready, he finished his beer and then leaned forward and put the barrel of the gun in his mouth.

Sweat broke on his forehead and he closed his eyes, fighting to control the shaking of his hand as his finger tightened on the trigger. He took a deep breath. Now. His finger squeezed the trigger slowly, carefully and just before the hammer released, he jerked the weapon out of his mouth. He held it in front of him, looking at it, and said out loud, "What the fuck am I doing?"

He was killing the wrong man.

He didn't deserve to die for what he had done.

Damon Taylor did.

Taylor had been home about an hour when the doorbell sounded. He checked it and buzzed the front door open. When the knock came, he peered through the peephole. A vaguely familiar man, holding a big package, was standing there. He opened the door and the man said, "Mr. Taylor, I've got a package for you from Roger Basile."

He couldn't place this Basile guy. The delivery man must have read the flash of confusion on his face. "Roger Basile. The tailor? Remember, Mr. Salmon brought you in?"

"Oh, sure. You're the guy who helped measure me."

"Right. Will you sign for this, please?"

"You know, I told Leo Salmon I didn't want a suit."

"I know. And he told Mr. Basile that you were desperately in need of one. May I suggest, sir, that if you have a problem with this, you take it up with Mr. Salmon? I'm simply the delivery man."

"Of course." He signed the receipt and tried to tip the man but he refused the five-dollar bill Taylor held out.

"I've been well taken care of," he said and scampered away as if he were afraid Taylor would chase him down and force the fiver on him.

He was opening the package when the front door sounded again. Thinking the delivery man had come back, he buzzed the front door open and a moment later, heard a fresh banging on his door.

"Hey, Damon," a voice called out. "Damon Taylor, you in there? Hell, boy, I know you're in there, you buzzed the door open. Let me in, will you?"

"I'm coming, I'm coming." He pulled the door open. "Hello, Woody."

"Look who's a free man? Charges dropped and everything." Guthrie's guitar was slung over his back, like always.

"Good. You on your way home?"

"Yeah. Pete and Lee wanted me to go out to Jersey and play a dance tonight but I got to see my family. Been a long time. Just came by to thank you for getting me out."

"No problem. Glad we were able to do it. Say hello to your family for me."

"I'll do that. You want to come along, have a little dinner with us?"

"This isn't a night for company, Woody."

"Reckon it an't, at that. Well, at least we can have a celebration drink before I go, can't we?"

"Fraid not."

"You ain't going to offer me a drink? Just one little drink?"

"Woody, I've seen you take one little drink. Most of the time it leads to another, then four or five more, and suddenly you decide to go on out to Jersey and play some music with the boys. You wind up going home to a disappointed wife the next morning. I can't be part of that."

"Well, hell, I reckon you're right. We'll have that drink another time, okay?"

"Count on it."

After Woody left, he finished opening the box, and then he picked up the phone and dialed Leo Salmon's number. After he'd gone through the secretaries and gotten Salmon on the line, he said, "Leo, I just got four suits delivered."

"You like them?"

"Sure. They're beautiful but that isn't the point. I can't accept four suits from you."

"What are you telling me? There's people you can take suits from but I'm not one of them?"

"Damn it, that's not what I'm saying at all."

"So you're saying you can't accept four suits from me. Well, how many can you accept?"

"You're enjoying the hell out of this, aren't you?"

"Of course, I am. Weirdest thank you call I ever got. You think the suits look good, wait till you put them on. You've never felt clothes this comfortable."

"Leo...."

"Look, Damon, don't think of it as a gift. Think of it as a thank you."

"You're thanking me? What for?"

"For bringing Terry Louvin into my life. Damon, I've never met a girl like her in my life."

"Sounds serious."

Leo Salmon paused for a second and then said in a quiet voice, "I think I'm in love, Damon. I think this is it."

At that moment, Taylor felt a tightening in his stomach and a rush to his brain that left him lightheaded. "How does she feel about it?"

"I think she feels the same way, Damon. That's the great thing. I believe she loves me, too. At least, I hope to hell she does."

He hesitated again, waiting for his stomach to relax. Then he said, "Good for you, Leo. I'm happy for you." After a moment, he said, "None of my business, but does she know what you really do for a living?"

"No. Of course not. You know, for the first time in my life, I'm beginning to have questions about the way I live."

"You'll work it out, Leo."

"Yeah, I guess I will. Fact is, there's only one way it can work out."

"What's that?"

"If I want things to be good with Terry, I'm going to have to tell her the truth about me."

"This really is serious, isn't it?"

"That it is. I'll let you know how it works out. Listen, I was going to call you. Word on the street is a couple of people would like to pop your balloon."

"I figured that. I'm getting close to a big story."

"You be careful, man."

"I will," he said. "Say hello to Terry for me."

34

Irish Jack figured there were two ways he could go: he could start a war, picking off Costello's men one at a time, sort of work his way up from the bottom, or he could just cut the head off the beast by getting Salmon and Costello. He glanced at his five men, his lieutenants, wondering that if he followed the war option how much it would cost him

to see it through. It would take a lot of time and effort and it would be very dangerous. Worse, it might not work.

Taking out Salmon and Costello would give him part of what he wanted, but that might be even more dangerous. But if he could remove those two from the picture, the Sicilians would know they couldn't just throw the Irish aside like garbage.

Still, he needed to stir up a little mischief, if only to serve as a cover, to divert Salmon and Costello from what was really going on. If he did this right, they'd spend their time swatting flies and not notice the swarm of bees coming at them.

He outlined the assignments and his troops left the office. Before he followed them, he tossed off the rest of his coffee and checked his gun, emptying the shells from the cylinder, swabbing the barrel and reloading the .38. Tucking it into his coat pocket, he left the building and headed uptown to Harlem.

He hated being in Harlem. The neighborhoods reeked of poverty and drunkenness. The crowded streets were layered with dopers and drunks who leaned up against the buildings like wallpaper. You couldn't walk half a block without some bastard hitting you up for change. The bums were aggressive in this neighborhood. If you told them "no" they were likely to grab you and hang on till you emptied your pockets.

He told one of the bums to shove off and the man reached for his collar, saying, "Come on, buddy, just a quarter. Big man like you got a quarter." His breath stank like a garbage dump. Irish Jack slugged him in the face and as the bum staggered away he sped up his pace down 125th Street.

The man he was looking for was just ahead of him. He could tell by the black book the man carried in his right hand. Irish Jack fell in behind him, keeping about five paces back. When the guy walked into the lobby of an aprtment building, Irish Jack hurried up and when he saw no one else was in the lobby, shoved his gun into the guy's ribs.

"You know what I want," he said.

The bagman froze. He was taller than Irish Jack, but what the hell, everybody was. He could feel the tension in the man's back muscles as the pistol made contact.

"You don't want to do this," the tall man said.

"Yes, I do. I want to do this."

"You don't know whose money you're taking."

"That's where you're wrong, my friend. I know exactly whose money this is." He laughed. "It's mine. Hand it over."

As the bagman held the envelope of money behind him, he said, "You're going to regret this."

Irish Jack started to make some wiseass comment but slammed the guy in the back of the head with his pistol instead.

Leo Salmon picked up the phone and dialed a number. When the person at the other end of the line answered, Salmon said, "For three days now, a gang's been holding up our numbers runners. First in Harlem, now it's spreading."

"I know."

"If you know, why haven't you done anything about it?"

"Well...."

"Forget it. I'm not interested in why. Here's what I want: I want them found and killed."

"Yes, sir."

"I mean it. I want them killed. Killed loudly and publicly. I want everybody in this city to know what happens if you touch one of our people. Got it?"

"Got it."

He cut the connection and then dialed another number. When Damon Taylor answered, he said. "Got time for a drink? I need to talk to you."

"Sure. What's up?"

"Rather tell you over a drink, in person. Meet me at P. J. Clarke's?"

"Sure thing. Half an hour?"

"Fine." He called Charles to bring the car around and then started downstairs.

Irish Jack watched Salmon get into his Cadillac. Leaning forward, he said to the driver, "Follow that car."

"What the hell," the cab driver said. *Follow that car*? Am I in a movie or what?"

"Never mind the wisecracks. Don't lose that Cadillac, there's an extra buck in it for you."

"This time of day, he goes to the airport or out to Jersey, it's going to cost you more than a buck."

As long as he was spending the money he took from the numbers runner, who cared? "Fine," he said.

When the Cadillac pulled up in front of P. J. Clarke's, Irish Jack had the cab stop half a block back. He paid the driver and slipped him an extra buck.

"What the hell," the cabbie said. "Where's my tip?"

"I gave you a buck."

"That wasn't a tip. That was for keeping up with the Caddie. Hell, man, that was a bonus."

"For Christ's sake." Irish Jack tossed another buck onto the driver's seat.

"Thanks, buddy. You want I should wait? I'll have to keep the meter running."

"I want you should get the fuck out of here."

The driver touched his hand to the bill of his cap and pulled away from the curb without checking traffic first. Irish Jack could hear brakes squealing as other cars slammed to a halt to keep from hitting him.

He hurried toward the bar but came to a stop as he saw Damon Taylor coming up from the opposite direction. Taylor opened the door of Clarke's and walked in. This couldn't be a coincidence: Taylor and Salmon being in the same bar might happen once by chance but twice? Were they friends? Was Taylor connected to Salmon's outfit? What was the deal between them? Irish Jack walked into the bar and saw Salmon greet Taylor warmly, shaking hands, slapping him on the back. They were obviously friends. Taylor must be a part of Salmon's operation. He wondered if the big blonde broad had known this when she'd hired him to slow Taylor down.

"Damon, it's good to see you," Salmon clapped him on the shoulder.

"Same here, Leo."

It was true, Taylor *was* glad to see Salmon and this bothered him.

You weren't supposed to cosy up to Mafia chieftains; all kinds of trouble could come from that. The only guy he'd ever known who could walk that line was Damon Runyon and even he'd had some doubts about his relationships. He was always telling Taylor how careful he had to be, how the simplest mistake could get him killed.

"You know," he said once, "I get offers every day, big money offers, to write my autobiography and I'd love to do it. All the crap there is about me out there, don't you think I'd love to see the truth printed? But I print the truth about some of the guys I know, I get my ass shot off. And if I can't write the truth then why bother?"

Taylor wondered if he was in danger of falling into the same trap.

"What's on your mind, Leo?" he said.

Salmon tossed off his drink and called for another one. "And a Jameson on the rocks for my friend here," he added.

There was that word. He was going to have to do some heavy thinking about things. "Thanks," he said when the drinks arrived.

"Damon, you're going to want to laugh at me, I swear you are, and if you do I'll kick your ass. Still, you're going to want to."

"Why am I going to laugh at you, Leo?"

Salmon turned to face him and his eyes pleaded for understanding, sympathy.

"Damon, I swear to God, I think I'm in love."

"With Terry, you mean?"

"Christ, man, who else would I be talking about?"

"This is big time stuff," he said, because he did not know what else to say. "I've got to say I wasn't expecting this."

He'd watched Terry turn from a helpless mess of a kid into a strong, capable and independent woman and he'd found himself, even as he told himself they were just friends, wanting more from her as she mastered each step of her journey. Before he got around to speaking up, though, Leo had made his move and now it was too late for him. The only way he could get Terry away from Leo would be to tell her the truth about the man and if he did that, he'd rip the happiness of two people to pieces. That wasn't the way.

And as much as he disliked the idea, he had to consider what Salmon might do in response.

"I know I asked you this before, but does she love you?"

"I think so. I hope she does. Hell, man, I don't know. What does a man like me know about love? All I l know is I want to marry her and have her with me forever."

"Jesus, Leo, you guys have only gone out, what is it, three, four times?"

"It doesn't take long to know when it's right."

"And you want to know if I think this is a good idea? Is that why I'm here?"

"Well, yeah, I guess so."

He finished his drink. "Leo, what does she know about you?"

"About the way I make my money, you mean?"

"Yeah."

"Nothing." He sounded like a sheepish little boy.

"Before you propose to her, don't you think she ought to know?"

"Up till now, Damon, I've never been bothered by what I do. I've always been able to divide the way I make a living from who I am as a person, you know what I mean?"

"I know what you're saying but I don't know if that kind of division is possible."

"Well, it turns out it isn't. All this time I've been deluding myself."

"What are you going to do about it?"

As he spoke, Salmon avoided Taylor's eyes, kept his face focused on his own reflection in the mirror behind the bar. "I don't need the rackets. Not any more. I got enough money to live three or four lives. I can get out." He looked around, as if checking to see who could overhear what he was about to say. "Damon, I chose the kind of life I've been living early, when I was a kid, you understand? And I didn't know what was open to me when I picked the road I walked down. I'm a smart guy, Damon, you know that, and I believe that given a different set of circumstances I could have had an entirely different life. Now the circumstances *are* different. Terry and I can take the money I've made, go to Europe or somewhere, and live happily, you understand?"

"Oh, sure, I understand, but don't you think she needs to know where the money came from? Who you really are?"

"Sure, she *deserves* it, but...."

"You said it yourself. You got to go into this thing honest. You can't build anything on a lie."

"I'm not going to lie. I just won't tell her."

"Come on, Leo. You know what you don't say is as big a lie as what you do say."

Salmon tossed off another drink and set the glass down hard. "You're right." He ran the back of his hand across his lips. "I have to tell her."

"You'll do it?"

"Yeah."

"I think that's good."

"But what if she won't accept it? What if she hates me when I tell her?"

"Then you'll know she wasn't right for you."

"Yeah, that makes sense." He grinned. "For a reporter, you're a pretty smart guy, Damon."

"Thanks."

Throwing a ten spot on the bar, he stood to go. "Oh, by the way, Damon. Nice suit."

35

"How was your day?" Terry Louvin asked.

This was living, Salmon thought, coming home to your woman and having her mix you a drink and asking how your day was. It was a simple and true way to live, being there in a small, ordinary apartment, not the huge and lavish place he lived in. Here, the *commonness* of the whole place was striking and, in some odd way he couldn't fully understand, wonderful. How could he have lived forty years without ever discovering this?

"My day? It was teriffic. How about yours?"

She sat next to him on the couch and told him about her work, how the kids had acted, how the pre-teens were improving and should be right on top of their routines for the recital that was coming up. She was still a little concerned over the teenagers, though. They weren't getting it and she was beginning to wonder if maybe she had choreographed the piece in a way that was too complicated for them.

As Salmon listened, his mind wandered. Actually, he couldn't say he was listening at all but her voice and her words had a way of relaxing him, making him glide into some unexplored area of his mind where everything was calm and perfect, where there were no mobs, nobody robbing his numbers runners, no takeover of the waterfront going on—nothing to fill his brain but contentment.

Yes, he should tell her about himself, tell her who he was and what he had done, because it wasn't right for her to think of him as just another real estate lawyer. If they were going to get anywhere, they had to walk on a road paved with truth.

And he would tell her.

But not now. Not while he was so completely under her spell, so totally wrapped in her mundane story of kids and dancing. It was funny. Originally, he thought he'd come into her life, fulfil the promise he'd made as part of his deal with Taylor that had enabled Costello's niece to avoid a first degree murder rap, and then walk away and never have to see her again.

Now the deal was complete. Terry Louvin owned the studio and this whole building. She was on her way to big time success. He'd done everything he'd promised but he found he couldn't walk away.

He'd discovered something unexpected. Here, next to this woman, was the only place on this earth where he really wanted to be.

Anywhere else in this whole wild and rich city, this town he'd always loved to be a part of, was now just an area of territory that on a map would be labeled *Not here with Terry*. When you got right down to it, being anywhere else was like being thrown into hell. How could it be that what he had loved all his life, this city, could now be so flat and empty, like an empty house?

As she continued to speak, he touched her cheek lightly and said, "I love you." It was the first time he'd ever said those words to anybody.

Irish Jack stood in the shadows across from Terry Louvin's studio, looking at the lighted window on the second floor. Once he'd decided that the best way to truly hurt the Costello gang was to cut its head off, he knew he'd have to get two people: Leo Salmon and Frank Costello himself. Frank never came out of his Upper East Side townhouse; you wanted to see him, you paid him a visit. Irish Jack needed a way to draw him outside, to fix it so the man had to leave his house. The best way to do that was to kill Leo Salmon first. The only reason Costello could hide himself away was because he had Salmon to run things for him.

So he'd been trailing Salmon, trying to get a look at his habits, trying to find his pattern. Leo ran most of the business from his Brooklyn townhouse and trying to get inside that place would be like trying to storm a castle. When he came out, at least two shooters walked him to his car. He'd have to get at him somewhere else. The main reasons he went out of the house were to see that reporter guy, Taylor, and to visit his girlfriend down here. He took his girl out to fancy restaurants, so that was a possibility.

Of course, he could always go upstairs, knock on the girl's door and blow Salmon away when he opened it, but then he'd have to do the girl, too. Oh, he would if he had to, but if he could get around it, he'd prefer it another way. If he did it here, it might look like a random street crime and that might not be enough to draw Costello out into the open. No, he had to do a big time public thing, something that would send the right signal.

He walked a block up Fifth Avenue and grabbed a cab, heading up to Hell's Kitchen where his guys were waiting for him. He'd figured he'd only need two for tonight's job, so he let everybody have the night off but McKnight and Connor. When he got out of the cab they came out of the bar to greet him.

"About a dozen guys have been in there tonight," Connor said. "None of the big guys have left, so the money's still there."

"All right, then. Ready?"

They crossed the street and walked over to the cigar store on the opposite corner. When they went in, the owner, a short, balding guy in a striped shirt, walked up to them, placing himself between them and the back door.

"Can I help you?" he said.

McKnight slammed him over the head with a blackjack and he fell like a slaughtered hog. They stepped over him and stopped in front of the door to the back room. They slid their masks over their heads and slammed the door open, rushing in with guns drawn.

"Nobody has to die," Irish Jack said. "All we want's the money."

One of the three men in the room, holding his hands up, looked at them and said, "You know what this is?"

"Sure do. And now it's mine. Pass it over."

The man nearest the door, a big muscular guy who didn't look too bright, frowned as if he were trying to think. McKnight put a gun to his head and said, "It ain't worth it. It's just money. Tomorrow you can go out and get yourself another bag of it but you can't never get your life back."

The big man lowered his head.

Irish Jack picked up the two pillow cases full of currency and said, "Appreciate it, boys."

36

Taylor could hear the music coming from inside the People's Songs office when he was still thirty yards from the door. It sounded good. A bass was thumping and a harmonica cut through the air like a knife through butter. Taylor opened the door and walked in. Up on the stage, Woody Guthrie was jamming with three negroes. One man played a mean blues guitar, another worked the harmonica while seeming to whoop and holler at the same time, and the third man, a young kid still in his teens, thumped out the rhythm on the bass. They made strong music, soulful and bluesy, a sound that spoke to Taylor's heart. He stood still and listened, his foot tapping.

When the song finished, Woody Guthrie threw him a smile and said, "What you think of that, Damon?"

"Wonderful. That's some fine stuff."

"Damon, this guy making that blues harp cry is Sonny Terry. That's my good friend Brownie McGhee on guitar, and this kid here tearing up the bass is Bill Lee. Guys, this is my buddy, the great reporter, Damon Taylor."

Brownie McGhee waved at him, while Sonny Terry—Taylor suddenly realized he was blind—nodded straight ahead. Lee, who appeared to be shy, concentrated on tuning his bass.

"You guys sounded great," Taylor said.

"These boys *know* the blues," Guthrie said. "You want to hear the music cry, they're your boys. We're going out on tour together."

"You are?"

"Yeah. Listen, if you had a chance to make music with these guys for three weeks straight, wouldn't you do it?"

"Absolutely."

The players began putting their instruments away. When they had packed up, McGhee said, "Same time tomorrow, Woody?"

"Sounds good to me."

McGhee guided Sonny Terry out the door. "Good to meet you, Mr. Taylor."

"Same here. Call me Damon."

"Sure thing. Till tomorrow, Woody."

When they were alone, Taylor said, "You're doing a three week tour?"

"Yep. I got to, man. That time in jail used up all my money. I can't be letting my wife and kid go hungry." He frowned, then appeared to realize what he was doing and smiled quickly, the cocksure grin of a man who knows he's on top of it all. "We're all going on the road. Pete and a few others are going out as the Weavers, playing some clubs. See, we got to put some money together. We're about to have to close this place down if we don't come up with a few bucks."

"Business not going well?"

"Well, we got ourselves a little cash flow problem. Don't nobody associated with this place have any business sense at all and running a booking office, a management firm and a music publishing house all under one roof calls for some business smarts, you know? I keep telling these boys to hire an office manager and do what he says but you think they'll listen? They're all too busy writing songs nobody wants to hear."

"You sound disillusioned."

Guthrie sat on the edge of the stage and polished his guitar with a cloth. "Nope. Can't get disillusioned of you never had any illusions to begin with. Fact is, Damon, this here People's Songs is going to make it, if it's meant to. If it ain't meant to make it, it'll go under. It's that simple. It'll be whatever it's meant to be."

"You're right about that. What's Marjorie think of you being gone for three weeks?"

"Well, naturally, she'd rather I stay home but we got to eat, man. Baby needs shoes, you know what I mean?"

"I guess you have to do what you have to do."

"That's the truth, son. How'd you like to buy me a beer?"

"Why not?"

"Hey, I saw the story you guys did on that cop, Murphy. He really that crooked?" Woody took off his guitar and placed it on a stand at the back of the stage. "I mean, he did a job on me but all the time I thought he really believed I did it."

"Once the first witness came forward, the dam broke. I was amazed at how brazen he was. He'd frame anybody to clear a case."

"What do you reckon's going to happen to him?"

"I can't say. Internal Affairs is investigating him. Best that happens is he retires from the police force and I hear that's already in the works. Worst thing is he goes to jail. I hear that's a possibility, too."

"I wouldn't wish that on a dog." Guthrie shook his head, as if puzzled by the vagaries of the world. "Come on, let's go get that beer."

They were waiting to cross 42nd Street when a police car skidded to a stop at the curb. It parked at an angle, blocking the lane, and the traffic began piling behind it. The door flung open and Danny Murphy jumped out, half running to the sidewalk. Grabbing Taylor by the lapels, he shoved him backward, slamming him against the wall of a building. The back of Taylor's head bounced off the wall and he saw spots in front of his eyes.

"Hey, you leave him alone," Guthrie shouted, grabbing Murphy by the arm and tugging.

With a backward swipe of his arm, Murphy brushed Guthrie off so strongly that the little folksinger fell to the sidewalk. Murphy slammed Taylor against the wall again.

"You son of a bitch," he screamed. "I'm putting you on notice! You're a dead man. You understand me? You're a fucking dead man."

"Murphy, you don't want to do this here. Look at the crowd. We aren't exactly alone, you know?"

Murphy hesitated, looked around and saw that a crowd of forty or fifty people had gathered already. Two of the spectators were helping Guthrie up. Others were staring at Murphy harshly, as if getting ready to physically go against him. He shoved Taylor back and as the reporter hit the wall, slugged him in the jaw. Taylor's head snapped back against the brick and spots danced before his eyes as slid down to his knees.

"You're on notice, Taylor. Just remember that."

He snarled at the crowd as he climbed back into his car and drove off.

"You okay, Damon?" Guthrie said. He helped Taylor to his feet.

Taylor shook his head in an effort to clear it but it only caused more pain. "Yeah, I'm all right."

"Come in the office with me, okay?"

They walked back to the People's Songs building. Taylor was surprised to find himself shaky on his feet, a little dizzy. He sat on the edge of the stage, cradling his head in his hands. He took light breaths, shallow ones, and concentrated on his breathing until he felt his head clear.

He looked up. Guthrie was watching him closely, a concerned expression on his features. When he saw Taylor's face, his expression relaxed and he grinned.

"Damn, he really did a job on you, didn't he?"

"You could say that."

"You going to be okay?"

"No lasting damage."

Guthrie scratched his cheek, his eyes thoughtful. "You know, Damon, I got a little present for you."

His guitar case lay at the back of the stage. Guthrie strolled over to it, unlatched it and raised the lid. Reaching in, he took out a leather bag that looked like a pocketbook and handed it to Taylor. He peered inside then reached in and took out a gun. It was a huge Colt .45, a cowboy gun, the type movie actors used in westerns. Taylor could smell the oil on the gun.

"Woody, where the hell did you get this thing?"

"Well, when I was out in California, trying to organize the farm workers, one of them gave me that thing to protect myself from the company bulls."

"He wanted you to kill the cops?"

"It wasn't that far out of the question. They were turning guns on the workers. It could have turned into a shooting war pretty easy. As it was, there was a couple of gun battles."

"You take a part in them?"

"Oh, hell, no. I told you a long time ago, killing ain't my style. Me, I can write you some songs about it, or I can try to get a union going, but shooting somebody? Hell, man, that's getting a little extreme, don't you reckon?"

"But you think I ought to use this on Murphy."

"I think if a man theatens to kill you on the street, you ought to be ready for whatever comes around the corner."

"I can't take this."

"Sure you can. Look, I'm hoping you won't ever have to use it, but it's nice to know you got it if a crooked cop starts shooting at you."

"Woody...."

"Just stick it in your pocket, man." He held his hands out as a barrier. "I ain't taking it back."

"Okay, I know when I'm beat." Taylor stuck the heavy pistol in his pocket.

"Now, what you say we go get that beer?"

37

"Before we get started, I want to thank you," he said, "for proving that Russell Wallace's murder didn't have anything to do with us or the work he was doing for us."

Ted Kirkpatrick, Ken Bierly and John Keenan were all gathered in Kirkpatrick's office. Kirkpatrick sat behind his desk, flanked by Bierly and Keenan. To Taylor, they looked like the defensive line of a football team, determined not to let any opponent through. Taylor thought Kirkpatrick was the one he had to win over. He was the heavy—the others were juniors and would follow Kirkpatrick's lead.

"Sit down, Taylor," Kirkpatrick said.

Taylor sat in an green overstuffed chair that looked like it was made of curtain fabric. "How you doing, Ted?" he said. "Ken, John."

The two flankers nodded. Kirkpatrick stared at Taylor for a moment and seemed to make up his mind about something.

"I wouldn't say it was proven," Taylor answered, "but you got to admit it's all leaning in that direction."

"Well, it's proven to the satisfaction of everyone that matters." He leaned back. "Now, what can I do for you?"

The three of them had drinks but no one offered Taylor one. There as no chit chat, no joking round; everything was serious business. Taylor wasn't happy with the tone of the meeting.

All he could do was make his case. "Ted, I'd like to convince you to rethink your attacks on Zero Mostel."

"Attacks? I told you before, we don't attack anyone, Taylor. We *report*. And what we reported about Mostel is true."

"True, maybe, but you have to admit it sounds worse than it is. Mostel's always been a strong American. He's never advocated selling the country out to Communism." He felt like an idiot, speaking in platitudes like this, but that was the only language these guys understood. Platitudes made up their everyday mode of speech. "He's as patriotic as you are."

"No Communist is as patriotic as I am," Ted Kirkpatrick snapped. "I've never advocated the overthrow of the United States government."

"Neither has Mostel."

"Certainly he did. It's the goal of every Communist."

"He worked with Earl Browder trying to seperate the American Party from the Russian one. He always said that communism and capitalism could coexist."

"This is beautiful, isn't it, boys?"

Bierly and Keenan joined Kirkpatrick in laughter, though it seemed to Taylor they had no idea what they were laughing at. All they knew was the boss thought something was funny, so they thought humor was in the air.

"Taylor, you come on here asking me to go easy on Mostel, and as proof of his patriotism, you tell me about his work with Earl Browder. Damn it, man, Browder's been in prison three times for anti-American activity. He opposed World War One and World War Two. He made two trips to Russia on a fake passport and the only reason he got out of jail for that was because Russia became our ally during the war. And that attempt to split the American and Russian parties, that Browderism I think they called it, hell, it got him thrown out of his own Party."

"Don't you see then, if Browder got thrown out of the Party for advocating a view that Mostel endorsed, then Mostel's not a Communist."

"Good try. Browder's still campaigning for the reds, even if they threw him out. Neither he nor Mostel have ever repudiated their Party memberships."

"You realize you're ruining Mostel's career? They canceled his TV show and he lost his night club bookings."

"That's not my problem. In fact, show business is better off without him."

"You said he hasn't repudiated his past. Is that what he has to do to get his life back?"

"That's not up to me. When he gets called to testify in front of HUAC, they'll tell him what he has to do."

"Look, Ted...."

"Ironic, isn't it, Taylor? The only leverage you ever had with us was the possibility of embarrassing us with the Wallace case and since you showed we weren't involved, you got nothing left. Nothing."

Kristen Eldredge was getting tired of all this hassle. What she wanted was the money. She was entitled to it; she'd earned it. She'd sacrificed three years of her life and whatever was left of her immortal soul for it. She'd paid for it in the past and was going to continue paying for it into eternity, so by God she wanted it. Now.

As she read Damon Taylor's story in *Crime Scene,* Eldredge was surprised at how good a reporter the man really was. He had it pretty close to right. What got her was that he mentioned that one hundred thousand dollars was stolen, but then later in the piece, when he was talking about the money being found, he only mentioned seventy thousand.

Kristen Eldredge had always done her best thinking in the bathtub. A good bath not only relaxed her, it refreshed and invigorated her. When she finished a good soak, she entered that relaxed but alert state that she loved so much. She stood, walked into the bathroom and turned on the water. There was a collection of oils and bubble soap big enough to stock a drug store counter and she studied the bottles and jars until she found the ones she wanted. These she added to the water.

After she had taken off her clothes, she stood in front of the mirror, admiring her body. She knew she was attractive to both men and women. She enjoyed that awareness but mostly, she enjoyed its strength, its magnificence: bold, striking, beautiful, muscular.

She stepped into the bath, sank into the warm water, leaned her head back and closed her eyes. Her mission was almost finished. This frustration she was feeling would end before long because now that she was in the tub and relaxed, she could see clearly and unmistakably, finally, that Damon Taylor must have the money.

Her money.

It couldn't be any other way. How else could he know that the original hundred thousand was now down to seventy thousand?

Oh, he had it all right.

And she would get it back.

If Taylor went down in the process, well, that was always a possibility. In fact, it was to be anticipated. She'd dealt with men like Taylor before. They thought that since they were, in their own eyes, virtuously honest, they were compelled to do what they felt right. The only problem was that what was right wasn't necessarily *correct*. He probably wanted to give the money back to its original owners or to the insurance company that had paid the claim after the robbery. How could it be in any way right for him to take her money, money she'd suffered for and would always suffer for, and give it to somebody else?

As she washed her breasts with a soft cloth, she said to herself,

"No."

There was only one way for this whole mess to come to its proper conclusion: the money had to wind up in her pocket and Taylor had to wind up dead.

38

"Damon," Leo Salmon said, "I'm getting out of the business."

"Sounds like you've made up your mind."

"That I have."

They were in The Corner Bookshop down on Fifth Avenue, in a neighborhood known as Book Row, where most of the city's used bookstores were located. They'd started down at the University Place Bookshop and were working their way from store to store, so that Salmon could search the stacks for hard to find psychology books. He had discovered an early translation of Jung's work on archetypes and was already a happy man. Now, anything he found was gravy.

"You told Frank yet?"

"Not yet." He examined the table of contents of a volume on the psychology of crime. Snorting in contempt, he put the book down.

"How's Frank going to feel about his right hand man coming in and saying 'I quit'?"

"Come on, Damon, it's not like the movies. That thing about how once you're in, you can never get out? That's a load of crap. People come and go all the time. As long as my place in the organization is covered, Costello won't have a word to say about it."

Taylor found a Cornell Woolrich book he hadn't read, one of the ones published under his William Irish byline. He decided to buy it. He'd read it and pass it on to O'Bradovich, who also liked Woolrich's work.

"Have you told Terry about all this yet?"

"No," he said flatly.

"We already had this conversation, Leo. You know you have to tell her. Look, what's going to happen if she finds out from somebody else? And you know she will."

"There's no reason she has to know. I'm not that man anymore. Why should I have to tell her about the guy I used to be?"

"I can think of two reasons. That guy you used to be? Well, you were him five minutes ago. This isn't the olden days we're talking about. It's fresh stuff. And then two, you got a lot of enemies. One of them is bound to make sure she finds out."

Across the street from The Corner Bookshop, Irish Jack waited impatiently, his hands in his pockets. It was getting cold out here. It was late afternoon and the sun was hiding behind the buildings and he began to shiver. His right hand was wrapped around the handle of his pistol, which, since it had been nestled in his coat pocket all afternoon, was still warm. And he smiled because the moment Leo Salmon came out of that bookshop—what the hell was he doing hanging out in a bookshop anyway?

Anyway, the moment he came out, he was going to get the surprise of his life.

The *last* surprise of his life.

"Look, Damon, we're going to be overseas, I'm thinking over in Ireland, where nobody's ever heard of Leo Salmon. How's she going to find out about me?"

A stool had been placed in the aisle they were in. Taylor sat on it and looked across at the mob lawyer. He sat still for a moment, letting the news Salmon had hit him with sink in.

"You told her she's going to be living in Ireland yet?"

"Well, no. Not yet."

"Leo, she just got the studio. Finally, she's where she's always wanted to be. She's got her life under control now. She's in control and you're going to ask her to just give all that up and move to Ireland? Just so you won't have to tell her who you are?"

Salmon looked sheepish. "Damon, this love crap is brand new to me. I don't know how to handle it. It's got me running around like I'm fourteen years old, you know? I'm a big dumb kid who doesn't know a damn thing." He held his arms wide, helplessly. "I get filled with these ideas that make sense at the time, you know what I mean?"

"I know. I've been there."

"I've never had to think about anybody but myself. I really don't know a damn thing about thinking of somebody else. You're right. Of course, I have to tell her." He glanced over at Taylor, gave him a searching look and said, "Or maybe you can do it for me?"

"You want to think that through for just a minute, Leo?"

"It's got to be me, doesn't it?" His voice was plaintive, making him sound like a little kid who didn't want to tell his mother about cutting school.

"That's right."

"How do you think I should do it?"

"You really are helpless, aren't you?"

Salmon laughed. "Come on, let's get a cup of coffee and I'll take you back to your office."

The door of the bookshop opened and Taylor came out, followed by Salmon, who looked up and down the street. Irish Jack stepped out to the curb and reached into his pocket, curling his fingers around the gun grip once more.

As he took it from his pocket, a black Cadillac pulled up at the curb. The chauffeur....

Taylor and Salmon climbed into the back seat and Irish Jack watched helplessly as the car pulled away.

39

Just after dark, Irish Jack got on a subway headed out to Brooklyn. As he hung from a strap, he saw down at the end of the car a little man in blue jeans, a flannel shirt and a sailor's watch cap, also standing. A guitar was slung over his back. Irish Jack recognized the guy but couldn't quite place him. He'd definitely seen him around, though.

He made his way down the aisle of the car and grabbed the strap next to the little guy. "Don't I know you?" he said.

"Could be," the little guy said.

"Yeah, I'm sure I do but I can't fiigure out from where."

"Maybe you seen me play. I'm a singer, work all around town. You a union man?"

"No."

"Well, then you wouldn't have seen me at any union rally. I play a lot of those. The working boys tend to like my stuff."

"That wouldn't be it."

"Used to have me a radio show. Maybe you seen my picture in the paper or something." The little guy flashed him a grin, held out his free hand. "By the way, my name's Woody Guthrie."

"I'm Ray Webster," Irish Jack said, using the name of one of his confederates. He shook hands with Guthrie.

"Good to meet you, Ray. You live out this way?"

"No, I'm just going out to visit a friend. How 'bout you?"

"Got me a place out in Coney Island. Heading home to see my lady now. See, I'm going out on tour, won't be at home for a few weeks, so I got to spend some time with her before I go."

Don't get curious, Irish Jack told himself, don't ever wonder about another person because if you do, you're going to talk to him and he'll just bore you to death, just like this hick's doing. He always made this mistake—he figured he should be interested in other people and then he'd go out of his way to make an effort. Within five minutes he'd be regretting it because the truth was other people just bored the hell out of him. Now he was trapped chatting with this guy until he reached his stop. All because he'd thought he recognized him from some place important.

He'd been right about that, though. He was sure he knew him, but why he'd know a country hick like this Guthrie guy was beyond him.

"You married, Ray?"

"No, I'm not. But you are, you say?"

"Hell, man, I been married more times than most people have had dates. But this one's the real thing. I found the right woman."

Irish Jack didn't know what to say. This guy with the guitar was turning out to be the most boring man in New York. "Good for you," he mumbled.

He'd had it. He couldn't stand another second with this guy. When the train rolled into a station, he let go of the strap and headed for the door.

"This is my stop," he said.

"Good talking to you, Ray," Guthrie said.

He ignored him and pushed a fat man out of his way so he could get out more quickly. Hurrying up the stairs to the street, he hit the sidewalk and stopped, looking around to see where he was. He'd penetrated deeply enough into Brooklyn; the neighborhood was residential, one where a lot of people used cars instead of mass transit and that was what he'd come out here to find.

After all, if you were going to shoot a guy while you drove by in a car, you first ought to have a car. *Shoot a guy*, he thought: that's where he knew Guthrie from. He'd seen him with his former target Taylor, who hung out with Leo Salmon.

Interesting. If the guy hadn't been headed out of town, he might have wound up shot himself. As it was, though, everything would be done and Irish Jack would be shaking up the Costello gang by the time that Guthrie guy returned to the city.

He found a brand new Kaiser unlocked on the street, hotwired it and drove it back to Manhattan. The car had less than a thousand miles on it and still smelled new. Who would be stupid enough to leave a car like this unlocked on the street? It responded with so much power it was like all he had to do was think about going faster and the thing would speed up. He'd never driven a vehicle this nice and wished he could keep it after the killing.

Leo Salmon had never been this content in his life. Stretched out on his back in the bed, with Terry Louvin's body crushed against his, her arm draped over his chest, he felt as though everything in his life had existed for no other reason than to lead him to this moment. If he were to die now he would go out a happy man.

Terry snuggled closer to him, sighing. He smiled. She was asleep and that surprised him. An old girlfriend of his had once told him that making love made men sleepy and woke girls up and he thought she probably knew what she was talking about because that had always been his experience. But here was Terry sound asleep moments after they'd finished, while Salmon was the one who was wide awake.

Maybe he couldn't fall asleep because he knew that when Terry Louvin woke in the morning, he was going to have to tell her the truth about himself. Funny, he'd never felt any guilt or remorse about what he'd done with his life until now, and as he thought of himself as if he were Terry, he tried to see him the way she would. He felt horrible about the way he'd lived his life. He wasn't a good man. The fact was, though, she was sure to look on him more favorably than he did himself.

She was that great a woman.

When he woke in the morning, she was already up and moving. He propped himself up in bed and watched her hurriedly down a cup of coffee as she pulled her hair back into a ponytail. Catching his reflection in the mirror, she smiled. "Hello, Bright Eyes. Sleep well?"

"Beautifully."

He climbed out of bed, pulled on his pants and walked out to the kitchen where he poured himself a cup of coffee. Returning to the bedroom, he watched her attach a ribbon to her ponytail.

"Listen," he said, "can we talk a few minutes?"

This time the smile she gave him was apologetic. "Wish I could but I'm running late. Got a class coming in ten minutes and I haven't even set up the studio yet. Can it wait till tonight?"

He was amazed at how relieved he felt. "Sure. Tonight's fine."

She let her fingers linger on his cheek after she'd kissed him. "Till tonight, then." Halfway to the door, she turned and said, "I wish I could tell you how good being with you is."

"Same here, babe."

After the door closed behind her, he continued to stare at it for a long time.

Irish Jack sat behind the wheel of the Kaiser, now stopped. Funny how quickly he'd begun to think of the car as his. He wished he could keep it but knew that was out of the question; falling in love with things you got your hands on only led to trouble. Every minute of your life, you had to be ready to walk away from your stuff, especially the stuff you took from somebody else.

He was parked across the street from the broad's dance studio, the one Salmon had been seeing. He wondered what it was exactly that drew Salmon to a girl like that. She was perky enough and, he guessed that in some way he couldn't appreciate, she was kind of pretty, but she definitely wasn't the type that attracted Irish Jack. He'd watched her when she'd come out to unlock the door and put away the garbage cans, dressed in a black skin-tight leotard with her hair pulled back and a long red ribbon hanging from it. The outfit she wore revealed the shape of her body but that did nothing for him. Everything was too little, there was nothing to get a good grip on. He preferred a little meat on his women—like that Amazon who'd hired him. She was ideal, perfect if she wasn't so damn scary.

The black Cadillac showed up at the door of the dance studio. The car blocked everything but Leo Salmon's head as he came out of the building, allowed his driver to open the back door for him before they drove off. As he fell in behind them, Irish Jack wondered what it would be like to have somebody drive him around.

Hell, he'd find out in just a few days. When he was big.

40

Taylor and Zero Mostel shared a cab uptown. Mostel had an audition for a nightclub appearance at a place on East 84th, one of the newer clubs that Taylor had never heard of. He suspected that because of the item in *Counterattack*, Mostel was having a problem getting booked in the same bigger, more important clubs he used to appear in. He was thinking that he ought to freelance a piece on the *Counterattack* people for one of the political magazines, but he wondered how effective it could be. Wouldn't he just be writing for people who already agreed with him?

The cab pulled up in front of the club. As Mostel climbed out, Taylor said, "Good luck, Zee."

"Damn it, man, never say 'good luck' to an actor. I thought you knew better than that."

"Sorry."

"You got the cab covered?"

"Yeah. Go in there and break a few bones."

"Better, better." Mostel looked at him for a moment. "Where you going from here?"

"Just home."

"How 'bout coming in and watching me work?"

After paying off the driver, Taylor followed Mostel into the club. It was small and dark, not much more than a long room with a makeshift stage at the far end and tables jumbled artlessly on the floor, no apparent thought given to room design. A bar ran the length of the south side of the room. After playing the Rainbow Room and the Copacabana, Mostel was going to work here? *This was all wrong,* Taylor thought.

The manager of the place, a short stubby man wearing a white shirt with his tie askew, came over to them, cigar burning in his left hand. He held his hand out and Zee shook it.

"I tried to call you, Mostel," the manager said, "but you must have already left your house. Look, I'm going to have to be honest with you."

Mostel turned to Taylor. "I hate to hear those words. No good news ever follows those words. A man says 'I'm going to be honest with you,' you know he's going to break your heart."

"That might be true, Mostel," the manager said. He had a dark stain on the front of his shirt. "The truth of the matter is I can't use you."

"You're rejecting me before I even audition?"

"It doesn't make any difference how funny you are, I can't use you."

"You can at least tell him why," Taylor said.

"Sure, I'll tell you both why. Soon as word got around that I was auditioning you, reservations started getting canceled. I began getting calls telling me how bad it's going to be for me and my club if I hire you. Damn it, Mostel, you didn't tell me you had all this Communist shit going on."

"I'm not a Communist. I haven't been involved with the Party for years."

"Yeah, I know how it is. You're not a Communist but I *am* a businessman and I can't go wrecking my business by hiring you. I'm sorry, Mostel, I'm not proud of what I'm doing but I got no choice."

"Can't you see I'm getting a bum deal here? I didn't do anything."

The manager chewed on his cigar and it bobbed up and down like a pencil balanced on a fingertip. "It don't make any difference whether you did anything or not. As long as these guys have you in their sights, nobody's going to have anything to do with you. It's not you, man, it's the times we're living in."

"You can take the times we're living in and shove them right up your ass," Mostel shouted.

"Sure," he said. "I can do that but you'll still be out of work. Try Chicago or Miami. Maybe it's a different world out of town."

Leo Salmon sat behind his desk, lost in thought. When he found himself in these moods, he usually just walked across the office to his library and roamed through the shelves until he found a comforting book. Today, though, he didn't feel like moving. Not being able to tell Terry the truth this morning had thrown him off balance and he couldn't get righted again.

He picked up the phone and called Damon Taylor. When Taylor picked up, Salmon said, "Are you busy?"

"No, I was just updating the Wallace story. What's up?"

"I tried to tell her this morning when we woke up," he said, "but she had to get out of the apartment too fast, didn't have time to listen."

Since both of them were adults, Taylor had assumed they were sleeping together, but to have Salmon talk about getting up with her in the morning caused his stomach to clutch, to tighten up like a biceps. He wasn't nearly as able to put his feelings on hold as he'd thought he was.

"What's the problem? Tell her tonight."

"The problem is how relieved I was. You know, she's making me look at the way I've lived my life through somebody else's eyes and for the first time I'm uneasy with what I'm seeing. Hey, when can you get free?"

"In about an hour."

"Good. Terry's meeting me at Le Pavillon at eight. If you could get there at seven, we could have a drink and I'll unload my sorry-assed story on you."

"What could be more of a thrill?"

Salmon laughed. "Thanks, Damon, you're a good friend."

After he'd gotten off the phone, Salmon found his mood had lifted. He had renewed energy for the paperwork he had to do, which he usually hated with a passion. He worked until six-thirty then went out and climbed into the Cadillac for the trip to Le Pavillon. As he relaxed in the back seat his driver navigated the way into Manhattan, Salmon did not notice the dark blue Kaiser maintinaing its distance half a block behind him.

Danny Murphy was lost in the act of cleaning his pistol yet again. It was the only thing that seemed to relax him now, along with the drinking. As he ran the oiled swab through the barrel, his mind floated free and he felt better than he had in days. It was funny how you could find your mind made up without really understanding how you got there, how there could be a sudden moment of clarity before an absolute truth was revealed to you.

Now that his decision had sprung into his mind, fully formed and ready to act upon, he took some time to reconstruct it. He knew his life was shattered, as broken as a dinner plate thrown onto a concrete floor. It had to be put back together. All the normal ways of reassembling a life—career, marriage, family—were closed to him. If he was to get back on track, he had to forget who he used to be and what he used to be. He wasn't a cop anymore and never would be again. That part of his life was over and done but with it went all of the restrictions being a cop put on a man. When he added it all up, if he was going to get back to himself, the only possible way was to take away the life of the man who had ruined his.

He reloaded the bullets into the chamber of his freshly cleaned .38 Police Special and slid the gun into his belt holster.

Now to go find Damon Taylor.

41

It was a cool evening but there was no winter bite in the air, so when three cabs in a row passed him up, Taylor decided to walk to Le Pavillon. It wouldn't be too long before stepping out for a walk would be impossible; the cold would drive you back inside. Why not enjoy it while he could?

It was a long way up to 55th Street, maybe three miles or so. He might have to grab a cab when he got further uptown but he loved this neighborhood. He walked toward Second Avenue, looking at the street as if it were brand new to him.

Park Row was located in the financial district and since long before Taylor had started working down here, it had been known as Chatham Street. People had once called it Newspaper Row because all of the city's major papers had offices here. They needed them, since it was important that they be located near City Hall, which was right down the road. Printing House Square was right across the street and in the old days the dailies were written, typeset, edited and printed right here on the block. As if to emphasize its history, a statue of Benjamin Franklin stood in front of 41 Park Row, one bronze arm holding out a copy of his newspaper, *The Pennsylvania Gazette*.

Now, though, the daily papers had all moved to midtown. During the real estate boom of the thirties, *The New York Times* discovered it could get much more space at a far cheaper rate by moving up to Times Square. Where the *Times* went the other papers followed, so pretty soon Park Row was just a shadow of what it had once been. His own boss had refused to leave; he continued to publish his dozen magazines from the building he owned next to the Potter Building.

When Taylor was on these streets, he felt as if he were part of a great tradition. If *Crime Scene* ever moved uptown or, as some businesses were beginning to do, across the river to Jersey, he'd have to quit.

When he hit Second Avenue and began walking north, it was like moving from one century to the next. He smiled.

Danny Murphy felt feverish, weak, as if he were suffering from a bad case of some new tropical flu. He couldn't control his dizziness and as he followed Taylor up Second Avenue he felt himself drifting from side to side; he would begin walking straight up the middle of the sidewalk and wind up over by the curb. He knew he wasn't going to feel any better until he'd done the thing he was here to do.

As long as Taylor was alive, he wasn't going to be able to put his life back together and he wasn't going to get over this sickness until he got himself centered again. Most people would think he was losing his mind; he was aware of that. People would look at him and what he was doing and they'd ask what killing Taylor had to do with getting his life back on track. Other than the revenge angle, he couldn't quite explain it, he didn't have the words. But he *knew*, way deep inside, he *knew* that this was the first step he was going to have to take. He trusted the rest of it would become clear after Taylor was blown away. That much he was sure of. But if Taylor didn't pay for destroying Murphy's career, his family life and everything else, if the bastard could just take away a person's purpose, his reason for living, and Murphy didn't do anything about it? Well, if he let this disrespect go by, he didn't deserve to have his life back.

He was no longer a cop.

He'd never be a cop again.

But, by God, he was still a man.

Leo Salmon had refreshed his cologne before he left his house and now in the confines of the Cadillac, he felt he'd put it on too heavily. The car smelled like a bordello. As he waved his hand before his face, trying to dissipate the odor, his driver caught Salmon's reflection in the rearview mirror and said, "Shall I take the long way to Le Pavillon, sir?"

"That'll be fine."

He opened his window, settled back and watched the tugboats chug up and down the East River as they drove over the 59th Street Bridge. It was a pleasant night, a gorgeous night, and soon he'd be with the reason it was so beautiful. If anyone had told him six months ago that a woman could turn his whole life around, could send him off in brand new directions, he would not have believed it. He would have said it was impossible for him to throw over his position in the Costello family—it had always been *his* family, too. He had never once doubted what he was doing, had never once felt that maybe the way he lived needed any kind of revision, but since Terry had come into his life, he saw that he wasn't the man she deserved and he wasn't willing to accept that.

Which meant he had to be honest. That was something new to him. He'd always taken his place in the family for granted, only now, faced with the need to tell Terry about himself, had he discovered doubt.

"You're very quiet, sir," his driver said. "Everything all right?"

"Never better."

They turned down Second Avenue and headed for East 55th Street where they would drive up to Fifth Avenue to the restaurant. They still hadn't seen the Kaiser.

A good plan was a simple plan. Complications always had a way of screwing things up. If you wanted to pull something off, you couldn't let it get all convoluted. Irish Jack had learned that fact in his early days running with the mob and he'd never forgotten it. What he was going to do was simplicity itself. As he followed Salmon's car down Second Avenue, careful to stay far enough behind that he would appear part of the evening traffic, Irish Jack reviewed his plan.

The driver of Salmon's car was going to pull over somewhere. By the time he had the car parked and had gotten out to open the passenger door for his boss, Irish Jack would be there. And when Salmon stepped out of the car Irish Jack would blow his fucking head off. That would be the end of part one of the plan. Part two was just as simple. In a few days, they'd bury Salmon. Costello would come out of his house to go to the funeral and Irish Jack would be across the street from the funeral home. When Costello climbed out of his car, Irish Jack and his boys—he wasn't going to take that one on alone; he needed to put on a show of force—would take his head off, too. Then the city would know the Irish were back.

It was going to be as easy as that.

What could be better?

When Salmon's car turned onto East 55th Street, Sheridan also made the turn. He didn't know where the man was going and didn't care. All he knew was that Salmon was going to have to stop somewhere and climb out of the back seat of that Cadillac and the moment he did, Irish Jack would speed up and blow him to pieces.

He felt like whistling.

At 14th Street, Taylor decided to pick up the subway. It was too chilly to walk all the way up to 55th. He walked down the stairs into the damp warmth of the subway platform, dropped his nickel into the slot, and went through the turnstyle to the tracks where he waited for an uptown train. It smelled like the locker room of a gym down there. The odor of summer sweat hung in the air year round, but he was thankful it wasn't oppressive in the way it would be come August.

When the train arrived he walked through the open doors into a car. Danny Murphy got into the car behind his. At the far end of the car, the window let him see where Taylor had sat, so he watched the reporter.

He could shoot him from here, he thought. He could get a clean shot through the windows. But the train rumbled and shook and he might miss. Taylor might survive and he would be goddamned if he had any intention of letting Taylor survive.

Murphy would be nothing if not patient.

He'd wait.

As they pulled up in front of Le Pavillon, Salmon said, "Charles, pick me up about ten, will you?"

"Yes, sir," the driver answered.

There was a crowd moving about the sidewalk as he came around and opened the door for his boss, holding it as Salmon climbed out among the throng. He didn't know it, but he stood between Salmon and the passing Kaiser. When his boss disappeared into the throng headed for Le Pavillon's doors, the driver climbed back into the Cadillac and headed downtown. There was a bar he liked that had a TV set where he could watch the fights while he nursed a beer.

Damn it, Irish Jack thought. His aim had been blocked by the driver and then that shuffling crowd. He hadn't been able to get a clear sight. Now he'd have to do it the hard way. He found a parking place on East 57th Street and, since he wouldn't be coming back, wiped the inside of the car down good and climbed out.

As he walked the couple of blocks back to the restaurant, he thought about how much he'd miss that car. It was a good one, but if he tried to make it back to it after he came out of the restaurant, he'd be committed to going in one direction only. That wouldn't do.

He'd need groups of people to fade into to cover his escape. He'd have to size up the crowds when he left Le Pavillon and go into the biggest one where he could disappear.

Always fade into a crowd, he'd learned early. Something went down, somebody saw you running up an empty street, you were a dead man. He didn't intend for that to happen to him.

Things had just grown more complicated but sometimes that couldn't be helped.

Where the hell did all these people come from, Murphy thought, as he followed Taylor off the subway. He took his finger from the trigger of his gun and shadowed Taylor through the mass of people, up the stairs and into the street. The Friday night crowds were out in force; couples debated where to go for dinner, daters made their way to the movie theaters and there were a lot of lonely men heading for the bars. He saw a couple of dopers slinking up the street, casing the buildings from the sidewalk and the thought of shaking them down occurred to him but that that just reminded him he wasn't a cop anymore.

You could shoot them, he thought. *You could just take them into an alley, blow their heads to pieces and help make the city a better, safer place.* He was astonished at how pleasant an idea this was, but he had other things to do. Maybe later for the vigilante stuff.

Irish Jack walked into Le Pavillon. The *maître d'* came out from behind his podium and, with a hand held out, asked, "May I help you, sir?" He looked as though he were smelling something unpleasant.

"Just going to the bar," Irish Jack said.

He walked past the man. The restaurant was jammed and he felt suddenly uneasy; never in his life had Irish Jack been surrounded by this much money. He looked around, quickly sizing up the room. Middle-aged women with dyed blonde hair and shoulders wrapped in furs laughed too loudly at things even their older husbands, all closed up and held together in their business suits, said. Glasses clinked and tuxedo-clad waiters scurried back and forth like mice. Everything was a little too loud, the gaiety a little forced as though the diners were trying very hard to keep the outside world at bay.

He spotted Leo Salmon sitting alone at a table off to one side. Salmon had a drink in front of him and was studying the menu. Irish

Jack walked past him then quickly turned back, pulling his gun from his pocket. A woman at the next table screamed when she saw it but Salmon didn't have time to turn around before Irish Jack shot him in the back of his head. Even though he knew Salmon was dead before his face hit the table, Irish Jack shot him again.

Everyone was shouting. All the rich bastards and their pushy wives were standing, yelling at the top of their lungs. Screams hung in the air like sirens. The woman at the next table began wailing in a foreign tongue as she tried to wipe Salmon's blood off of her mink coat.

Irish Jack pushed his way out of the restaurant.

As Taylor approached the awning that hung over the sidewalk in front of Le Pavillon, a spate of panicked people came flooding out the door. Immediately, he knew what had happened inside. He sped up, intending to fight his way through the crowd into the restaurant.

He came to a dead stop as the little man with the gun came out the door. The little man halted too, recognition flaring in his eyes. He raised the gun and was about to fire when a the flat pop of a gunshot, followed by two more, came from a spot off to Taylor's left. The man with the gun grabbed his side with his left hand and fired back at the man shooting at him. Taylor looked over and saw Danny Murphy sink to his knees and empty his gun into the other shooter. Both of them collapsed.

Taylor rushed to Murphy's side. The cop's chest was covered with blood—it looked as if he'd been hit three times. His eyes already cloudy, Murphy looked in Taylor's direction although Taylor didn't know whether the cop really saw him or not.

"God damn it," he said, in a small voice punctuated by coughs. "I had to be a cop. Couldn't stop being a cop. You son of a bitch, I couldn't stop being a cop."

Before he could find an answer, Taylor saw the life go out of the man's eyes.

42

"Quite a story," Marsczyk said. He poured them both a drink and slid a glass across to Taylor. "Let me see if I got this right. Danny Murphy follows you uptown to put a slug in you and winds up saving your life instead?"

"Yeah, that's the way it happened."

Marsczyk tapped Taylor's copy. "This is one fine piece of reporting. I don't think you've ever written this honestly before."

"You know, somehow that doesn't make me feel any better."

"I know. You lost a friend. I sympathize with you, Damon, but you got to realize the business he was in, that's the risk, you know?"

"He was getting out of it."

"He said he was." Marsczyk took a drink. "Maybe he would have, maybe he wouldn't have."

"He would have. He was in love."

"I'm going to edit out the girl's name, how she got her business, the rest of it. She sounds like a good kid. We don't need to throw her to the wolves."

Taylor nodded. "Thanks."

"And you know," Marsczyk tapped the pages again. "Runyon would be proud of you for this piece. You might be the first person writing for a piece of crap rag like this to win a Pulitzer."

"It's not worth it."

"I know. Go home, Damon. Go home, get drunk, sleep in tomorrow and then come in and we'll start all over again."

"You know something? I wish there was something else to do."

"I know. But there isn't. This is it, Damon. All we can do is try to keep our fingers in the dikes."

"Exactly."

Around two in the morning, just as he was dozing off sitting on his couch, he heard a sound in the bedroom, a soft, muffled noise that sounded like someone bumping against the bed in the dark. Without getting up, he reached and turned on his lamp. Then he waited.

When the bedroom door opened and the figure eased into the living room, he said, "Figured you'd be dropping by."

"Hello, Damon," Kristen Eldredge said, her knife held loosely by her side. "There's a little matter of my hundred thousand dollars. "You got it, I want it."

"No."

"Taylor, I'm not screwing around here. You know what I've done to get my hands on that money, don't you?"

"You've killed four men."

"And one more won't make any difference to me. Where's my money?"

"In a safe deposit box."

"We're making progress. Just give me the key and I'll be on my way."

"Can't. The money's going back to the insurance company."

"Bullshit. The money's going back to me."

"'Fraid not."

When he stood, she raised the knife, held it in front of her like a charm. He stopped moving, so she relaxed her arm again.

"The key," she said.

"I'm not giving you the key, Kristen."

"You know my real name, huh? Maybe you're a better reporter than I thought you were. Tell me, where'd you find the money?"

"Under the floor in Wallace's apartment."

"Under the floor." She nodded. "Who would have thought it?" She raised the knife again. "Good as it is to chat with you, I'm kind of in a hurry, so if you'll just hand over the key…."

"No."

"Look, Taylor, you don't hand me the key, I'm going to start cutting you. You of all people know what I can do. And the cuts'll get deeper and longer till you give it to me. We both know I'm going to wind up with the it, so why not skip all the bloodshed?"

He reached behind him and pulled Guthrie's .45 out of the waistband of his pants. Pointing it at her, he said, "Why don't you put down the knife?"

She drew back a step when she saw the gun. Then she laughed. Her nostrils flared and very quickly, almost imperceptibly, her eyes widened and then narrowed again.

"I don't want to shoot you," he said.

"Don't worry about it," she said. "You won't."

"You don't think so?"

"No." She smiled. "I know you, Taylor. You were in the war, weren't you?" When he didn't answer, she took a step toward him and continued. "You did horrible things, terrible things. And when you came home, you took a vow you'd never do any of those things again. You swore to God you'd never kill again, didn't you? Took a solemn vow." She took more steps.

"Fact of the matter is, I've already broken that vow. Shooting you won't change anything. Stop there and put the knife down."

Holding up the knife, she rushed him. He shot her in the stomach. A .45, he thought, is a powerful weapon, designed to knock a victim off their feet. It carries enough stopping power to drop the person who catches the bullet flat on the floor.

Except for Kristen Eldridge. She staggered back a step or two, her eyes confused. She looked down at her stomach, eyes wide in disbelief, and then at him, questioning, as if she wondered how anyone would be rude enough to do something like this to her. Then she got angry, letting out a horrible scream as she charged him again. He shot her once more, this time the bullet hitting her upper chest. Still she didn't fall. Instead, she took two small steps forward, saying "Not possible" as she slashed at him with the knife. He held his left arm up to block the blow and felt the knife slash his forearm.

He shot her a third time, right between her perfect breasts.

43

He was trying to decide whether or not he wanted a drink when the banging started at his door. He decided against the whiskey and walked across the room to open the door.

Terry Louvin stood there. Her face was bloated and swollen, her eyes red from crying and her hair hung in limp, untended curls. Under her overcoat, she wore sweat pants and a sweatshirt that didn't match. As she came into the apartment, she glanced at the sling holding Taylor's left arm in place but didn't say anything.

"You want a drink?" he asked.

"No." After a pause, she shook her head and said, "Yes. Sure. A drink would be good."

He poured them both a shot of Jameson, added ice and handed her one. "Good to see you, Terry. I've been meaning to call you."

"I had a visitor today," she said as she walked over and sat on the couch. She looked as though she expected to leap up suddenly. "I was sitting in the office, getting ready for my next class and a man walked in. He was familiar. I looked at him, knowing that I recognized him, but I couldn't place him. He stood in the doorway, looking at me and I finally realized who he was. It was Frank Costello. He was staring at me and it was like he was wondering who I was and why he was here. You know what he said to me?"

"No, I don't."

"He said I was not to worry. Everything was going to be all right, he said. The deal stood and would continue to stand. I looked at him and said, 'The deal?' He said, 'You don't know?' When I told him I didn't, he said he meant the deal that you and Leo Salmon had negotiated for me. He said the studio and the building were mine, the mortgage had been paid off and I'd be receiving the paperwork in a few days. Damon, what the hell did you do?"

"Terry," he said and took a long swallow from his glass. "You were in a pretty bad place. I tried to take care of you."

"By putting me in bed with gangsters? By making me partners with a gang of murderers and thieves, the worst people in the world?"

"Terry...."

"And what was worse, Damon, is that I thought you were my

friend. My very best friend. I thought you were on my side. But you brought Leo Salmon into my life and when I started falling for him, you didn't say a word. You knew who he was and what he'd done but did you warn me? Hell no. You just sat there and let it happen."

"I just wanted you to be happy. I thought I was doing the right thing."

"Damn it, Damon, in what world is making me a member of the Costello gang the right thing to do?"

"You weren't a member of the gang."

"Right. Because to be a member of the gang, you have to actually know you're in the gang and I never did, is that it? Because you didn't tell me."

"Terry...."

"When you saw me falling in love with Leo, didn't you think you had an obligation to tell me what he really was?"

"He was a man who was willing to give up everything for you. A man who would turn his back on his whole world because he was in love with you. He was going to quit."

"Is that supposed to make me feel better? Make everything all right?"

"Terry, I wanted to tell you. I started to a dozen times but Leo talked me out of it. He wanted to do it himself. He was going to tell you that night."

"You don't understand, do you? By the time he was going to tell me, I was already in love with him. I should have known from the beginning. I should have been able to make a decision about it early, but I couldn't because you—you, Damon—didn't tell me." She put her drink on the table, stood up and headed for the door. "You should have told me. You say you were trying to help me. The time to help a person is before she's in a place where she can't do anything herself. The time to help is before she makes a bad decision, not after it's made. And you didn't do that. I needed you and you weren't there."

"I'm sorry, Terry. All I can say is I meant to do the right thing."

"I just don't think that's enough, Damon," she said as she walked out the door, pulling it closed behind her.

She didn't slam it but the closing of the door sounded very loud to Taylor.

The apartment was a lot colder after she'd gone.

THE END

Afterword:

In the late forties, the black list moved through the entertainment industry like a plague. Groups such as the ones depicted in this novel published the names of Communists, real and suspected, and pressured advertisers not to use them in television or radio work, which at that time were wholly owned and developed by sponsors for licensing to the networks. The House Un-American Activities Committee held hearings aimed at driving the Communist influence out of Hollywood. The major studios, who simply wanted to keep the money flowing, rolled over and cooperated with HUAC.

Performers, writers and directors who were not willing to cave in to the Committee by branding themselves as Communists and providing Congress with the names of their associates who had anything to do with left wing politics found themselves blacklisted, unable to find work in this country. The Hollywood Ten, a group of screenwriters who defied the Comittee, were sent to prison.

Actors such as Will Geer and Zero Mostel, who appear in the novel as fictionalized versions of themselves, found their thriving careers suddenly ended. Mostel, unable to work in the United States, spent several years in England and touring Europe. During the sixties, he managed to come back big in Broadway musical comedies like *A Funny Thing Happened on the Way to the Forum* and *Fiddler on the Roof.* Will Geer returned to California, where he operated a commune for blacklisted performers who needed a place to wait, hoping for the political climate to change. Geer scraped by until the seventies, when he landed the role of Grandpa Walton on TV's *The Waltons.*

In 1942, Pete Seeger joined the Communist Party, USA, but in his own words, drifted away from the group by the late forties. Regardless of the fact that he was no longer active in the Party, Seeger and the folk band he was in, the Weavers, were blacklisted. Club owners wouldn't hire them and radio refused to play their records. Seeger himself was called to testify before HUAC. Most leftists took the Fifth, claiming their testimony might tend to incriminate them. Seeger, however, refused to go that route; instead, he questioned the Committee's authority and refused to answer any questions on the grounds that any inquiry into his political, philosophical or religious beliefs would violate his First Amendment rights. He was indicted for contempt of Congress and sentenced to ten years in prison. An appeals court later overturned his conviction. At the time of this writing, Seeger is over ninety years of age and is enjoying the love and respect of all of the folkies he influenced.

The period of time depicted in this novel represents pretty much Woody Guthrie's last healthy moments. He declined quickly, his behavior becoming increasingly erratic and, without a proper diagnosis for his illness, was thouight to be alcoholic and schizophrenic. When he was no longer able to control his muscle movements, he was admitted to Gretystone Park Psychiatric Hospital, where he was correctly diagnosed as having Huntington's disease, a genetic disorder that ran through his family tree.

While he was still capable of communicating, he claimed to love being in the psychiatric hospital because, he said, he could be as openly left wing as he wanted to—people thought he was crazy anyway. He died of complications of Huntington's on October 3, 1967.

In 1939, Herbert Huncke hitchhiked to New York City. When he asked someone how to find 42nd Street, he was told to walk right down Broadway. He did, found Times Square and became a regular there, eventually becoming known as the Mayor of 42nd Street. He was a bum, a poet and writer, a street hustler and a drug addict. He was also the man to see if you needed anything in Times Square. When he did his landmark study of human sexuality, Dr. Alfred Kinsey sought out Huncke to help him find interview subjects. Huncke became friends with the Beat Generation writers and appears in Jack Kerouac's *On the Road* as Elmer Hassel. He authored a few books, most notably his autobiography, *Guilty of Everything*, and died in his sleep at the age of eighty-one.

All of the restaurants, bars, clubs and shops the characters frequent are real. They all existed during the time in which this novel takes place but, of course, as is the case with the characters who actually lived, I am using fictionalized versions of them. Although I've tried to stay true to their characters, I've always kept foremost in mind the fact that I am writing fiction, not fact.

Michael Scott Cain Bibliography

Fiction:
Jason's Song (1974)
False Starts, Sudden Stops (1979)
What the Night Will Bring (1995)
Midnight Train (2003)
Arbuckle's Dance (2014)
Damon Runyon's Boys (2018)
A Net of Good and Evil (2020)

Non-Fiction:
Co-op Publishing Handbook (1978)
Book Marketing: An Intelligent Guide to Book Distribution (1981)
The Community College in the Twenty-First Century: A Systems
  Approach (1999)
The Americana Revolution: From Country and Blues Roots to the
  Avett Brothers, Mumford & Sons, and Beyond (2017)
Folk Music and the New Left in the Sixties (2019)

Short Stories:
Crazy Old Man (*Alfred Hitchcock's Mystery Magazine*,
  Mar 3 1982)
The Custody Thing (*Alfred Hitchcock's Mystery Magazine*,
  Nov 11 1981)
The Next One's for Real (*Mike Shayne Mystery Magazine*,
  Dec 1981)
On Different Tracks (*Alfred Hitchcock's Mystery Magazine*,
  Aug 19 1981)
Retirement Job (*Alfred Hitchcock's Mystery Magazine*,
  June 24 1981)
The Stray (*Alfred Hitchcock's Mystery Magazine*, Feb 4 1981)
Willie Meets the Man (*Mike Shayne Mystery Magazine*, Aug 1982)

Michael Scott Cain was the author of seven books of poetry, most recently *East Point Poems*, and three novels, including *Midnight Train*, a country music novel. After teaching popular culture and literature at the collegiate level for forty years, he covered the topic in the Frederick *News-Post* while also serving as jazz, blues, poetry, and folklore editor for *Rambles*. Cain's final project was a social/political history of the Folk revival of the 1960s called *Folk Music and the New Left in the Sixties,* as well as this, his second Damon Taylor mystery. Cain passed away on January 30, 2018.